Names
and
Addresses

Diana Gruffydd Williams

Diana Gruffydd Williams

OPENING CHAPTER
Creative Media

First Printing, 2023

ISBN 1-904958-79-6
EAN: 9781904958796

published by

Opening Chapter

openingchapter.com

for Meleri and Gwen

Acknowledgments: to Derec and Rhian Jones for their kindness and especially to Peter for his careful help and support in producing this book.

Chapter One

Cardiff 2007

The parcel was slim even though it had been placed inside a recycled Jiffy bag. The sticky label said 'I'm helping to save the planet.' Megan recognised the neat handwriting underneath and smiled. The last letter of the postcode was incorrect but it was easy to mistake an H for an N. It somehow enhanced the whole thing – fallible with a fountain pen was much more reassuring than perfection from a computer.

She took the parcel back into her flat and felt inside. Solid. Rectangular. A book. The trouble with receiving books was that everyone knew her interests so she got duplicates. Art, Poetry, Mysticism. Environmental matters. Megan had once been given four copies of the Green Guide to Everyday Living – which seemed a strange irony. She had kept one, shredded one and given the other two copies to different charity shops. She had enough books on Michelangelo and Leonardo to start a small library.

Megan took the paper-knife from the letter-rack and slid it along the line of the parcel tape. She'd have to discard the Jiffy bag. It had already made several journeys and there was a hole in one corner where the bubble-wrap had burst open. Could she tear away the bubble-wrap from the paper and use them separately? What for? She had no intention of moving again. No more need for packing china. She crumpled the bag into the waste bin and looked at the gift. The sender knew her well enough to have forgone the customary gift-wrap and decorative ribbons.

It was a telephone and address book. Attractive

enough – lightly padded front with a good reproduction of a Renoir on its cover. There they were, the cheerful, rosy-cheeked, plump women with open lips inviting seduction. Warm flesh tones, breasts like apples, dimples. Luscious. Or, as everybody was now in the habit of saying – lush.

She looked inside the new book. It was good quality paper. Plenty of space. A generous allocation for the 'A's, then the 'B's and so on. They had tucked the 'I's, 'J's and 'K's in together like the 'X's, 'Y's and 'Z's. These general purpose books didn't take ethnic minorities into consideration. In Wales, for example, there were the Joneses and the Jenkinses. Lots of them. There'd be people somewhere who had the same problem with the 'X's, 'Y's and 'Z's – the Greeks, maybe?

Megan took out the card that had been placed neatly inside the book and opened it. She'd recycle the envelope. She smiled softly at the splendid reproduction of a Berthe Morisot (The Bowl of Milk). All the shades of green and cream – so pleasing to the eye. The card was good enough for her to frame later – the wall in the hallway of her flat was still cold and clinical-looking. It would be an uplifting thing to see when she opened the door – and it would please Annie too.

Dear Annie – she always remembered birthdays. She read the message inside in the comforting, familiar hand-writing. 'Have a lovely day, Megan. All my love, Annie'. Then there was a P.S. There was always a P.S. with Annie. 'See you soon. Come round anytime – Wednesdays are usually free for me. And please give me a ring if you need a chat.'

Megan stood the card up on the mantel-piece. Then she smiled back at the Renoir girls before going into her bedroom and placing them in a plastic bag in the cupboard. With the others.

Megan had worked with Annie at St. Anne's School. She would wait another week or so before ringing her. Then they could fix up a time. On a Wednesday. They'd do what they'd always done since they'd retired.

Last month, they went into Cowbridge, browsed around for a while before going to the café for lunch. 11.45 on the dot to make sure of a seat. They both chose the soup and chatted away until it arrived.

Abuse. An over-used word – abuse. Like bullying. This easy tripping off the tongue of powerful words does no-one any favours. It undermines the suffering of the real victims.

It hadn't been abuse when Annie's husband lost his temper. Went berserk. Hit her. For the first time. Annie was the first to admit that they were both hot-tempered. They'd fallen into a familiar, dysfunctional rhythm over the years. Comparative harmony for a while then the sparks would suddenly fly. They'd kept together for their son's sake but, once he'd gone to University, well, that was the time that he hit her. They called it a day. Annie regretted it all, said they never should have married in the first place, but they were young. They were in love. Yes, it was love but they couldn't live together. Regrets were no good and she would never have wanted to be without her son, who was the apple of her eye.

They'd said that they wouldn't eat much – Annie and Megan. Annie was constantly on a diet. Megan looked at her friend's generous curves. Maybe that's why she had chosen the Renoir address book. Annie joked that, now that her brain cells were dying at an alarmingly fast rate, she might benefit from some fish. Two fillets of plaice arrived on oblong plates, duly battered, adorned with a slice of lemon and fresh sprig of parsley. With peas and chips. What was it about chips that made them so satisfying? The fat? Childhood associations?

Megan seldom ate chips these days. There was something so sad about putting a portion for one on a baking tray.

Megan always had been a good listener but Annie was sensitive enough to move on from her own problems. They talked about the children at St. Anne's. The dreadful year that she'd had with a class in 1984. Those children had moved on to Annie in the September of 1985. Annie had a hearty laugh that silenced the place for a moment. It didn't come from a cruel sense of humour – just that open laughter that you find with very young children. And sometimes with the very elderly when they've let go of the world's struggles and hover somewhere between Heaven and earth.

They hadn't intended to have a dessert but the café was crowded and the waitress was clearing their plates. There was a small queue desperate for a table. 'A lemon meringue for me!' Annie had announced cheerfully. 'With cream?' 'Yes, please'. And Megan had asked for rhubarb crumble. It was delicious – not too sweet – with a lingering but not overwhelming tang of ginger. Again, something she wouldn't bother with at home.

The café was still heaving so they ordered coffees. A latte for Annie and a cappuccino for Megan. Annie asked again how her friend was managing but Megan didn't want to impose her feelings on Annie – and she didn't want to spoil the occasion. The dreadful year back in the eighties continued to amuse. 'Did Annie remember Willie Thomas?' 'Ah, yes.' There was more laughter that silenced the place for a moment. Not surprising that Annie had no discipline problems – she

4

was such an expansive personality.

'Cheeky little chap!' she conceded. 'Do you remember the bleeding finger?'

'The bleeding finger?'

'He didn't try that on you?'

'I don't think he repeated his jokes,' Megan had chuckled. 'He was too canny for that. It was the ears with me. He'd stuck these rubber ears on top of his own – horrible, grotesque things with hairs sticking out of them. And he put his hand up and said 'Miss, can I be excused?' I said yes and he put his hand to his 'ear' and said 'Pardon, Miss?' He had the whole class laughing with him and I had an awful moment when I thought I'd lost control. Do you remember Susie O'Leary – the nose-picker who kept the snot on her fingers and examined it at length? It was the best thing she could manage – concentration wise.'

It had been a lovely day. Megan was looking forward to seeing her again. But she wouldn't use her address book with the buxom wenches.

Megan was out when the next batch of cards and parcels arrived on the following day. She had taken a leisurely breakfast, listened to Radio 4 for an hour or so, looked out of the window to get an idea of what the weather was doing, put on a thick cardigan and topped it with a striped scarf. It was late summer but felt more like autumn. She slipped a folded umbrella into her handbag and an empty jute bag in case she bought anything.

As she walked across the streets to the park, she met a few acquaintances and passed the time of day with them. Acquaintances. People who knew her name. But not people who knew that it was her birthday. Gone were so many familiar handwritings – from her parents, her husband and most of her cousins. Childhood links had loosened with the sheer busyness of everything. Relatives had moved away. There were exceptions, such as Annie, but, on the whole, most of her former colleagues had lost touch. From Down Manor School and from St. Anne's. If she met them now, they might not even recognise her. Today it was her two children who remembered her – Tom and Susan. Her grandchildren – Stevie, Bella and Catherine. Her brother Sam. And new friends who were her neighbours in the sheltered accommodation complex.

As she focused back on the present moment, she was glad that she had decided to wear her flat shoes with the thick soles. The ground was damp underneath with an early patchy carpet of fallen leaves after the rain. She enjoyed scuffling them as she walked and tried to recognise the trees from their autumn farewells. Horsechestnut she knew, of course, and oak – but her knowledge was scant about the others. She decided to make it a task for the winter. Learning about trees. She still had an old Observer's Book of Trees at home in the flat. It showed pictures of individual trees with their general overall shape and smaller inset drawings of the fruits, leaves and any other common features. She had referred to that book for her own children and all those she had taught. But she had completely forgotten the information now.

Megan hadn't noticed the man walking towards her so it was a shock to see him standing beside her. She didn't recognise the face – eyes red and slightly watering from the wind, generous mouth and balding hair that had once been dark. She didn't recognise him yet there was something vaguely familiar about him.

When he placed his hand on her shoulder, Megan felt afraid. It was the kind of fear that resulted in muted numbness rather than the desire to run away. Her mind was doing several things simultaneously, automatically. Looking around her, she realised that there was no-one else nearby although there were several lads on bikes and a woman walking her dog. They might hear a scream. But a scream might be silenced by some act of violence. She had meant to carry her old school whistle in her pocket but she kept on putting it off – she didn't want to give in to anxiety just because she was living alone. She hadn't re-written her Will since Hugo had died. Should she have done?

'I'm sorry to trouble you,' the man was saying. 'You're Mrs. Roberts, aren't you? From Down Manor School?'

Yes, Megan had taught there before the children were born. Could this man have a sinister motive for the question? She had heard about strangers with evil motives who assumed familiarity.

She replied with a cautious 'Yes'.

The man smiled at Megan. She saw his teeth. There was a little piece of food lodged on a couple of them. He had been eating salad – or something green, at any rate. He withdrew his hand from her shoulder and said gently, 'I thought you'd want to know – you may know already, that Miss Stafford has passed away. She was Headmistress when you were . . .'

Megan relaxed and gave a smile that was intended to convey the sympathy that she felt. But she didn't know this man's connection with Cicely Stafford. A nephew – or a cousin? A close friend?

The man picked up her confusion and explained. 'I don't expect you to remember me,' he began. 'My son was at Down Manor School all those years ago. He

7

thought a lot of you.'

Megan was genuinely touched. 'How kind!'

The man began talking quickly then, satisfied that he had made the right introductions, added 'I used to help Miss Stafford out – with her garden, odd jobs in the house – you know the sort of thing'.

Yes, Megan knew the sort of thing. She hadn't had a Christmas card from Cicely Stafford for a few years and just assumed that she had died. She tried to phone in the January after the first card had failed to arrive but the number was unavailable. "How old was she?" Megan asked gently, trying to compensate for her frosty start to their conversation.

'Eighty-six.'

'I thought it was something like that. Do you know what happened?'

The man screwed his face up, as if in pain; he had obviously been very fond of Miss Stafford. 'Donations in lieu of flowers to Alzheimer's. Need I say more?'

It was Megan's turn to show distress. 'I'd have called to see her if I'd known. We could have talked about the old days at Down Manor. I assume that she couldn't look after herself at the end?'

'No. She went into a nursing home – oh, about three years ago. I went in to see her quite often. I had one of those long photos of the school that you have to roll out. The pupils, the staff and her in the middle as proud as could be. It gave her so much pleasure. She remembered all their names. Well, almost all of them. And she loved talking about her staff. She always had a fond word to say about you, Mrs. Roberts.'

Megan found herself blushing at this unexpected flattery. She looked at her shoes that were now dark with the wetness underfoot. 'Has the funeral gone?'

'Yes, I'm afraid so. Last Tuesday.'

'Well, thank you for telling me. I knew something was amiss when the Christmas cards stopped.' Megan felt a warmth towards this strange messenger. He was earnest and honest. She just knew it. Intuitively. 'Tell me about your son,' she said. 'It's hard to remember everybody.'

'I wouldn't expect you to. Ronald Price. Everyone called him Ronnie.' And he looked at her with a parent's yearning that the teacher might remember.

Megan knew that feeling too and she was kind. 'Ronnie' – she said slowly, with a smile as she tried to picture him. She recalled a brown-haired boy, small eyes but dark. A slight squint that rectified itself. He hadn't stood out in any way. He wasn't brilliant or naughty. One of those children who have to try hard just to be average. 'Ronnie', she said again. 'Yes, I remember Ronnie. How is he?'

The look of gratitude on the father's face was moving but marred by some sign of distress. 'He did really well,' the man said. 'For Ronnie. He was no genius, I know. He was a plodder. He got himself into an estate agency and everybody respected him. He was reliable.'

Megan was waiting for the 'but'. What had gone wrong? She helped him out.

'Has there been a problem, Mr. Price?

The man looked at her. His eyes were sad. Like Ronnie's. Eyes that had struggled. 'Well, he got himself involved with a woman. They were going to get married. He'd left it late in the day, hadn't settled with anyone before. And I was so pleased for him. I encouraged him. But she was greedy. She wanted it all. A nice engagement ring. A big one, top quality. It was like some kind of emotional blackmail, really. She wouldn't get

9

married before they'd looked at a little house. That's hard these days . . .' The man hesitated but Megan had already guessed what was coming next. 'It's hard dealing with money at work with that sort of pressure . . .'

Megan put her hand on his shoulder. 'I can imagine'.

'You know what I'm going to say, don't you?'

Megan nodded. She kept her hand on his shoulder to encourage him, to let him know that she understood.

'He was sent down. Not for long. Released early for good behaviour.'

'I'm sorry. So very sorry.' And she remembered the little boy with the brown hair and the squint that had rectified itself. She could see him now, pleading for attention, wanting to have ticks in his book and 'Good' written on his work. 'And now?'

'Well, it's hard. The woman disappeared off the scene. It's hard to get a job when . . . He's back living with me. Does a bit here and there. Casual work.' The man brightened up as he looked directly into Megan's face. 'He used to go and see Miss Stafford too. Took the old school photo as well. Went through all the children – and the staff. He'd say how he found the teachers and Miss Stafford giggled if there was a bit of a clash. Not that there was one with you. 'Mrs. Roberts always had time for me,' he said. 'She made me feel I was worth something.' And Miss Stafford said that you were one of the best teachers she'd ever had . . .' He trailed off. His eyes were watering again and this time it wasn't because of the wind.

Megan found herself saying 'Would it help if I dropped Ronnie a line?' – then worried that it sounded like a grand gesture.

The man looked at Megan in amazement. 'You'd do that for Ronnie?'

'Of course.'

'That would really make a difference. He gets no encouragement, you see. His mother left years ago. Friends fall away. Colleagues didn't want to know him after . . .'

'Have you got a paper and pen?'

They both started to fumble about – Megan in her handbag and the man in his trouser pocket. She found a pen but neither of them had a slip of paper. The man tore a part of the front cover of his cheque book and scrawled down the details. The writing was spidery because he had nothing to lean on. He handed the blue scrap to her and Megan put it carefully in her handbag.

'Tell Ronnie I'll be in touch,' she said, smiling.

Megan felt that she knew the man well after such a short meeting and wondered whether to give him a peck on the cheek. But that would send the wrong message. She held out her hand and shook his. There was a quality about the handshake. Gratitude and openness from him and a heart that had been touched from Megan.

She walked away and turned back. The man had turned back too. They waved. Little Ronnie Price. And his dad. She'd have walked past him, not knowing that he was carrying deep personal tragedy. Some people asked for little in life and were profoundly grateful for whatever small blessings came their way.

Megan had lunch in one of her favourite cafés. It served food that was locally sourced and, whenever possible, organic. She chose a leek and potato soup that arrived with a warm, home-made roll and a little rectangular piece of butter wrapped up in gold paper. She preferred butter to the spreads and margarines but she never ate much. There was something wonderfully indulgent about unwrapping the little piece of butter and scraping it with her knife onto the edge of the plate. Knob by knob, she let it melt into the bread and ate most of it on its own as the soup was too hot. It was a shame to have a warm roll and wait until it was cold. The soup had cooled down enough for her to dip the last of the buttered bread into the bowl. She liked simple soups. Leek, potato, seasoning, stock. That was all she could taste. And all she wanted to taste.

The café was half-full and there was a gentle buzz from the other customers. She didn't turn around but she could hear a voice, shrill and loud, above the others. It was a young woman talking to her carer. She had that delightful laugh that can so often be heard in people with mild learning disorders. Laughing at simple things. Something that the rest of us tend to lose. Who were the disabled and who were the carers? Megan often wondered. And she thought of Bella. Her beautiful granddaughter. Bellissima Bella. She felt the feelings that would have led to tears if she were not on medication. Megan quite enjoyed eating alone. She could concentrate on the food and her thoughts. It wasn't easy to chat and eat at the same time. Poor Ronnie Price. And the pain his father must have gone through. Understated, almost apologetic. Mediocrity in every aspect of his life, a wife who'd left him, a son who'd tried hard to make the best of himself and then the bad relationship, prison and the aftermath: no-one trusting Ronnie, difficulty getting references . . . Yes, that was something she could help with. She knew intuitively from what the father had said that Ronnie was essentially an honest and hard-working man. Yes, of course she could offer to be his referee. She was sorry to hear about Cicely Stafford – but glad in a way to know what had happened to her. There was something so unfinished about not knowing what had happened at the end of a friendship. Cicely had been a sound, sensible woman.

Megan ordered a *tarte au citron*. She often asked people how their cakes were made – so much potential for factory-farmed eggs and dubious fats. But she didn't ask that day. The café was good on the whole – and adapting to green, ethical living was a process. She was still on the journey. And so were they.

The *tarte au citron* was not up to the usual standard, and she left the pastry untouched. She didn't complain but only left a small tip.

Megan caught a bus into town for the cinema. She'd be back in time for supper and then she'd open the cards and parcels. And phone the family to say that she'd had a wonderful day. They worried about her.

This was her sixty-ninth birthday. Her husband Hugo had died four years earlier. Too young. It had taken her a while to make the decision but a flat in a sheltered housing complex had been a sensible move; the thought of moving again was unlikely; her arthritis was already causing her problems,

She had difficulty with the door of her flat when she got back from the cinema as it was partially blocked by a little cluster of cards pushed in by hand during the day. She put them all on the little side-table in the hallway. As she closed the door behind her, she mused about the right level to hang the Berthe Morisot. She took off her shoes and carried the cards into the living-room. The three-piece suite was too big for the flat but she couldn't bear to part with it. She had compromised by putting one of the armchairs in the small second bedroom. She and Hugo had gone to choose it and they had spent hours testing items of furniture for comfort and style. They decided on the brown leather suite – a classic design – because it was hard-wearing, a delight to sit in and it would never date. It was showing signs of ageing now but that was part of its charm. Megan slid her hand over the brass buttons that held the leather in place along the front part of the arms of the chair. Handling them reassured her – it was something she had done over the years. In stressful moments or when a difficult decision had to be made. She did it now and the familiar action brought her in touch with the past.

When Hugo came home after the first legal complaint, they sat down and she had listened. That under-estimated gift – the willingness to just listen. Not being judgmental. She had fingered the brass buttons then over and over again – like worry beads, a rosary. And she had prayed for the grace to restrain her own feelings until later.

Unless Hugo noticed her little habit – and she doubted that he had, he had been spared from knowing the extent of her own anxiety. She just sat there, listening, absorbing his sense of shame, injustice, anger. Like blotting-paper.

Yes, the three-piece suite was too big but she'd bought a patterned Axminster carpet that drew the eye's attention to the floor and she had hung several brightly-coloured paintings fairly high on the walls. She no longer had a Dado rail but the two Gauguins, one of her own (painted when she was a student) and a Paul Klee, helped to balance the room.

Megan had the day's post on the matching leather footstool and, as she knew all the senders, she placed them in the order in which she wanted to open them –

the cards first, then the parcels. Even the cards were placed in a particular order – there had always been a degree of obsessiveness in Megan's behaviour. She understood it well. It was to do with order, being in control. Most of the residents on her floor had sent a card. Megan had mixed feelings about this. There could be strong feelings, jealousy, an unhealthy desire to please in enclosed communities. There were three people there she counted as friends – Harriet, Myfanwy (Myf) and Albert. Even with them, Megan tried to keep a bit of a distance. 'Falling out' became hot gossip.

Harriet's card was written in her beautiful hand – every word an aesthetic joy to behold. The old curves – the capital Ts and Fs – came from another age. How sad to think that, with the tap of a couple of keys, this could all be produced by a computer. Soon, children would be unable to write – they wouldn't need to. Harriet's message was warm and loving. Her daughter was going through a very disturbing marriage break-up. Harriet did her best to be positive and remain calm. But she often unloaded her worries onto Megan. Other residents found Harriet demanding. A tiff over something trivial, raised words in the laundry-room. That was why Megan wanted to be as pleasant and polite with everybody. It was the easiest way.

Myfanwy, known to everybody as Myf, sent another attractive card. She had obviously chosen it with care and that meant a lot. A painting by a minor French artist from the Barbizon School of Painting on the front and, inside, was Myf's careful, rather pedantic writing. 'With my kindest thoughts on your birthday, Myf,' That was typical of Myf – straightforward, slightly formal. She had never abandoned the discipline of the Civil

Service, for which she had worked for over forty years. They had given her a silver tea-set which she displayed but never used. Did anyone use a silver tea-set? The trouble with Myf was her partial deafness. It got in the way of having a two-way conversation for any length of time so, when she had a gap in the afternoon, Megan went over to her flat and simply listened.

Megan opened Albert's card with interest. She by-passed the cover to concentrate on the message – 'I hope that you have a wonderful day' it read 'You deserve it. With best wishes, Albert' – and, then, in brackets, '(Evans)'. Megan smiled – with affection but relief. She had visited Albert in his flat one day earlier in the year – she needed the address of a mutual friend. Megan was fond of Albert – who was a gentleman – and they had exchanged their usual continental-style kiss on both cheeks. It didn't mean anything, this greeting. It was just an affectionate, modern way of saying hello or goodbye. But he had placed his hands on her waist. A little too tightly. She sensed that he was about to let them slide lower down, softly, and she stood back. He placed his hands by his side like a corrected child. She looked at his hands. They were sensitive, well-manicured. Part of her yearned for a caress. But not yet. Probably never. And not from Albert. They had been polite and pleasant with each other after the incident but the friendship had cooled.

Megan looked at her watch. After she opened the cards and gifts from the family, she popped a ready-meal from Waitrose in the microwave. She didn't like the idea of ready-meals – she didn't much like the idea of microwaves – but Waitrose was the most ethical of the supermarkets. And they gave her the opportunity of eating family food. Baby new potatoes with peas and a salmon and leek pie in its own herb-scented sauce. And a miniature apple tart.

After the meal, she phoned the family briefly to thank them – and cheerfully told them what a wonderful birthday she had had. And then she phoned Harriet, Myf and Albert. Yes, it was an indulgence to ring up the other residents – but when she called personally, they tended to keep her. That is how it is with the lonely. A simple invitation to come and share a birthday drink with her in the flat was on offer. Nothing more and nothing less. She called Harriet first, then Myf. If Harriet hadn't been able to come, she would have called it off. But, yes, she had been free. It was settled.

Megan smiled at her visitors. 'Thank you so much for coming to celebrate my birthday with me!'

She and Harriet had been drinking red wine – a pleasant Bordeaux. Albert had a couple of whiskies and Myf had been tempted to have a sherry. Megan disliked sherry but kept a bottle in her cupboard. It was still the drink of choice for many of the elderly – especially the women. Memories of Harvey's Bristol Cream in its heyday and prim little receptions with the distinctive glasses on a platter. With a doily. Salted peanuts before everyone knew that too much salt was bad for you. After Eight mints.

When the glasses were empty and they'd had ample time for a conversation, Megan hinted that the party was over. Any sensitive guest would pick up the message. Harriet took her glass into the kitchen and offered to wash up.'

'No, honestly, there's hardly anything to do,' Megan insisted.

Albert shifted awkwardly and took his own glass into

the kitchen and placed it in the sink. Megan noticed that he was probably the only one who had changed his clothes to come over. She'd seen Harriet wearing the same dress earlier on in the corridor and Myf was not the sort of person to change except for a formal occasion. Albert wore a white crew-cut, long-sleeved Tee shirt under an open black shirt; his casual trousers had been ironed. But he seemed smaller somehow, bent, older. Maybe it was just seeing him out of his own personal space. It was surprising how this could diminish people. He had the air of an animal trying to settle down in the lair of another.

Myf had not heard Megan's comment, but she realised that it was time to go. She was a little awkward socially and noticed that the other two had taken their glasses into the kitchen. She placed her glass on a coaster on the coffee-table then removed it in case it would damage the wood anyway.

'Here, let me take your glass!' offered Albert, kindly.

Myf smiled at him gratefully and said nothing.

Harriet was busily telling Megan about her daughter's most recent dilemma in the kitchen. There had been more fireworks . . . She knew that Myf couldn't hear the conversation and she discounted Albert because he was a man.

Megan yawned and stretched her arms above her head, as if to relieve back-ache. She lowered them and rubbed them along the small of her back in a movement that was almost massage.

'I'll catch up with you tomorrow,' she promised Harriet.

'Righto!' Harriet was always grateful for Megan's input but knew when she was pushing her friend's good-will too far. She walked towards the hallway and passed the little table. She gave Megan a generous kiss on the cheek and took Myf by the hand. 'Come on, Myf!'

Megan would explain to Harriet – but not then – how demeaning it was to treat the deaf as though they were stupid. Albert hovered by the door and Harriet hesitated, checking that Megan was happy about this before leaving.

Megan looked into Albert's eyes and perceived something that shook her. It wasn't lust or longing. It was fear. It was there in the dilated pupils. But there was something more that she couldn't discern. Eyes – those little windows of the soul. He was very scared about something.

Megan closed the door, leaving the two of them on their own in her flat. 'What's wrong?' she asked.

'How do you know there's something wrong?'

'I can see it in your eyes.'

'I'm sorry about that incident earlier in the year,' Albert confessed. 'I shouldn't have done it.'

'It's past. Gone,' Megan reassured him. 'Tell me what's wrong.'

'I went to the surgery a couple of weeks ago . . .'

'And?' she asked gently.

'Spread everywhere. It's metastases par excellence. They've done a good job.'

Megan was shocked and a shiver streaked across her body. Like lightning but chilled.

'What treatment are you having? Why didn't you tell me?'

'There was the incident – and I haven't told anybody else. I know that I can trust you to keep it to yourself.'

'The treatment?' Megan repeated, calmly.

He gave her a resigned smile. 'There's nothing they can do. Liver, lungs, bones – I've scarcely got a clear

19

organ in my body. Oh, they offered me chemotherapy. It would keep me alive a few months longer but what for? I know what it all does to you. Strange for me to reject pharmaceutics, isn't it?'

Megan had known Albert for a long time. Not well. He had been a pharmacist.

'There's nothing?"

'I've gone the way of complementary medicine.'

He held his head back and laughed heartily. He had needed to vent his feelings and it was strange how laughter came to the rescue. Often. Even in the saddest of circumstances.

Megan approached him and lifted her head to let him know that she was waiting for a continental-style kiss on both cheeks. He leaned down to let it happen. And she put her arms around his waist. To let him know that he was forgiven. And she kept them there. To convey her sorrow at the news.

On her own, Megan decided to finish off the bottle of red wine. She had a gadget somewhere that was supposed to keep it fresh for a day or two but she wasn't sure where it was. She might have given it away. She didn't really like gadgets – most of them just complicated life. They took one further and further away from the essence of the task in hand. The bottle needed to be finished. And it was her birthday.

She tried to recollect her thoughts. It had been an odd day with so many unexpected surprises. Maybe she was getting old – well, she was getting old but days seemed so muddled and cluttered, merging into one. It was difficult to remember the chronology of events. She had heard younger people saying the same thing so although the ageing process might be a factor, the chaos came from the pace of life – the over-burdening of the mind and senses with too much information from too many sources. The brain just couldn't deal with it.

She had had a light breakfast – cereal and yogurt with a cup of tea. She was aware of an obligation to tell her family again how much she had enjoyed herself. She had invited her friends over for a drink – the family would like that. She had gone to the cinema; she wouldn't tell them that she had gone alone. Looking back, the fresh air in the morning had done her good. The westerly wind hadn't brought the rain until the evening. There'd been that strange meeting with Ronnie Price's father. Learning about the death of Cicely Stafford.

Albert. She could see him quite clearly in her mind's eye. The way she had noticed his frailty; the apology and then the news of his illness. He had a few hairs that had fallen onto his shirt – he must have combed his hair after brushing his clothes. He'd not checked in the mirror. Unusual for him, a meticulous man. She imagined him undressing in his own flat afterwards and being upset at discovering the hairs. He would be determined to get his grooming immaculate in the future. But maybe he had let go of such concerns? Or was in the process of doing so? She doubted it. It's difficult to change the habits of a lifetime. He had always been well-presented. Not that they'd known him well. He and his late wife, Doreen, were on the periphery of their social circle. Sometimes he was the pharmacist on duty when Hugo was on call. She wondered how Albert would cope with the disease that he understood so well. Megan found that upsetting memories of Hugo were interacting with her thoughts about Albert. She undoubtedly had unresolved grief.

The family had made a fuss of her for almost a year after Hugo died. She spent some time in London with Tom and Alice and then a couple of months in Mid-Wales with Susan and family. They had wrapped her up in cotton wool. Not that she had objected at the time! But then she suspected that there had been a family consultation – to which she had not been invited. They were well-intentioned but she had resented the exclusion. She decided then that she would make her own plans before they started dropping more explicit hints and suggestions.

It was certainly true that their house – their home – was far too big for one. A delightful, Victorian house on three storeys – with a cellar. She could take in lodgers or house-share but neither option appealed to her. She wouldn't be able to maintain the place either. There was a limit to the amount of time and effort that could be put into employing gardeners and cleaners – odd-job men. For many years, it had been too big for her and Hugo anyway, but they had never got round to doing anything about it. And then he became ill.

Megan announced to the family that she had found a flat that was easy to care for in a sheltered-accommodation complex. There was safe parking. It wasn't too far away so she'd be able to keep up with old contacts. It was on a bus route.

Now, in her living-room, late in the evening of her birthday and mind fuzzy with the wine, she considered going to bed. But she decided to wait until her head was clear. Otherwise she might have upsetting dreams. One of the most frightening things for her living on her own was waking after a ghoulish dream and believing that it was real. And having no-one to put an arm around her. No reassurance from the presence of another human being.

She reached for her old address-book. Her beloved address book. She sometimes thought that it acted as a substitute for human companionship. If ever she were asked what luxury she'd take with her on a Desert Island, it might well be this little book. It had been given to Hugo as a Desk Diary by some drugs firm in 1984. He already had one and it seemed a shame to waste it. She fashioned it to suit their needs. There was a big section for the 'D's, 'E's, the 'J's the 'R's and the 'S's. This was Wales, after all. And it had served them well. It still served her well. So many memories.

She found the torn piece of paper from the cheque-book cover belonging to Ronnie Price's father and made a new entry. PRICE, Ronald (Ronnie) and father. And she copied the address down carefully, guessing at the final letters of the post-code. She would write the letter formally in the morning though she made a mental draft of it. 'Dear Ronnie, I was so pleased to meet your father in the park yesterday. I was sorry to hear about Miss Stafford's death but glad to know that you and your father' – maybe she should put, 'you and your Dad?' – yes, 'that you and your Dad had been so kind to her in her final years. I am sure that this gave her great comfort. I would have attended the funeral if I had known about it. Miss Stafford was such a good woman and an excellent headmistress. I have very fond memories of her. When I asked your Dad about you' (this covered her if Ronnie accused his father of 'telling' on him. She had been the one to ask the question and he had just supplied her with the honest reply.) 'I was so sorry to hear that things have been difficult for you recently. I remember you in my class. You were always eager to do your best and I'm sure that this still applies.

I hope that you have success in finding a job that will challenge and stimulate you. Please be in touch if I can help in any way. I would be happy to act as a referee. Yours sincerely, Megan Roberts.'

She turned to the 'S's and found the entry she was searching for. STAFFORD, Cicely. And just above the name, she wrote R.I.P. Again. Another one.

It was not a depressing thought to go to bed with. *Requiescat In Pace.* What a wonderful thought for Cicely. Cicely who had never married. She never fell out of love with the fiancé who had been killed in the War. Now, at last, they were united again. She had waited a long time.

A sudden thought came to Megan. She would support Albert as much as she could but she was glad that she hadn't succumbed to that incident when he had put his arms around her waist earlier in the year. A bit of selfishness. In us all if we dare to face it. Megan acknowledged the feeling – and let it go.

Chapter Two

She knew that it had been a mistake to settle on meeting at the Italian café in town at 1p.m. Every table was taken but, just as she made her way inside, a small group got up to leave. Their place was taken smartly by three people who came in just after Megan. She was standing in the way of the dapper waiters who were carrying their platters of pizzas and pastas with acrobatic skill. She sat on the bar stool by the till – which was rather high for her – and asked one of them who was busy with the coffee-machine if he could keep an eye out for the next vacant table. 'Just a small one!' she explained. 'I didn't want to take up the big table in the corner.'

The man smiled vaguely – a professional smile that he put on with his working clothes. 'Am I ready now – hair tidy, shirt clean, order pad, pen, the smile that stays, however rude the customer or ignorant. Just smile at the lot of them.' She realised that he probably hadn't heard her but, before he glided off with his lattes, he asked her if he could get her a drink while she was waiting.

'No, thanks,' she replied. 'My daughter's due any moment.'

It was demeaning to have to eye the tables like a hawk, but she had no alternative. The waiters were clearly too busy to do it for her. There were several tables for two along the edges of the room and she'd have to rush to take the next one. Her feet didn't touch the ground on the bar stool, so she'd need to be careful not to hurt her back in the process.

Most of the tables for two were occupied by people who were still eating a main course. Two more were still browsing through the menu. The greatest hope was in the young couple who were taking their time over a coffee – but lovers were notorious lingerers. She looked across at the three people who had taken the large table in the corner. Extroverts, bags on the spare seats, wrapped up in the world that they loudly inhabited.

It looked as if the young couple were preparing to go and she lifted herself down from the bar stool so that her feet were touching the ground. They were smiling at each other and seeing if they had enough money to pay. The woman took a note out of her handbag and her lover checked to see how much change there was in the coins he had lifted out of the pocket of his trousers. They whispered together – they hadn't yet received the bill – and checked the prices on the menu. The man shrugged and walked towards the till as he reached for his piece of plastic.

Megan took the table. She checked her watch. It was 1.06. Susan would undoubtedly be late – she *was* already. Defensively, she placed her bag on the other chair and began to study the menu. She already knew what she was going to order so she was only playing a game. Her eyes wandered. The plates were smaller than they had been on her last visit. Square-shaped with curved edges. Undoubtedly, the prices had gone up. Yes. It was these small changes that were so insidious. £5.95 had become £6.25. Market forces. Dark forces.

She liked the café though and usually ate here on the few occasions when she came into town. A good meal at lunch-time meant that she didn't need to bother with much in the evening. A sandwich or just a bowl of cereal.

Susan came down to Cardiff from time to time. She bought clothes for the whole family – usually in Marks and Spencer's. At first, they had spent the day together shopping but Megan found it too tiring. It was hard to maintain enthusiasm for someone else's shopping – even if it were her own daughter. Susan then started to come over to the flat for a chat and a cup of tea after shopping, but it made *her* day too long. She had to get back for the children. And so they had settled on meeting in town for lunch. It worked out well – even though Susan was seldom on time.

One of the waiters waltzed in front of Megan, carrying two plates of salad. Somehow, he managed to look at his watch at the same time. The glance was too short to have properly registered the time but the message was clear.

'Excuse me!' she called out. 'Can I order a drink while I'm waiting, please?'

The waiter delivered his salads and came to Megan's table. 'What can I get for you, *signora*?' he trilled. The accent and Italian mannerisms were exaggerated. But everyone loved them. Almost as good as going on holiday, they cooed. Shame about the weather!

Megan ordered a herbal tea. They were low on everything but she settled on chamomile. She knew exactly what would happen. The tea would arrive and, instead of being able to enjoy it, Susan would come in and they'd order their meal. But she had been there for almost a quarter of an hour. Peak time.

'Hi, Mum!' Susan walked into the café with her back pushing the door open as her hands were weighed down with bags. She came up to Megan's table, put her bags down, gave Megan a kiss and removed her bag from the seat that she now occupied. 'Sorry I'm late!' she said. 'I'd have rung you but you've never got your mobile on.'

What good would it have done if she had? She'd have

spent fifteen minutes wandering around a drizzly city centre instead. In spite of the hassle, she had at least been in the warm.

'How are you, darling?' she asked.

'I'm fine! Got a load of things for the kids in M&S. And a jumper for Paul. I'll show you in a minute. Shall we order first?'

Susan looked at the menu and screwed her face up. 'Spoilt a bit for choice, aren't we?' And she answered her own question. 'Paul's seeing to the children today so he'll probably not get much of a chance to eat. We'll have a proper meal when I get back. Something light for me then. The soup sounds nice – or shall I have a Cesar salad?' Again, she answered her own question. 'I'll go for the soup. What are you having, Mum?'

Megan smiled. 'I'm having a *risotto ai funghi*. They do it well here.'

Susan had no problem in catching the waiter's attention because he approached their table with the pot of chamomile tea.

'Odd for you to have a drink before your meal, Mum!'

'Show me what you've bought.'

A lot of her energy went on making the right sort of response to each item. The jumper for Paul was, indeed, very nice. Sensible. A soft fabric but hard-wearing. Useful for most occasions. Then out came the things for the children. Trousers for Stevie and socks – two Tee shirts, one red and one white. And two dresses for Catherine. One pretty and feminine – a party dress, And the other was a patterned corduroy. Standard. Easy to wash. A little long but she was in between the two age sizes and it was better to buy big. She would take the hem up. The trouble with corduroy was that, when you take the hem down eventually, it's hard to get

28

rid of the crease.

When she wasn't listening to the constant flow of words, Megan observed.

Susan was always in a rush – but then *she* had been when her own children were small. She had to avoid making judgments. But had she, herself, been so cavalier with her own mother? Possibly – though the circumstances had been so different. Hadn't it occurred to Susan that she'd ordered the tea simply to keep the table? Now she was going to be laden with the pot on a table that was barely large enough to take two plates. But now that the plates were smaller, maybe it wouldn't be so much of a problem. The comment about the mobile phone had been a reproach. Weren't mobile phones a symptom of the times rather than a solution to its disease? All they seemed to do was to make life more complicated, provide more choices. They said they would meet at one. That should have been enough.

The food arrived and the two of them began to eat. Megan listened as Susan continued talking. A sip of soup then 'Stevie's doing really well at school. He's much happier now. Which is a great relief.' A couple more spoonfuls of soup. 'And Catherine's so happy at Nursery. The girls there are like 'second mothers' to them. She loves them all, especially Cindy. I do feel guilty sometimes, though.' More soup.

Megan wondered what all this was doing to her daughter's digestive system. Food, gas, food, gas. She'd be taking a Gaviscon tablet on the way home. If she had time. In tablet-form for people on the move. Susan looked like Hugo – slightly fragile, a high forehead, curly, light brown hair. She was proud of her but worried about the frenetic life-style. All the younger generation appeared to be trapped in it. Sad.

'Thank you all for the birthday presents!' Megan said, fondly.

'Oh, there's no need for more thanks, Mum. We had your letter. Ours weren't very imaginative, I'm afraid. But I know that they'll be useful. And the children chose their own little presents.'

'I didn't know that you have a Neal's Yard shop in Powys . . .'

'No, Stevie ordered it himself on-line, would you believe? We gave him a bit of help, of course, but he went through the different types of soap and Catherine was nodding at the sound of some of them. I don't think they had a clue what they actually meant but Stevie liked the sound of the Rose and Geranium. And Catherine agreed.'

Susan looked up at Megan with genuine concern. 'How are you, Mum? You don't give a lot away, you know. I worry about you.'

'I'm fine. I really am! I've adapted more easily than I thought I would. Not that I don't miss Daddy!' she added hastily.

Susan's eyes misted up with tears which slightly smudged her eye make-up.

'When are you coming up to stay with us?' she asked. 'The children love having you. Half-term would be a good time,' she added before Megan could reply.

'Give me the dates. I'll see how they fit in with my commitments.'

She had no real tying commitments, but she felt better for saying that she did. The older generation was just expected to fit into a suitable slot in the diary of the younger ones.

Susan wrote the dates down on a piece of paper for Megan and ordered a latte. 'Sure you won't have one?'

Megan was still drinking the chamomile tea which was very strong now as she had left the teabag inside. And tepid.

Susan asked for the bill when the waiter brought the coffee. 'This is on me!' she said firmly.

'No, really! I had a more expensive meal than you.'

Susan smiled. She had a charming smile. Slightly crooked. Like Hugo's. 'I've got a favour to ask you so there's an ulterior motive.'

Megan's heart sunk.

'I saw a lovely dress for myself in Next,' Susan explained. 'I didn't have time to try it on – and anyway, I had all these bags . . .'

'Why don't I look after the bags for a bit so that you can go back? Is that the favour?'

'Are you sure you don't mind?'

'Not at all.'

'What shall we do then? Shall we meet back here in, say, half an hour?'

'No.' Megan wanted to get out of the café. The solution came to her straightaway. 'Let's walk over to St. David's Cathedral. I'll be happy to sit there quietly for half an hour or so – and the bags will be safe.'

The two women made their journey to the church. Megan carried one of the bags. The one that contained Paul's jumper and Stevie's socks.

The bags were lined up on the pew at the back of the church like worshippers – some sort of a bargain between God and mammon.

Megan moved to her right to the copy of Michelangelo's Pietá. A man was kneeling before it. Foreign. Spanish – or Italian maybe. Odd how British men found it hard to pray. His lips were moving silently in some private petition. Probably about his mother.

And, if his mother had died, the Madonna would be taking her place. The perfect Mamma. A series of little candles had been lit on three layers. Some were almost burnt out – others were new. Most of them were somewhere in-between. A morning's worth of pain placed before the Virgin and her crucified Son. Megan wondered about the candles that had obviously been lit early in the morning. What happened when the last flicker faded? What mystical happening? Had the prayers been taken up and were held in Heaven, in the ether? Did they stop being received when the flame went out?

The man was weeping unashamedly. She stood behind him but at a sensitive distance. What greater sign of human agony could there be than the Pietá? And yet it was a statue of hope. There had to be hope. Mary had been told – 'a sword will pierce your heart.' She could feel the dreadful nature of those wounds. But Mary had also been visited by the angels; she had heard the words of Simeon and Anna in the Temple. They were wonderful things to hold on to – beyond the pain. Many people couldn't believe in the Resurrection or in life everlasting. They dismissed it all as myth, a fantasy to sustain the feeble. It was illogical mumbo-jumbo. She had no answers to the hottest questions. Why doesn't God intervene in terrible disasters where the innocent are killed? Why is there suffering? She didn't know but she believed anyhow. In the mystery.

The kneeling man wiped his eyes with the back of his hand and fetched a tissue from his pocket to wipe his nose. When he stood up and turned to face Megan, he smiled. He felt better about whatever had been troubling him. And the smile was intimate. 'It's your turn now!' – it was saying. 'Thank you for not interrupting. Whatever your problem is, we're in this together.'

Megan acknowledged him, then lit a candle and placed some coins in the box. She knelt on the little cushion that was warm from the man's body. She had to hold onto the bar to help herself down.

At first, she stared at the beautiful image before her. Then she whispered out the names of people who were close to her heart. Susan. Paul. Stevie. Catherine. She took her time with each name, savouring it, giving God a chance to listen. Tom. Alice. Bella. The bane of meditation was distraction and, for a moment, her mind lost its focus.

On the autistic spectrum. Under its umbrella. Grim phrases. And she saw, in her mind's eye, a woman opening an umbrella. A multi-coloured umbrella. She was a healthy woman, a blooming woman. A Renoir *mademoiselle*. And, as she opened the jolly umbrella, little pieces of torn paper fell out of it – all grey and floating down forlornly to the ground. There was a name on each shred. When they reached the pavement, they became blurred and the rain broke them down.

She recognised that the distraction was significant – it was telling her something about repressed inner feelings; she would explore it all later. Megan returned to focus her eyes on the figures before her. '*Maranatha*,' she whispered, breathing the word in again and again like fresh, country air without the threat of rain. 'Maranatha.' And then she left the world and entered that place where time is no more. A place beyond words and emotions. She was out of touch with her body and the statue faded from her sight.

When Megan became aware of her surroundings again, she remembered the bags that were in her care.

She stood up – with difficulty – and turned round. In the pews of the back row, the bags were still there. So was Susan. With an additional bag from Next.

It was well into the afternoon before she picked up the day's mail. Most of it was junk. Someone trying to sell hearing-aids, another trying to lure her into a Saga holiday.

A catalogue of fair-trade clothes – she would look at that later – and another telling her that she had won some money, a bargain offer on a time-share. Two charity requests.

There was one real letter. It was handwritten with a local postmark. First-class stamp. Although Megan was intrigued, she had kept it until the last. She opened it with interest.

"Dear Mrs. Roberts," it read. "Thank you so much for writing to me. My father said that he had met you. I'm sure that you were distressed to hear about Miss Stafford. It was very kind of you to offer to be my referee when I apply for a new job. I especially appreciated it because Dad told you about my problem. It is difficult to get into regular employment after being in prison. I would like to meet you some time in the near future, if you have the time. At the moment, I'm not thinking of applying for a new job. However, there is another matter that I would like to discuss with you.

Yours faithfully,

Ronald (Ronnie) Price."

Megan read the letter carefully and then re-read it. It was well-written, if a little pedantic. She liked the way he had been straight and honest about 'getting employment after being in prison.' He had used the word prison and that was a strong thing to do. Her intuition told her again that Ronnie was a good man. He must be now in his thirties, she thought. If not older. Forty, perhaps. She'd guessed that his father was in his sixties, which would fit. She noticed how Ronnie had referred to him as 'my father' and 'Dad'.

She wondered what he wanted to talk to her about. Could he be going through some deep psychological trauma after his experience in prison? Did he need a sympathetic ear? Was there some conflict between father and son? She faced the possibility that it might concern Cicely Stafford. When Ronnie's father first mentioned their involvement, Megan had housed the suspicion for a moment that there might have been some ulterior motive. It was a fairly classic situation. An elderly spinster with no close relatives. Megan recalled that Cicely had a brother and a sister, but they were older than her and had already died. There had been a few nieces and nephews but, as the years went by, they had hardly featured in her conversations. She owned her bungalow, of course – though that might have been sold to pay for the Nursing Home fees. She had a generous pension – Megan remembered her talking about that and saying how grateful she was that there would be no financial worries in her old age. As a spinster, she must have accrued a fair amount of money in her life. She was a prudent woman. Yes, she had liked to go on holidays of cultural interest but she didn't smoke or drink. Like many people, she enjoyed a glass of wine with an evening meal – but that was all.

Megan decided to write back to Ronnie and suggest a meeting in a neutral place – she didn't feel sure enough of herself to invite him to the flat yet. She'd leave it a day or two so that she appeared interested – but laid-back.

She looked at her watch. Albert had said that he'd call over at about eleven. He was late but she knew that he'd been to the doctor's. She filled the kettle with enough water for two cups and brought the green tea out of the cupboard.

It was twenty to twelve by the time Albert knocked on her door. She opened it to him and gave him a continental-style kiss on both cheeks. 'I'll put the kettle on,' she said. 'Take a seat!'

As she made the tea in the kitchen, she watched Albert in the living-room through the open door. He looked tired and was already losing weight. His trousers were held up by braces and his blue woollen jumper hung in the place where he had had a slight paunch. She noticed that he was making little circular movements around one of the brass buttons. Seeing him do that made her feel the feelings that would have led to tears if she were not on medication.

'Here we are!' she said breezily, bringing in a tray with a teapot and two cups and saucers. No-one bothered with teapots anymore, but they made the simple sharing of a hot drink into an occasion. There was something calming and comforting about the process. There was a delicacy to the ritual. It was something to do with old-fashioned courtesy and hospitality. The tea-set had been a wedding present from Hugo's parents and she had only broken a couple of cups and the sugar bowl. It had actually been Hugo who broke the sugar bowl. She'd handed it to him and he'd misjudged the distance. It fell onto the ceramic tiles and they had stared at it for a few moments – needing a little time to interpret what had happened. Hugo had been upset at his clumsiness and Megan had tried to reassure him. It was, after all, only a sugar bowl.

She poured the tea for Albert first. He placed his cup and saucer on a little slate coaster that Tom had bought as a gift when he'd gone on his first trip away with school.

Megan poured her own cup and did what she did best – she listened. 'How did you get on today?'

'Oh, alright. They want to get the Macmillan nurses out to me – but I'm not ready for that.'

Albert had thought everything through very carefully. He was keeping his illness a secret for the time being. No-one apart from Megan knew about it. He'd talked with the doctor about the possibility of going into a hospice when the time came. That's the way he wanted to play it. Manage as long as he could. Then, when the struggle became too great, he'd admit himself to the hospice. He hadn't even told his sons yet. Megan knew that he had to deal with the pain of it in his own sensitive way. He didn't seem close to his sons though they came to see him from time to time and he occasionally visited them.

'I've been to Boots!' Albert confessed.

'Oh?'

'Yes. I wanted to be anonymous. It's the only pharmacy big enough to allow me to do that – apart from Tesco's, of course.'

She waited for him to continue. He needed a bit of help.

'What did you get?'

Albert laughed and rested his head on the part of the chair's back that had darkened the leather over the years with the pressure of heads. Heads resting like Albert's. Heads weeping. Heads relaxing. Heads thinking.

'I've spent a lifetime advising anxious mothers not to waste their money on vitamins and minerals,' he said. "Make sure that they eat well', I've said, 'and they'll get all the vitamins they need."

'You bought vitamins?'

'Yes. Loads of them. In doses I've always frowned at. They might help and . . .'

He looked at Megan directly, his expression half-way between amusement and indifference. 'I've got nothing to lose, have I?'

'Nothing at all.'

'I sometimes feel as if I've achieved nothing, you know. I despised all those women – it was always the mothers who came. I looked down at them, I patronised them. I thought that they were stupid. But they were just worried, wanting to do the best for their kids. I felt ashamed when I bought them – the vitamins, today – ashamed of the way I dismissed them. It was almost as if, well, I know this sounds crazy but it was almost as if I could hear their voices speaking in unison, like some chorus out of a Greek tragedy. And they said 'So you know now, Mr. Evans. You know now.'

Megan got up and stood behind his chair. Her right hand massaged his shoulder. She said nothing but kept the movement going. Rhythmic. Reassuring.

Albert lifted his hand to touch hers. Then he stood up, ready to exchange the usual kiss. But their eyes met and their lips puckered. There was a brief but intimate kiss and then Albert leant down and wept on her shoulder.

Chapter Three

It was time to discard, re-use or keep the birthday cards. She looked through them again before deciding on their fate. There was just one from a former colleague at Down Manor. There were a few from colleagues at St. Anne's including Annie's. She had already decided to frame the Berthe Morisot, and she propped the card up on the table in the hallway to remind herself to take it with her to the charity shops to find a suitable frame. Some of Hugo's patients still kept in touch and there were cards from neighbours in the Avenue where she and Hugo had lived for so many years.

Then there were her new neighbours in the sheltered housing complex. Harriet's in her lovely writing, Myf's thoughtful card with the reproduction of a painting by a minor artist from the Barbizon School on the front. Who was anybody to decide what was major and what was minor in art? Major tended to be a well-known name, minor was not. As she looked closely at the painting, she thought that it was charming with a lively talent in the brush-strokes. She would keep Myf's card. She had to be very selective about keeping things as there was not a great deal of storage space in the flat. In spite of the flowing hand, she placed Harriet's card on the pile to be recycled. She had already kept a letter from Harriet – a loving, appreciative one. Megan kept it in the shoe-box that was full of things to brighten her up when her mood was low.

Several of the cards were small enough to be re-used for her to make her own cards. She could easily paste the covers onto another piece of blank card that would fit into a standard-size envelope.

She decided to keep Albert's too. She looked inside at the formal message and the signature – Albert (Evans).

The other cards didn't fit into any neat category. Her hairdresser always sent her one – reciprocated, easily remembered as they shared the same birthday. A couple she and Hugo had met on holiday. The weather had been unusually bad in their secluded spot of Majorca that summer and they had found themselves in each other's company often throughout the fortnight. They had made the effort to come to Hugo's funeral – a gesture that she had appreciated as they had had to stay in a B&B overnight.

Although she didn't come from a large extended family, there had been plenty of cards. Some relatives, who had let the habit go, took it up again after Hugo's death. Extended sympathy cards in a way. Her brother, Sam and his friend Jack. She'd heard from one of Hugo's cousins – they'd always been close.

Then there was a Gwen John painting from Susan and Paul with two little drawings from the children inside. Catherine's was little more than a scribble, but Stevie had drawn a pot of flowers which was quite impressive. She wondered if he had copied it. Susan's infant school teacher handwriting wrote the message in Catherine's card but Stevie had written his own. *Penblwydd Hapus i Mami, oddiwrth Stevie.*

His writing was improving with every card, and she smiled at the Welsh. She, herself, had more or less lost the Welsh she had as a child. Her parents, like so many people in the Valleys, had seen Welsh as a hindrance rather than an asset. They wanted the best for the next generation. It was a shame and Megan regretted it deeply. She had gone to college in Bristol. And then she had met Hugo, who was English. But Susan and Paul had been keen for the children to go to a Welsh-language school and, situated where they were, that was no problem. Stevie just adapted to either language, according to the person he was with. It was as simple as that. Bilingualism. Stevie quite enjoyed talking to his Mami in Welsh. Especially when she made a mistake. He loved to correct her.

The trouble with the Gwen John card was that it was too large to be made into another greetings card. She had a special stash of items that were kept in a foolscap envelope. They were kept 'in reserve' – a sort of longish-term in-tray. Susan and Paul's card went into that envelope. She always kept the children's cards – and any drawings that they gave her – in a Scrap Book. She gained a great deal of satisfaction from looking at them – another thing that lifted her spirits. She'd give the Scrap Books to the children when they had their eighteenth birthday – if she lived that long. How right Hilaire Belloc had been when he said,

'Child, do not throw this book about;
Refrain from the unholy pleasure of cutting all the pictures out!
Preserve it as your chiefest treasure.'

Play, drawings, spontaneity, were as important as league tables and continuous assessments.

Tom had sent a L.S. Lowry card. It was signed inside. 'With our love, Tom and Bella'. She knew how busy he was but he had taken the trouble to get her a special card; she appreciated that.

Alice had sent a card of her own work. It was not to Megan's personal taste – Alice knew that. They had often joked about it. She had chosen one that she thought would appeal to her this time and its colours were certainly impressive and bold. Fortunately, it was small enough to be made into another card and she looked at the message. 'Hope you have a smashing day, Megan. I'll be thinking about you. Don't don't do anything that appeals to you, Lots of love, Alice and Bella'. She laughed softly. Alice and she had had a discussion about double negatives once – it had become quite heated and they had both had a glass or two of wine. Ever since, Alice had been in the habit of using the double negatives in letters. She never used them in conversation. She was far too spontaneous to be slowed down by something like that. Megan decided against using the card to make another card after all and placed it in the foolscap envelope.

Alice had included a card from Bella too. It showed a line of buildings very intricately drawn with people walking in the foreground. Each one was an individual with different clothes and facial expressions. One man was walking with a stick, another old lady wore a hat – there was a little group of children playing with a ball. And in the background, there was a sky that was all blue without a cloud in sight. On the autistic spectrum. Lovely. Very Bella.

She decided against putting Bella's card in the Scrap book. She would keep it in the shoebox for ever.

In a gesture that by-passed her conscious mind, she put Bella's drawing in-between the folded card that had come from Albert. When she realised what she had done, she wondered what her psyche was telling her. Somehow, she must have felt that Bella was protected in the safety of Albert's arms. She needed no reminding about her love for the child. But what was it telling her about her feelings for Albert?

Chapter Four

The arrangement had been to meet at 10.30 am in a cafe about a mile away from the flat. She feared that she might arrive too early and she didn't want that to happen. On the other hand she didn't want to be late. She needed to wander into the café promptly but casually.

At 10.20, she slowed down and browsed in a charity shop. They had several picture frames in a huge plastic box and one of them was a possibility for the Berthe Morisot. However, she needed to have the print in her hands to be sure. She didn't want to take the risk. She glanced at the women's clothes. She had often picked up the most wonderful bargains. A Laura Ashley skirt, a Jacques Vert jacket and a couple of Monsoon dresses. Why did people discard their clothes so quickly? Why did they let themselves be dictated to by high fashion? Why didn't they realise that it was all a sophisticated marketing game? Miniskirts and fitted jackets were bound to follow if the last season had been full of kaftans and skirts skimming the ankles. Her bargains had all been perfect except for one of the Monsoon dresses. She hadn't noticed the tear at the side where the pocket joined with the main part of the frock. That had been her own fault and, though she had tried to repair it, the damage was too great and the design too fine to disguise it. Brightly-coloured dusters were always an asset.

She lifted a blouse out from the rail and looked at it as it hung on its black plastic hanger. It had an Italian designer's name on it. It seemed to have been well-made, but the problem was that an Italian or French name could merely be a marketing ploy. Maria Borelli could be their equivalent of Primark, for all she knew.

She looked at her watch and realised that she didn't have the time to try it on. Just as well. She didn't really need another blouse.

Megan walked into the café at 10.30 precisely but floundered for a moment. Would she recognise Ronnie Price? She had last seen him in Primary School. There were a number of long and narrow tables, and, for a moment, she panicked.

Then she saw him. She wouldn't have recognised him from those early days, but he bore quite a resemblance to his father. He was sitting on the last table, next to the toilets, fiddling with a button on his jacket – staring into his coffee. He brightened up when he noticed her, and she walked up to him confidently.

'Ronnie!' she said. 'How nice to see you again!'

He stood up, still nervous, and shook her hand. 'Thank you for coming, Mrs. Roberts.'

His hand was wet with an excessive amount of cold sweat. Tension or even a physical condition.

Megan withdrew her hand and hoped that her face did not give away her slight sense of unease. She brushed her hand against her jacket very discreetly as she sat down opposite him.

He had hardly touched his coffee so she said brightly, 'Excuse me for a moment. I'll just order a coffee.'

'No, absolutely not, Mrs. Roberts.' He was on his feet. 'This is on me. What would you like?'

She smiled at his earnestness. 'A latte then, please. Decaffeinated.'

She watched as he went to place the order. She did remember the boy. It all came back to her. He'd been in the habit of lifting his hand to answer questions before he had worked them out. Just in case he came first.

Just in case he was chosen. And she recalled the laughter there had been when he got it wrong. It was the last time he ever put his hand up. She'd been trying to get them to do simple mental arithmetic. She couldn't remember what the sum was – 9 and 3 – something simple like that. There'd been an array of eager arms waving in the air and she'd said – 'Yes, Ronnie?' It had been so important to him. And he got it wrong.

In the café, he'd left his satchel-type bag hanging over the back of the chair. She'd noticed lots of them around – presumably a fashion trend. Canvas but well-made with sound sewing.

He came back with the coffee and placed it in front of her.

'Thank you.'

'It's the least I can do.'

There was a short silence then Megan said 'I'm sorry you've had such a hard time.'

His eyes were as dry as the bone that lay behind them but his lips quivered. Just a little. 'I got what I deserved.'

She reached down for her cup, sipped the froth and licked her lips. It was still too hot to drink.

'I really loved Donna, you know, Mrs. Roberts. I thought that I was in with a chance. At last. Well, I know she wanted things – but so do most women, it seems to me.' He gave a humourless grunt that was supposed to sound like laughter. 'I lost her anyway.'

'I'm sorry. I really am. I remember how you used to put your hand up.'

'You remember that?'

'Yes, I do.'

His eyes became moist. 'You remember that?' he repeated.

She thought that he was going to cry but he hardened his tone, beating his right side with his right fist. He continued to pound away for a while as he spoke. 'I always wanted to do well. But there was always some-one else – in my case, three-quarters of the class – who did better without trying.'

'You're not drinking your coffee. It must be cold.' She felt maternal as he took his cup and drank it down obediently. All of it. Like a man who is used to taking orders.

'Did it change you – the experience?'

'It made me bitter. I'd lost Donna, I lost the flat that I'd been renting. I wanted to be independent. I had to move back in with Dad.'

'And you're still there . . .'

'Yes. He stood by me, did Dad. He was the one who got me out to help him doing odd jobs. Painting, decorating. Dog-walking. I was surprised how many things I could turn my hands to. That's how I got to know Miss Stafford. I'd known her at school, of course, but that was different. I weeded her garden and painted her ceiling. She'd had a small leak that had left a large brown stain. I'd work away then she used to say 'That's enough for today, Ronnie. Come and have a cup of tea.' She praised me, Mrs. Roberts. She knew what had happened to me and she said that it was all past and gone. She'd trust me with her life, that's what she said.'.

She smiled gently to herself. She could just hear Cicely saying those things.

Her thoughts wandered for a while as he continued to sing Miss Stafford's praises. He was trying hard to look attractive. A casual shirt over a dark brushed cotton jumper. It was a little bit big for him, but it must be hard to find the right size for all parts of his body. He was trying to hide his paunch. With men, it was always their bellies. Some almost had the word 'beer' written across them, others came from sheer enjoyment of good food and wine and there was a third kind. It came from unhappiness. From a body that had known some sort of hardship – biscuits had been gorged to ease the pain. That was what Ronnie's well-concealed paunch was telling her.

'So, I could really say that it's due to Miss Stafford that I've got my confidence back.'

'I'm really pleased. She was such a kind woman. And so sincere. You're a tribute to her, Ronnie.'

She placed her left hand under the table so that she could glance at her watch without seeming rude. The last thing she wanted was to rush him. But the fact was that she had limited time.

'You said that you wanted to discuss something with me,' she said, softly.

'Yes.' He looked down then built up the courage to face her directly. 'You see, Mrs. Roberts, Miss Stafford has made me Executor of her Will.'

She leant back in the bath, letting her head rest on an inflated cushion that supported her neck. The water was comfortably hot and softened by an un-perfumed moisturising baby bath lotion. Its bubbles were gently floating on the surface, and she felt completely relaxed.

She had allowed herself to focus on all her current concerns – and then she had let them go – lost in the calm of meditation. Distractions – the bane of contemplation! The first one came from the sound of the telephone ringing. There was nothing she could do about it. She wasn't fond of the cordless receivers that wandered around the place with their owner, losing signals and clarity. She had her phone in the hallway. An extension in her bedroom was her only concession. She couldn't bear the thought of being constantly available to everybody.

It was difficult to re-immerse herself in contented detachment. Maybe the call was urgent? But, no, she wouldn't let herself think like that. She could pick it up later. Pick it up later? That expression had filtered in to her consciousness. 'Pick it up later' – at the time of your choice! Probably something else that had come from America.

She circled her feet around in the water, drew her legs up to her body then let herself slide to the far end of the bath so that she could push herself forward and create a wave. As the water splashed her, she remembered how she had always loved doing that – even as a child. A simple pleasure.

She knew that taking baths was frowned upon as they used more water than a shower. But that was based on the premise that a bath was taken daily. She took a bath once a week. On the other days, she simply had an all-over wash, standing at the bowl. She never used the shower. Anyway, as it was a power shower, it probably used up as much water as a bath. Who, in their right mind, had designed power-showers in a sheltered housing complex? Most of the residents had trouble with their eyesight and many had mobility problems. She, herself, was one of the fittest residents but even she found it difficult to manage its force and variety of knobs. There had been a small flood the previous year. One of the men on the top floor had taken his glasses off then gone into the shower. He couldn't see the controls and the water that had spurted out was far too hot. He climbed onto the other side of the bath panel to avoid getting burnt. He had struggled to find his glasses and, in the process, he slipped. Fortunately, he hadn't hurt himself but, while he was on the ground, he paused to get his breath back. By that time, the water had found its way down to the next floor. He hadn't been able to reach it to turn it off. Power showers were not a good idea for the elderly.

The elderly? She supposed the term could be applied to herself but, in many ways, she still felt young. Youngish. Middle-aged. But not elderly. Not yet.

The bath was beginning to cool a little and she resisted the temptation to turn the tap on for more hot water. She watched the gurgles as they whirled down the plughole for a moment, then she felt a bit chilly. The towel was large, and she patted her body dry. It took her some time to rub in the body butter that smelt of vanilla – a present from Susan and Paul. She massaged it into the dry areas – hands, feet, elbows. It wasn't late, but she decided to put on her nightdress and dressing-gown. She had no intention of going out again and the body butter – however carefully she applied it – tended to rub onto her clothes.

She had grudgingly accepted a telephone-answering machine and had to concede that it was useful. The call had been from Tom. 'Hullo, Mum,' it said. 'Tom here. Can you get in touch with me – asap.? Bye.'

She didn't like abbreviations. What was the matter with 'as soon as you can'? It took a few seconds longer to say. But that was the problem. Everyone was in this crazy rush.

As she was going to sit down on a small chair by the phone, she noticed that a note had been slipped under the door as well. She reached down to pick it up. It was from Albert. He had tried knocking on the door when she was in the bath and had assumed that she was out. He wondered if he could call around later.

Megan had had to search out Tom's number in the Address Book. She found it hard to remember – especially as he had moved twice recently. Then, there was the probability that she couldn't get him at home anyway so she'd have to try his mobile. Tom had tried to get her to put all the numbers in the 'memory' of a mobile, but she refused. She rang until the answering-machine took over. 'This is Mum returning your call. I'll try your mobile.' She sighed in frustration. There was no way of telling where people were these days. Tom was sometimes at home during the day, working. But he wasn't there. She didn't know what his working hours were. No-one had nine-to-five jobs anymore. It was early evening – just gone seven. He could be in the car, and she didn't really want to trouble him on his mobile. He had a 'hands-free' facility, he assured her – so she dialled the number. It rang for some time before appearing to go onto some kind of extension – another line?

At last, she heard her son's voice.

'Hullo, Mum. Thanks for ringing back.' He knew that it was her because her number shone a light onto his mobile.

'What's the matter?' she asked.

'Oh, nothing's the matter,' he assured her. 'It's just that a colleague has got a lap-top going. He's upgraded and will sell it to me for a song!'

'What's that got to do with me?' Megan asked, mystified.

'Well, I thought that I'd buy it for you. But I don't want to get it if you're not going to use it. You know what you're like about these things.'

'Exactly!' She laughed softly into the phone. 'It's sweet of you to think about it but I'd have no use for it.'

'You'd be surprised at how useful it is. Honestly. You can learn how to e-mail. It's easy and you can get in touch with anybody – whenever you want to.'

'I don't want to e-mail people.'

There was a pause then Tom's tone changed. It was softer – and persuasive. 'Do you still have that old typewriter?'

'Yes.' It was true that she had brought it to the flat in its case that zipped up neatly over its body. An Olivetti. A name once said with pride.

'What do you use it for?'

'Well, I haven't used it for . . .' She probably hadn't used it for years. Before Hugo died. Before he was ill. Before she retired?

'Why are you keeping it then?' I thought you got rid of things you don't use. You hate clutter.'

'Well, it might be useful if I get back into writing. I haven't done an article – or written a poem for . . .'

'Why don't you try it all again, Mum? And a word-processor would be ideal. It's easy and the work looks so professional. They'd think you're out of the Ark if you submitted anything that's typed.'

She smiled fondly. Tom had always been bright – and persuasive. Hugo used to say that.

She realised that he was making sense. 'Alright Tom. As long as you're not out-of-pocket. And thank you.'

She could hear the triumph in his voice. 'When you're next up in London, I'll go over it with you. You can take it back with you on the train. Unless you'd like it sooner?'

'No, darling. I can wait.' She hesitated then asked cautiously, 'How are you?'

'Me? I'm fine.'

He certainly sounded as if he was fine.

It was strange how people's ideas of urgency differed. She wouldn't have dreamt of ringing anyone with a 'get in touch as soon as possible' message about a laptop. Had it not occurred to him that she might have been worried about his well-being?

Looking down at the open address-book, she saw the muddle of entries she had for Tom. Changes of addresses, different phone numbers. Only the mobile had been a constant but he'd even changed that now. For security reasons.

Remembering Albert's note, she turned to the 'E's and found his number. She rang it.

'Hullo, Albert. Sorry to have missed you. I was in the bath. Yes, call over. Just give me half an hour or so to get myself something to eat.'

The bath had taken the edge off her appetite, so she settled on a sandwich. She cut two thin slices of multi-seeded bread then took out the last bit of salad from the fridge. A little grated cheese was all that she needed to add. It tasted good and she finished off her meal with an apple. She decided to wait for her cup of tea. It would be something to share together. It was a useful way of diverting attention if things became very distressing. 'Another cup of tea? I'll just put some fresh water in the pot.' Solved a lot of problems.

She wondered whether she should change back into her day-clothes. But she'd told him that she'd taken a bath and they had agreed that honesty should be at the heart of their friendship. They were two mature people. How could you give the wrong messages to a dying man?

Hugo's illness had been different. Same disease, different pattern. At the beginning, there had been hope for Hugo. Hope of recovery. If a glass is half-full of water, they say that there are two types of people – those who see it as being half-empty and those who see it as half-full. Hugo had struggled in his early years but, once he began practising and, with the security of his own family behind him, he'd become a quiet optimist. He knew that he was an effective doctor – respected. With a good bed-side manner. Then medicine had changed into a jungle of targets and an open field for anyone who wanted to sue. Sue for the fact that good people do their best and life is not perfect. Refusal to believe that life has an end, and that end is death.

It had altered Hugo's personality and she had worked hard with him to regain his dignity and balance. To see the glass as being half-full again. Not long after she had succeeded, he had become ill. Her own mind had sunk into dark places, but she had to play the game of optimism for his sake. He had been positive about things at the very beginning. His spirits were high. He'd got in touch with a colleague who'd become a leading oncologist. They were going to fight it together. He'd been able to look on it in an academic way – as though he were treating someone else. Then, at the end, he'd become depressed. In those last couple of weeks, if he bothered to get up at all, he sat on the very leather chair on which she was now sitting. And, with a smile on her face as she gazed at him, she had inwardly broken her heart. His head no longer rested on the part of the back that he had dented from regular use. There was a new patch – lower down, where he looked at her like a frightened animal. Cornered. Defeated.

She had once seen a deer stagger after it had been

shot. She had never forgotten its terrified eyes as it found somewhere to lie. Hugo had the same look. She had not cried then – or since.

Someone had accused her of being cold. People could be so cruel. She had spent time with the family in a daze. They said that Stevie had 'got her through it'. Maybe he had.

She knew that Albert would give her more than the half-hour she'd suggested and it hadn't taken her long to eat the sandwich and an apple. She filled the time by shredding paper manually into a green bag. Another gift she had received recently had been a paper-shredder. She had taken it to a charity shop immediately after writing the 'thank-you' letter. Paper-shredders! Another symptom of a restless society – strained and stressed by its own incessant activity. Paranoid about security.

'What is this life if, full of care, we have no time to stand and stare?'

Over-quoted, but true. W. H. Davies had been so right. What would he have made of things as they were at the beginning of the twenty-first century? There was something satisfying about shredding the paper. A simple, repetitive activity, good for her hands that were stiffening up a little. And it was a way of getting rid of negative emotions. She realised that she was shredding with some force. There was something troubling her, but the problem had no name. She vowed to identify it later in the evening when Albert had gone. These things helped her to understand herself better and, without self-understanding, human beings tend to get into terrible messes. They get into messes anyway – but to be aware makes them easier to deal with – even if it's more painful in the short-term.

When her bell rang, she opened the door, having forgotten that she was in her night-clothes and wondered why Albert hesitated.

'Are you sure it's convenient?' he asked, looking down at the towelling of the dressing-gown and then averting his eyes to focus on the unappealing wooden veneer of the door.

'Of course it is!' She stepped out and initiated the kiss on both cheeks. She placed her hand briefly on his waist to reassure him – and ushered him in. He had bought new clothes. They were identical to the old ones – but in a smaller size. So that no-one would notice.

'Take a seat!' she said. 'I'll go and make the tea. You'll have a green tea, Albert?'

'That would be lovely.'

Everything was set in the kitchen, and she only had to wait for the water to boil before pouring it into the teapot. Should she mention why she was wearing her night-clothes? She didn't want to draw attention to them, but she probably needed to clear the air.

Back in the living-room, she placed the tea on the coffee-table and looked across at Albert. He had chosen to sit on the armchair, so she settled on the settee. 'I hope I haven't embarrassed you!' she said brightly. 'As I told you on the phone, I took a bath and it seemed pointless to stay in my day-clothes. Then I saw your note.'

'I'm not embarrassed if you're not.'

Yes, it had cleared the air. She wondered how Albert had got on with his aromatherapy session. He had already changed his diet radically as well as taking all the supplements. He'd been to a Cancer Centre at

Bristol and seemed to be taking on board all the approaches that he had ridiculed as a pharmacist. He'd been to see a Macmillan nurse a couple of times – a lovely girl. He'd even gone to look at the hospice and enthused about its location overlooking the sea.

'How was the aromatherapy?'

'Wonderful!'

There was a shining glow on his skin that had begun to turn grey. A slight hint of yellow. It could easily be mistaken for a healthy tan at this stage.

'Have you told the family yet?' She was worried that she was still the sole person who knew. If anything happened . . .

'I need time. I need to do this thing on my own. For the time being. I don't want their input. Not yet.'

She understood his feelings. He was on the biggest adventure of his life. Well-meaning relatives could be intrusive and directive.

They sat together for a few minutes in silence. It was an easy silence – and she was good at discerning such things.

He leaned back in his chair, and she noticed that his head rested somewhere between the dent that Hugo had made in his healthy years and the smaller dent that he'd made in sickness. This was a new space.

'Do you really believe?' he asked suddenly. 'Really, really believe?'

'Believe in what?' She enquired gently even though she knew what he was getting at. Allowing him to put the words and ideas together would help him.

'Believe in God – in Jesus? And life-after-death?'

'I do,' she said. 'Do you?'

'I don't know. I've struggled with it all my life. It's never seemed more important. I need to know.'

56

'There are no certainties. Faith demands the acceptance of mystery.'

'I can't. I'm a scientist.'

'So are many believers. Can anyone count the stars – or the grains of sand in a desert? Will science ever end?'

'What do you mean?'

'Well, will science ever solve everything – and will research come to an end?'

'I doubt it.' Then, provocatively, he added. 'You don't always go to church.'

'Faith is bigger than the Institution. It gets in the way sometimes, the Institution.'

He looked at her directly and, for a moment, she saw the look of the falling deer.

'I want to go to church!' he said emphatically. 'Or chapel.'

'What would you want to find there?'

He laughed with his mouth wide open. 'If I can't find certainty,' he said 'I'd like to find beauty – and sincerity. Will you come with me?'

She went to different places of worship. Again, she was criticised for this. People said that she should make a commitment and become involved in a community. She had been deeply hurt in the past by getting too closely involved in a particular church and had come to the conclusion that her only commitment was to God.

'Yes, of course. If you want beauty and sixty-five per cent sincerity, we could try St. Michael's and if you want sincerity but twenty-five per cent beauty, we could go to Ebenezer.'

He laughed again, heartily. 'Let's try both!'

In a sudden, impulsive action, she found herself standing up and putting her hands out over his as they rested on the arm of the chair.

'Come!' she said. 'Sit on the settee with me.'

And she gently pulled him up. He sat a little awkwardly, unsure of himself and the situation. She kissed him on the lips and put her fingers through his hair. The white hair that was soft with a subtle fragrance of cedarwood. Or maybe sandalwood. Or both.

'I'm so frightened,' he moaned as he nestled his head against her breasts.

She kissed the crown of his head where he was bald. 'I know you are, my love!' she whispered.

Chapter Five

Confused, she half-opened her eyes. She wasn't in her own bed – the pillow was too hard. It was dark. She fumbled with her left hand to try and find a light switch so that she could see what was happening. There was a body beside her, rumpling her duvet. Little hands were tickling her.

It was then that she remembered. She was in Mid Wales, spending a few days with Susan and her family. By the time she found the switch, she had rightly guessed the tickler: Catherine.

'Catherine!' she exclaimed. 'You frightened me!'

Delighted at her power, the small child chuckled. '*Stori*,' she demanded. '*Stori. Mami, dw i'n isio stori.*'

For a moment, hearing the Welsh language again disconcerted her and she realised, with sadness, how far she had grown away from her roots.

She propped the pillow up behind her head ready to put her arms round the child for a cuddle, but Catherine was already impatient. She jumped up and down on the bed, using it as a trampoline. Megan moved to the far side, worried that the child would fall. Jump so vigorously that she'd land on the floor and hurt herself. She'd seen it happen so often. That scaringly fast transition from infant enthusiasm to sobbing.

She was still struggling with the sluggishness of a brain that had been woken too early. It felt like the middle of the night but the clock on the bed-side table told her that it was nearly six. Her mind returned to that place that still haunted her. Children out of control. Children, canny, cruel, taking advantage. Sensing the fear.

'Stop it!' she shouted at her granddaughter. 'If you

want a story, you've got to sit down quietly.' Then, by way of a diversion, 'What story do you want?'

'Wela! Wela! Wela!'

It was possible now to understand most of her speech but there were times when she needed a bit of help. 'Wela? Paddington Bear? With his wellies?'

Catherine was stamping her feet on the bed in frustration. 'Wela!'

'Do you mean Cinderella?'

It was an inspired guess and the child beamed.

'Wela,' she said triumphantly.

The door opened and Susan walked in swiftly. She took hold of her child and whisked her away, holding her tightly in her arms.

'You mustn't disturb Mami like this!' she said. 'Mami needs her rest.' Once she had calmed the protesting child, she turned to Megan. 'Sorry about that, Mum.'

And they were gone.

Megan had been disturbed by her slow reactions, then the acute feeling of panic – even though it hadn't lasted long. 'Mami needs her rest'. It made her sound like an invalid. Yet it was true that she needed her rest. It was these small experiences that reminded her of her age. The short intrusion had exhausted her. She loved them all – they were her family – but dealing with little children and their needs was no longer something that she could manage easily. She had resented the intrusion.

She placed the pillow flat against the bed again and rearranged the duvet so that it fully covered her. That was the kind of thing she disliked about being away from home. A pillow that is too hard and uncomfortable. She hadn't been sleeping well with them. She'd looked in the wardrobe to see if there was an extra pillow, but it was stuffed full of junk – the sort of thing that accumulates when people are too busy. Bags of children's clothes, old newspapers, a stock of Bibles, some vestments and a box of candles. The candles had been squeezed into a box that was too small so that a few of them had fallen out where the cardboard had burst. The elastic bands around the box had also burst and were dangling like dirty little pieces of spaghetti.

She turned the bedside-lamp off and lay with her head resting on the uncomfortable pillow. She knew from experience that she wouldn't go back to sleep.

It had been a successful visit. She had had the chance to be with the children. Although Catherine had exasperated her sometimes, she loved her. She was a pretty little thing – a bit precocious, very responsive. She had gone to watch Stevie playing football with his friends. He was quieter – though not worryingly so. A bit sensitive. With his new second teeth at the front, his face was changing shape and he'd become lanky after a series of growth spurts. When she'd watched him playing football, he fell and cut himself. She knew that he wanted to cry but the pressure from the other boys – most of whom were older – was telling him to brave it out.

She had had the chance to talk to Susan and Paul at some length. They'd all had a drink after supper on the day she arrived, and it had helped them relax. She hoped that she had convinced them that they needn't worry about her. Ever since Susan had found her in front of the Pietá at the end of the shopping trip, there had been more phone-calls than usual. It had partly irritated her and partly mystified her. Of all people, shouldn't a vicar and his wife have been pleased to know that she had been at prayer? Wasn't it the most natural thing to do?

She didn't envy Paul his job – his vocation. Neither did she envy Susan in her role as the Vicar's wife. Susan's supply teaching had not gone down well with the parishioners at first. But Susan had proved to them that she was more than capable of getting the balance right. She managed to juggle parish affairs with caring for the children and working. The attraction of supply work was that she had the school holidays off, and she could make choices. They were already thinking of the future and hoped to buy a house in West Wales the following year.

It would provide them with holidays in the short-term and then, when Paul retired, they could either sell or move up there to live. In the meantime, they had a very substantial vicarage. But their pillows were too hard.

Paul had been tired on the Monday night but talking about his on-going problem in the parish seemed to have helped. After a glass of wine, he was even able to laugh about it.

Joseph Blunt, a member of the P.C.C. and a generous giver financially, was an autocrat – a difficult man. Strange how some people are attracted to power. At the point before the Eucharist when everyone is invited to exchange the Peace, Joseph had refused to shake hands with Jack Perkins. He'd gone up to Paul after the Service for a 'confidential word'. He'd refused the gesture because Jack was 'carrying on' with a married woman. The confidential chat had been overheard by several other people, so it had become common knowledge. When Joseph said that he couldn't possibly condone adultery, Paul suggested that he could sit elsewhere in the church. It had been a big mistake but, as Paul said, he'd been trying to sort out the date for a baptism at the same time as well as saying good-bye to parishioners who were leaving the church – one of whom was about to go into hospital for surgery. He'd just said the first thing that came into his head, but it had produced an outraged response. 'Was he, the Vicar, suggesting that he Joseph Blunt, should move when the other man was at fault?' 'No, no, of course not!', Paul had replied. Joseph began to introduce theology into the argument. 'Our Lord didn't condemn the woman taken in adultery, but he said afterwards 'Go and sin no more.'

Paul had become really miserable about the falling-out. This sort of argument always ended up by being a point-scoring game. 'If I'm sympathetic to Jack, I'm accused of being a liberal. Preach about forgiveness, tolerance and that upsets someone else. Everyone else in the village knows that Jack and Sheila have been together for ages.'

'Sheila's one of the school cooks,' Susan had explained to Megan. 'Her marriage has been dead for years. Her husband always had an eye for the ladies. I don't know how she put up with it all these years.'

'Have you evidence that they're in a relationship?' Megan had asked. 'It's surprising how many people value companionship in later life. And, is it the business of the Church to interfere anyway?'

Paul had sighed. 'Some say yes and some say no. Jack's such a nice man – much more of a generous, caring man than Joe, I have to say. And Sheila – well, everyone's got a good word to say about Sheila. Whatever I preach about, someone will start reading things into the sermons that simply aren't there. It's all so ugly – I sometimes wonder why people come to church . . .'

Susan had taken the bottle of wine in her hands at that point and offered to re-fill their glasses. No-one had refused though Megan had cupped her hand over the glass so that she only took a little more.

By the end of the evening, Susan had come up with an idea. They were planning to print a little book full of recipes and household hints along with a brief history of the village in the near future. Susan would ask the 'fallen woman' to volunteer a recipe. This would give her the chance to have a word with Sheila and she might open up.

Yes, it had been good to get to know Paul a little better too. Sleep is such a strange mystery. The next thing Megan remembered was Susan coming in with a cup of tea at 8.15.

She pulled up into the lay-by on the Brecon Beacons that she always used to break her journey. It was a beautiful spot, and it only took a very short walk along the pathway by the wiry grass to give her a sense of solitude in the midst of the stunning scenery. It offered her a kind of controlled freedom. She would never have gone walking there alone. The moods of the weather were too violent and unpredictable, and it didn't take long for a human being to be reminded of its limitations. But to have a little wander with the safety of a car and a road nearby was another matter.

She moved her hand to open the door, but something stopped her from getting out of the car. Her mind had been wandering as she drove. From the moment she'd said good-bye she'd struggled to keep her concentration. She didn't dare let her thoughts overwhelm her as she found driving difficult and needed to use her full concentration when she was at the wheel. There had been a couple of accidents in the past. Now that she had stopped the engine, she tried to work out what was troubling her. Yes, there had been that isolated moment of panic when Catherine had jumped on her bed but, otherwise, the visit had been pleasant. Paul and Susan were dealing with their problems. There'd been nothing disturbing about the visit. Or had there? Catherine resembled Paul but Stevie was very like Susan and she, in her turn, resembled Hugo. There'd been a few occasions when she'd felt Hugo's presence very close to her. Stevie had a strange combination of quiet confidence that could easily be mistaken for arrogance. He'd had that look about him after the football game. They'd walked along together for a while – just the two of them – and, she hadn't allowed herself to dwell on it but she now realised that it was as if she were walking with Hugo. And an awful thought occurred to her. She had forgotten what Hugo looked like! Yes, she had photos, but how could she forget the exact features of the partner with whom she had spent the bulk of her life? She hadn't forgotten them – they had become vague.

She pressed her head and neck hard against the back of the seat and made a fist on the steering-wheel. Why had he died so early? He was 62. She'd told herself that many people had had worse experiences. She had made mental lists of them and forced herself to think of them whenever she felt sorry for herself. Like some kind of cognitive behavioural therapy. But it hadn't worked. As she banged her fist repetitively on the steering-wheel, she realised that she was angry with Hugo. Angry that he hadn't pulled through. Angry that they had worked so hard to overcome problems and then, just as things were getting better, he had had the diagnosis.

'Hugo, why did you have to die?' she called out inside the car. 'Why did you have to die?'

This was anger. She knew all the bereavement processes, but anger had by-passed her. It had to emerge sometime.

There were advantages to being on your own. Hugo had been a very early riser. She was not. They hadn't always agreed on everything. There was the time when Hugo had insisted that the children were old enough to go on a holiday to France. They had argued about it, but he had had his way. Susan had been sick on the boat and then they'd lost Tom one afternoon on the beach. She'd run the full length of the sands with Susan in tow. She had imagined the worst and could still remember the anxiety as she passed row after row of sun-bathing French families who seemed to show no interest in her plight. *Les Anglais? Un enfant perdu?* And all they did was carry on reading their copies of Ouest France and applying more lotion to their brown bodies. By the time she got back to Hugo, Tom had returned. He'd only wandered a few yards away and then went back to his father's spot. 'I told you there was no need to worry!' Hugo had said. That was all he could say! They had been distant with each other for a day or two. It had spoiled the holiday for her. Nevertheless, he shouldn't have died so young.

She relaxed her hands and began to laugh. It was hearty laughter, slightly uncontrollable, as she shared an unknown joke within the confines of her car. Laughter doesn't always have a direct cause. Maybe it was just a sense of relief. When she calmed down, she looked at the two other cars that had parked on the lay-by, one on each side of her. On the right, the people inside were eating and drinking from cans; they had the radio on and were obviously oblivious to her. To her left, the driver and his front-seat passenger were looking at her, puzzled – probably uncertain as to whether they should intervene. She smiled at them. They smiled back and turned away.

She wondered whether to get out of the car and soak up the atmosphere of the mountains as she always had done, but it was drizzling. They had forecast heavy rain for later on, and she wanted to get home. She began to smile again. Home. Yes, she wanted to get home. Not just to the flat that she had taken on as a sensible venture after she was widowed. Not just to the sheltered accommodation complex that gave her a degree of protection in her widowhood.

Home. Somewhere that she was happy to be.

Something had lifted inside her. She wanted to ring Annie and meet up for lunch. She wanted to put finishing touches to the décor of the flat. She had promised to meet up with Ronnie Price and his father. She had missed Harriet and Myf when she was away. And she had missed Albert. How she had missed Albert! One of her recurring thoughts when she had been away had been concern for him. There were times when she couldn't get him out of her mind.

She started the engine and continued her journey.

Chapter Six

Sycamore Road – leading to Sycamore Drive and Sycamore Avenue. She took the turning into Sycamore Drive. After a hundred yards or so, there was a choice. Sycamore Avenue 1-31 to the left. Sycamore Avenue 32-68 to the left. She took the left turning. She wanted number 46 but it was hard to see the numbers. People had given their bungalows names – *Maes-yr-haf, Swn-y-Mor*. Odd choice that – 'Sound of the Sea'. Perhaps the residents had moved up from the coast – it reminded them of home. Nostalgia. Perhaps. She noticed a number. It was 58. She had gone too far.

Megan parked the car and decided to keep it where it was. The bungalows all had garages and a second car was in the driveway of number 58. It would only be a short walk back. She sighed. She seldom drove the car anymore, but she had used it a lot recently. There were some trips that offered her little option.

She got out of the car, checked her parking, locked the door and was ready to make her way back. She had visited the bungalow many times before, of course, but they all looked so similar from the outside and the residential site was quite confusing. The man from Number 58 came out into the garden and she thought that he was going to object to her using his patch.

She decided to speak first. 'I'm terribly sorry!' she said, pleasantly. 'I'll move the car.'

'No problem. It's really no problem.'

'Oh!' She looked at him closely, trying to guess why he'd approached her. He was a man in his late forties, maybe a little older.

'Mrs. Roberts? It is Mrs. Roberts, isn't it?'

She smiled in a way that was playing for time. One of

68

Hugo's patients? Too old to have been one of her pupils. Or maybe not.

'Hilary Benson?' he prompted.

'Ah, Hilary!' Again, she played for time. 'Hilary . . .'

His rounded, clean-shaven face was not at all familiar but the name Hilary Benson rang a bell. A distant bell but it was there somewhere in her brain. She took a fairly safe risk. 'I taught Hilary!' She smiled as if she remembered her well; he helped her out.

'That's right!' he began. 'St. Anne's. It must have been, well, about fifteen years ago.'

'And how is Hilary now? What's she doing?' Megan asked kindly – sincerely – although she still couldn't recollect the girl.

The father beamed with pleasure. 'She went on to University – Bristol – and got a good degree. A 2.1. We were so proud of her!'

'Excellent!'

'We never thought she'd get there. She had such bad asthma.'

Megan suddenly recalled the girl. There was nothing like suffering to help nudge the memory. She had been a highly-strung child, sensitive, and her asthma had not been well-controlled at the time. She had a spray but, when she was in Megan's class, she hadn't grasped the technique. The responsibility had troubled her and she remembered talking to Hugo about it.

'How is her asthma now?'

'Oh she's grown out of it. Well – 'Touch wood!" He had that irritating habit of pointing to his head to imply that it was made of wood.

'Good.' He hadn't mentioned anything about a career, and he was the sort of parent who would, if there had been anything impressive to tell so she avoided asking any further questions.

'Have you come to visit someone?' he asked. 'I'm sorry. I've been keeping you.'

'Not at all. I'm going to Miss Stafford's home. Cicely Stafford.'

'Oh?'

She studied his face as he moved towards her, close enough for his substantial pot-belly to brush against her body. She took a discreet step backwards then he leaned his head forwards. A confidential exchange was evidently about to take place. 'Funny business!' he said. 'Funny business!'

She knew what he was referring to, but she didn't make it easy for him.

'I was so sorry that Cicely deteriorated at the end,' she said. 'It must have been very distressing for her. She was always so meticulous about things. We taught together at Down Manor . . .'

'Did you know that Bill Price and that son of his, Ronnie, have got involved?' he persevered.

'I know that they were both very good to her.'

'But to take advantage of an old lady like that!' he said with disdain. 'You know about Ronnie, I suppose? Not that I'd be the first one to cast a stone . . .'

'Ronnie made a mistake – a serious mistake – and he paid a heavy price for it,' she said, hoping to shame him into silence.

'Well, I'm not the only one who's saying it. They were just after her money. She's got family, you know.'

'She had a few nieces and nephews,' she continued evenly. 'Were they close?'

'I don't think they were that close but, after all, blood is thicker than water.'

Megan's goodwill had frayed. 'I'm going to meet Bill

and Ronnie Price now,' she said. 'In Cicely's home. We've got business to discuss. Please give my regards to Hilary – and I'm glad that she's done so well.'

As she walked down the Avenue, Megan suddenly felt a knot of panic. She had placed a considerable amount of trust in Ronnie Price and his father. She didn't really know them at all. She'd only just learnt the father's name. Bill. Yes, he seemed like a Bill. A Bill who'd always been called Bill. Not a Bill who'd ever been a William.

When she reached the bungalow, she remembered it. Lavender and Rosemary bushes were still in the front garden but they were overgrown. The bench that Cicely liked to sit on to do her sewing was still there. But there was a sense of neglect everywhere. Some of the paving-stones were loose and cracked. Weeds had grown in the spaces, creating unstable bulges. She was surprised that Bill and Ronnie hadn't kept it in better order for her. The net curtains were that sort of sallow grey colour that comes with neglect and the passing of time. If they were touched, they would probably rot in her hands. And the name. The name that Cicely had loved. 'Green Pastures'.

Some of the letters on the plaque had peeled away and it had been removed from where it had previously hung from a hook between the front door and the porch. She bent down to look at it. She and Cicely had laughed about the name. 'Not very original!' Cicely had said. 'But that's how I want it to be. The image of green pastures is so appealing and, at the end of the day, everyone turns to the 23rd Psalm. 'He maketh me down to lie in pastures green, He leadeth me the quiet waters by." And, to hide the tears of which she had been ashamed, Cicely had added, 'I could have called it

Shangri-la, of course or . . .'

And the two of them had exchanged highly improbable suggestions until Cicely had regained her composure.

For a few moments, Megan held the plaque in her hands. The wooden background – a dark hardwood bought before everybody became conscious of the problem of disappearing rainforests. The carved incisions had been highlighted with gold leaf but the G and the two Es in the word Green had disappeared, as had the A, the S and the T in the word Pastures. Little flakes of gold leaf had remained on the wood in forlorn streaks. There was a dent in the wood at one end. The chain that had held it in place was broken. Sawn off.

Megan could see Cicely's figure in her mind's eye standing proudly below the name-plate. 'Have you been well fed in Green pastures?' she always asked, pointing to it. And she always had been. No-one was allowed to leave without a cup of tea and some cakes. Whatever had been eaten or drunk, Cicely had the gift of nurturing – of offering, giving.

And she had always said in reply, 'I've been very well-fed, Cicely' before giving her a gentle kiss on the cheeks.

And now, here she was, holding the damaged nameplate with Cicely dead and buried. She felt immensely sad as she knocked on the door. The bell was not working.

'Would you like tea or coffee?'

She wasn't particularly thirsty, but the two men were facing her with thermos flasks. Bill had the tea and Ronnie had the coffee. They were going to use the top of the thermos as a cup for themselves, but they had brought a china cup and saucer for her. She didn't have the heart to refuse. A lot of thought had gone into the gesture – she was sure that neither of them used a china cup. Where had it come from? Was it one of Cicely's?

'That's kind of you. I think I'd prefer tea, please.'

Bill poured the drink out and it had that thick appearance that she expected. The same colour as an old-fashioned lisle stocking. He handed her the cup and saucer and she noticed that his hand was shaking.

For a moment, they were silent as they drank the tea. It was an opportunity for her to look around the room surreptitiously. They were sitting in what used to be the lounge. Large items of furniture were stacked together to one side and covered with an old sheet; there was a stack of boxes in the other. The once-loved three-piece suite with washable covers looked odd now, crushed up together as it was. They'd shown her to the arm-chair – Bill moved a kitchen chair to face her, and Ronnie sat on one of the boxes – the labels attached to them.

'Yes,' said Bill. 'Some of it went before she retired of course – the bigger stuff. Miss Stafford wanted the family items to stay in the family – and the jewellery. Her nieces and one of the nephews are coming tomorrow. I think they've hired a van.'

The light wasn't good and Ronnie took her empty cup and saucer and placed them in bubble-wrap inside a plastic bag. There was such a feeling of pathos in the room. She could sense it. The two men, – slightly awkward, the furniture bundled together ready to be despatched to other people, the fading of a very grey day.

Bill seemed to pick up her mood and began to apologise. 'I'm sorry about all this. We disconnected the telephone straightaway. We kept all the other things until there was no chance that Miss Stafford would come back. At the beginning, she thought she was on holiday and she liked to come back here for the day. Ronnie or me used to bring her over and she liked to have a cup of tea here . . . Then, when she got worse – more confused – well, we came here from time to time to pick up more clothes for her . . . But, apart from that, well . . . We kept the gas for a year or so, but it was wasting her money. We kept the electric so that the place wouldn't get damp.'

Ronnie added 'And we've kept the insurance going. We've done our very best.'

She looked at Ronnie. The little boy again trying to do his best. Wanting to be acknowledged. Wanting to come first – just once. Ticks on the pages of his exercise book. 10/10.

'You've both done an excellent job!' she assured them. 'Will the bungalow be up for sale?'

She said it gently – casually – but Bill was tight-lipped.

'You see, Mrs. Roberts, I would have come over in the past year or two to keep the place tidy. But we had trouble with the neighbours.'

'I'm sorry to hear that.' She waited for one of them to explain more but Bill changed the subject.

'You see those boxes – just to the left of where Ronnie's sitting?'

She nodded.

'Well, they're the ones that have got all her stuff from school. Piles of it. She loved that place – Down Manor was her life.'

She smiled generously. There was something touching about the way these two men were so protective and concerned about the deceased woman even though they might have benefited from her estate.

'Yes, it was!' she agreed. 'And all the pupils were as dear to her as if they had been her own.'

She noticed a large, framed, picture on the wall, partially hidden because of the re-arrangement of the furniture. She stood up, moved towards it and screwed up her face as she tried to recognise the faces without her glasses. 'Isn't that you, Ronnie?' she asked, pointing to a lad in the second row.

Ronnie smiled, delighted that he had been identified in the sea of children's faces. 'Yes, that's me.' His voice began to falter, and he looked down.

There was a short silence then Ronnie said, 'I'm sorry. I miss her so much. Do you mind if I go out to tidy the garden up a bit? It's not the best thing for a buyer to see it as it is. And, after all these years of a buoyant market, trust us to have to deal with things now that things have fallen flat. We'd have got the asking price easily last year.'

He stood up and left the room. She saw him outside as he went into the garage to get the tools and begin the work. Buoyant market? Yes, of course. He had worked for an estate agent.

'Ronnie obviously thought the world of Miss Stafford,' she said to Bill.

'We both did.' Bill Price lowered his head as he continued to speak, as if ashamed to face up to his feelings. 'You must think it very strange how we got so involved. But she needed some-one. Her family – such as she had – sent presents at Christmas and on her birthday but do you know something?' he asked, facing her with red eyes. 'I loved that woman. I really loved her. And so did Ronnie.'

Megan stood up and went over to him. 'Don't be ashamed of that.' She put an arm on his shoulder – not for long. Just long enough for him to know that she was sympathetic.

'We want you to have all those boxes, Mrs. Roberts – like I said. They were her real treasure – the jewellery meant nothing to her really – not compared with them. We've put in a couple of other things too. Her address-book. We don't need it anymore. We did our best at the time – we got in touch with her family and asked one of the neighbours who's nice to us to tell the rest. I rang the school. We should have rung you. But you do your best at the time. We were upset. We put it in the Echo, we had to sort the funeral out – her niece insisted on changing the hymns.'

'I know what it's like,' Megan assured him. 'Don't worry. Don't worry.' She put her arm on his shoulder again briefly, reluctant to offer anymore. Yes, she did know what it was like.

'It was as if it was meant to be, me meeting you like that in the park.'

Meant to be? So Bill was one of those people who believed in 'meant to be' too. The quiet people who change the world. Who let the world be changed through them. People who fooled the opinion polls, followed their instincts and intuition. People who knew about the movement of the Holy Spirit and the gifts of knowledge and wisdom. People who just 'knew'. She was one of them but she hadn't expected Bill to be one too.

Although Ronnie was still weeding in the garden, she noticed that he was looking sideways into the bungalow, through the net curtains that would give him just an opaque view. Bill began to weep openly. She was glad that she had gone back to the armchair, but she now felt the need to move. But not towards Bill again. Not with him crying. She went over to the boxes and opened one of them. She felt like crying herself at the neatness and order inside – every item catalogued and filed. Separated into years. The class photo for every year. She lifted one out of the box and looked at it. It was before her time but, attached to each one, was a list of the names of each person. Every member of staff and every child, row by row, from left to right.

'I'm touched that you've asked me to take these. But are you sure that there's no-one else who should have them?'

'There's no-one. The Head couldn't even remember her. Do what you like with them – get rid of them, if you want. But please go through them first. And, if there's anything else you'd like . . .'

'What's the plan?' she asked suddenly, surprised at her directness. 'The relatives are coming tomorrow for the furniture and the jewellery. And then?'

'We'll get a house-clearance done soon. I won't be sorry to see the back of this place, to be honest,' he confessed. 'It's been a nightmare.'

There were so many questions that remained unanswered. She forced herself to ask one of them. 'Tell me Bill – I can call you Bill?'

'Of course. I didn't want to sound too familiar.'

'Tell me, what happened to the nameplate above the door?'

Bill drew up his chair so that he was sitting closer to her.

'I've been coming here for years,' he began. 'First it was just the garden. Miss Stafford didn't want me to do the main gardening. She liked doing that herself – the planting and so on. But she couldn't do the heavy work. The digging. As time went by, she needed more help and not just in the garden. I was happy to do it – and she was always very generous. I used to be a painter and decorator before I fell off a ladder and busted my legs up. Well, I can still do things – but not professional, if you know what I mean?'

She looked at him carefully as he tried to tell the tale. As if sensing that something important was being discussed, Ronnie had come indoors. He had taken his shoes off and slipped into the room. Megan hadn't noticed him at first. Not until he blew his nose with a floral linen handkerchief. He noticed that she was staring at him and explained.

'I got upset earlier on,' he confessed. 'Before I went out into the garden. I didn't have any tissues on me. Miss Stafford had loads of hankies – in little boxes, pinned down. We couldn't think of anyone who'd want them so they were down for the charity shop. I needed them just now. I don't think she'd mind.' He smiled fondly, as if to himself. 'No, she'd have been the first to say – 'Help yourself, Ronnie.'' He used the handkerchief again.

It looked so odd to see Ronnie using the dainty handkerchief. She had an awful feeling that she had sent Cicely a box of handkerchiefs for Christmas once. A box of handkerchiefs – the perfect present for an elderly spinster. Linen, fine, tastefully embroidered, lace-edged. Boxes of six. Maybe she had given the very handkerchief that Ronnie was using. But no, it wasn't her taste. She wouldn't have chosen something so loud. The roses were a vibrant pink and the greenery too strident.

Ronnie went over to sit on one of the boxes again. He

looked fragile somehow in his socks. Grey with blue at
the heels and toes. His feet were a medium size for a
man but he had long big toes that had strained the
cotton.

'I was just telling Mrs. Roberts about the sign,' Bill
said.

'The sign? The 'Green Pastures' sign?'

She noticed a bit of tension between the two men as
they looked at each other. Ronnie was saying a silent –
'How much have you said?'

Megan came to the rescue quickly for her own sake as
much as theirs. 'Your Dad hadn't really begun to
explain,' she said. 'He just said how he began coming
here.'

The anxious exchange between father and son had
resulted in Ronnie taking over. He spoke in little spurts
and it was difficult to discern whether this was coming
from his lack of ability to describe the situation or from
his own emotions – which obviously run deep.

'The neighbours turned on us. It was to do with me
being in prison at first. Everyone knew about it. They
didn't, well, they didn't like it.' He paused. 'She, Miss
Stafford, told me to take no notice. She said that I'd
paid the price. I . . .' Ronnie stopped, overcome with
emotion again. He had filled the handkerchief so he
went into the other room to fetch a second one.

'It wasn't just about Ronnie,' Bill explained. 'There,
there were a few neighbours who used to come in. To
have a chat and so on. But they started to drop off when
she began to get ill. She repeated herself all the time.
She couldn't remember what she'd just said.'

'What happened?' Megan's voice was firm but kind.
'What happened?' She felt a little chilled sitting in the
room with the two men now and just wanted to know

the story about the nameplate.

'That woman, she started out alright.'

'What woman?'

Bill spoke. 'She and Miss Stafford had got on very well. They'd both been teachers. You know, 'teachers' talk."

'What went wrong?'

Ronnie could see that Megan wanted them to finish the story and he did it as clearly as he could in a firmer voice. It was as if he had rehearsed the words several times.

'The neighbour became bossy when Miss Stafford started losing it. She came in – when we were here – and she just told her how to organise things. What to eat, how to pay her bills. It didn't go down very well, and Miss Stafford said she didn't want to see her anymore. One day, we were helping out changing some lightbulbs and so on when she knocked at the door. Frances, Miss Stafford called her.'

Bill pointed to the chair that was backed up onto the wall. 'Miss Stafford sat in her chair and looked – well, frightened. 'Please don't let her in!' she said. I told Ronnie to stay in the bungalow and I went to the door. I was polite. I just said 'Miss Stafford can't see you today.' She blew her top, this Frances. She said I was lying and I just said it again. 'Miss Stafford can't see you today."

He paused, looking across at Ronnie. 'I thought she was going to force her way in.'

'So I went to the door,' added Ronnie. 'I tried to be polite, but she shouted out 'Cicely, your jail-bird friend won't let me in.'

'She started to get really nasty. She was going to hit Ronnie, so I pushed him out of the way, hard.' Bill was sweating. There were shiny streaks on his forehead and, when he lifted his arms to speak, there were dark, damp circles around his armpits. 'We didn't know that Miss Stafford had come to the door by then. She had her stick. She had trouble walking and needed it to get around. Well, before we knew it, there was a fight.'

'A fight?' Megan was still convinced that the men were genuine but the light was fading fast.

'Where I'd pushed Ronnie aside, there was a sort of gap and Miss Stafford came out and started poking this Frances with her stick. Ronnie lifted her up – she was no weight. To protect her. She was having none of it and kept on shouting 'Get out! Get out!' ' Bill wiped the back of his hand across his forehead.

'She wouldn't let go of the stick. She really wanted to aim it at Frances but, because I had her in my arms, she hit the nameplate,' Ronnie added. 'We took it down afterwards. It upset her so much. She wasn't herself by this time, of course. It was the illness – it made her like that sometimes. If she was crossed.'

'We got her back inside. That Frances walked away, crying. We slammed the door. We tried to calm Miss Stafford down. After that, she wouldn't open the door to anyone,' said Bill. 'That's when she gave us her keys.'

Chapter Seven

Megan checked that she had all the ingredients before she made the cake. The free-range eggs were fresh from Driscoll's and came from hens that had not been fed on antibiotics or hormones. She had bought the flour, the organic lemon and the butter from Pulse Wholefoods.

She weighed the dry ingredients, then put them in a bowl and sifted them. There was something comforting about adding the butter. She had been given a food processor once but had given it away. What was the matter with hands? Admittedly, her own were getting stiff, but the manual preparation was good exercise. She watched as the lumps broke down until they just added texture and colour to the mixture. She tapped the eggs on the side until their shells broke and the healthy yellow yolks fell into the bowl with their slimy whites. A quick whisk with a fork to make sure that there was no flour left on the edges or at the bottom and it was ready to be poured into the greased tin loaf.

Everybody seemed to like lemon teabread, and it was fairly easy to bake. There was no point in making a cake just for herself, of course, but there were times when it was the right thing to do.

There was always a strange tension in the sheltered housing complex after a death. For some, there was profound grieving. Friendships tended to become deep in people who shared dependencies. The next-door neighbours were always shocked. The night before, there had been thirty-two residents. With the dawn of a new day, there were just thirty-one. Death had been on the other side of a wall. They had grown accustomed to the coughing, the particular idiosyncrasies, the movements. Taken away in the night. It was more common these days for the person to have been admitted to hospital beforehand so everyone had been prepared – had been given some sort of time to get used to the idea. This death had happened in the complex itself. It was a reminder to everybody of their own frail mortality and this rendered them even more fragile than usual.

Megan decided to offer a slice of cake around to the other residents on her floor. She'd keep a bit for herself, of course, but she would give the rest away. There were several residents whom she just knew by sight. Then there were the diabetics. She counted them – there were five. Disease is so cruel. It hits several times. Firstly, there was the illness itself to bear – the fear of complications. Then there was the deprivation of those little treats that make life so good when taken in moderation. She'd have to leave the diabetics out but she'd make a point of explaining why. They shouldn't be denied the chance to share memories and feelings.

She herself had gone out for a walk in the morning when she heard the news. She'd bought a newspaper, a sympathy card and then went into Brava to have a latte. That was where she had the idea for the cake so she bought the ingredients on the way home.

She picked up the card and hesitated for a moment before writing a message. These messages were so important to the bereaved. Painful at the time but such a comfort later.

'Please accept my deepest sympathy,' she began. 'Molly was a lovely lady and I have wonderful memories of her. Even though I only got to know her in recent years . . .'

Molly had been very popular. A real family woman, she never had a bad word to say about others. A typical old-fashioned Welsh 'Mam'. Her three children were dotted around the country and the daughter who lived in Cardiff had emphysema so was unable to look after her. Molly had regular visits from her huge extended family. There was nothing quite like a large functional family to highlight the disorder in that of others.

Megan realised that it could take her a few hours to give out the pieces of cake. There might well be some relatives in Molly's room and she would offer slices to them first. People might want to talk. She'd leave Harriet and Myf till last. There was no point in offering any to Albert as he was now on a strict diet.

She poured the lemon glaze on the cake and waited for it to cool. There was no point in hurrying things as it would be impossible to slice so she sat down and listened to a CD. Music was such a great pleasure, and the Chopin Nocturne fitted her mood. Maybe subconsciously, she'd chosen it as a way of saying farewell to Molly. 'Goodnight'. Suddenly, a wave of emotion swept over her and she felt the feelings that would have led to tears if she were not on medication.

One or two of the residents invited Megan in and shared their own memories of Molly. Then they moved on to their own fears. 'You never know what's round the corner.' one had said, and another voiced the common saying that 'Thank God we don't know what's ahead of us.' One of the men had talked about his own health problems and a couple of people were out. Either they were out, or they were deaf, watching the television or simply not in the mood to answer the door. She had considered leaving a slice outside those doors, but they might not be picked up until the following day. She explained what she was doing to one of the diabetic women who then proceeded to cry. She'd just been to have her eyes tested and there was some evidence of diabetic-related problems. Megan had ushered her into her flat and tried to reassure her. Yes. A death affected them all.

Harriet took her time in answering the door. 'Oh, hello!' she said in a dull voice.

'I've made a cake and thought you'd like a piece,' Megan explained.

'Oh, thanks. Are you coming in or are you too busy?'

Megan went inside and sat on one of the armchairs. Harriet was clearly annoyed. 'Are you too busy?' She knew Harriet well enough to know that she would soon thaw out.

'How's Sheila?' she asked.

'She's fine.'

Harriet took the piece of cake and placed it on one of her own small plates. 'I'll have it later, if you don't mind.'

'Of course I don't mind.'

After a short, tense silence, Megan asked, 'What's the matter, Harriet?'

'Me? I'm fine!' She stroked her legs, following the weave of her skirt.

'You don't sound fine!'

'Well, if you must know!' Harriet's sulk was over and replaced by anger. 'If you must know, I'm fed-up. I haven't seen you for ages. At least, not to talk to.'

'I'm sorry. I've had quite a lot of things on lately.'

'Not so many things that you can't see Albert!'

So that was the problem. She should have guessed. 'Albert's a good friend – but so are you, Harriet.'

'You're in and out of each other's flats all the time,' Harriet complained. 'It's not that I mind. But, if you ask me, Albert looks a bit peaky these days. I could have sworn that he's lost some weight though his clothes still seem to fit him. If you're not careful, Megan, you'll be propping up some sick old man. I thought you'd had enough of that.'

Megan thought hard about her reply. 'We all get off-days at our age,' she said. 'I've known Albert for a long time. Not well but . . .'

'Well, you're making up for it now.'

'I know what I'm doing, Harriet.' Then, softly, 'Why don't we go out for a meal? Just the two of us. We'll have a glass of wine with it and celebrate. Celebrate friendship.'

'It's just that it's so hard sometimes.' Harriet was back to normal.

'Sheila?'

'She's decided to split up after all. The rows were getting so bad. The children have been very upset. I'm sorry that I go on and on about it but I've got no-one else. Not for a really helpful chat. There's Myf, of course, and she's very sweet, but her deafness doesn't make it easy. And what does she know about it all?' She paused. 'I feel so inadequate! You never share your problems with me. Perhaps you haven't got any?'

'Of course I have! Listen, we're just different personalities. When I heard about Molly this morning, I went out for a walk. It was my way of dealing with it – and making the cake. When I was waiting for it to cool, I listened to some Chopin and it was only then that I felt something. It hit me then. Writing the sympathy card helped me too. In a way, you're more fortunate. You let things out. It's healthier.'

Harriet moved over to sit on the arm of the chair beside Megan and she burst into tears.

Megan was too tired to take the slice of cake in to

Myf. It would have to wait until the evening – or even the following day. Once she was inside her own flat, she placed the rest of the cake in a tin and then reached for a rug that she kept in a cupboard. She put it on the floor of the living-room and lay on it. On her back. Experience had taught her that, if she used her own bed or the settee for meditation, she was inclined to fall asleep.

A familiar text came to her and it seemed right for her that day. *'Come to Me, all you who are weary and heavy-laden and I will give you rest for your souls. Learn from Me for I am gentle and humble of heart.'* She mouthed the words and repeated them from time to time when distractions came.

It had been a busy day. First there was the upset with Molly. Then she had gone for a walk. She'd baked the cake and spent more than two hours going round to share it. She hadn't expected Harriet to be so wound up. She hadn't realised how dependent Harriet had 'd become on her. Hopefully the meal at Cibo's would soothe her wounds.

'Come to Me all you who labour and are heavy-laden and I will give you rest for your souls. Learn from Me for I am gentle and humble of heart.'

For a few moments, she lost herself in the words and went to a state beyond them.

The business with Bill and Ronnie Price was odd. She had the boxes from Cicely to sort out and . . .

'Come to Me all you who are weary and heavy-laden and . . .' The peace that came from those words. Handing everything over to a higher Power.

Alice had tried to phone her while she was out. She'd wait until she had time for a good chat before.

'Come to Me . . .'

She couldn't get Albert out of her mind. How was he today?

'*Come to Me* . . .' She handed him over too.

She should have soaked the cake tin.

'*Come to Me* . . .'

She hadn't forgotten Myf. When would they have Molly's funeral? She'd like to go. Perhaps she and Myf could go together . . . She'd have to invite Harriet, of course . . .

Someone knocked on her door and she knew that it was Albert.

She used her hands to lift herself up from the floor and then squatted on all fours before she was able to stand. She opened the door and showed him in.

'Come in, Albert!' She laughed when he looked at the rug. 'Meditation!' she said before kissing him. 'How are you today? I was just thinking of you.'

He sunk into the armchair. He was tired. 'Started well, I felt quite positive,' he said, then, simply, 'To be honest, I think that Molly's death has affected me. I'll be the next one to go.'

'None of us knows what lies ahead.' She heard the triteness of her words but there was nothing else that she could say.

'If I weren't ill, you'd be a friend at a distance, wouldn't you?'

'Oh, let's not go over that again.'

'Do you know something?' he said softly. 'It's almost worth being ill – yes, even with this cancer, just to have the pleasure of being with you. I've never been so happy in my life.'

She stood behind him, caressing his shoulders, feeling the blades, massaging her fist down his back. 'Oh, Albert – please don't say that. Were you never happy with Doreen?'

'Not really.'

They both looked at the rug on the floor at the same time. 'We're a bit too old for the floor!' she said and, making sure that he understood, she added, 'I had quite a job getting up to answer the door.'

The bed offered them more comfort. She had kept the double-bed because she thought it would be more useful in the long-term. Extra space for the time when the arthritis became very bad. It was the bed that she had shared with Hugo for so many years. At the end, they had had separate beds. She'd given his 'sick' bed to Track 2000.

At first, she felt a sense of betrayal to Hugo but she overcame it. There was something beautifully delicate and innocent about the two of them lying there – her with her stiffening joints and him wasting away from the disease that had taken Hugo. Was it total madness to deepen a relationship that was doomed to be short? What were they seeking from each other? He'd spoken about her tenderness. And her? He was not strong enough – and she wasn't agile enough – for youthful passion. She, too, had found tenderness as well as . . . companionship. He waited for her to take the initiative and she opened the buttons of his shirt and loosened her blouse. He placed his hands on her breasts then rested his head there. She stroked his hair that smelt of sandalwood. Or cedarwood. Or both. There was something about Albert that she – that she loved. Yes, loved. Deeply. More so because she knew that it wouldn't last.

She ignored the telephone call.

Much later, when Megan had a piece of the cake herself, she was pleased with it. It was always worth being generous with the lemon glaze.

The following morning, she went over to see Myf. She cut her an enormous piece. She had a sweet tooth and no-one to spoil her.

'Hullo, Megan. Will you come in?' Myf was always hospitable.

'I've brought you some cake that I made yesterday.'

'How kind! Please come in.'

Myf showed her into her lounge and directed Megan to a comfortable chair. The furniture was rather dull and old-fashioned but it suited its owner.

'Can I get you a cup of tea?'

'No, really! Thank you for the offer but I've just had breakfast.'

Myf sat directly opposite her friend and Megan guessed the reason. She was already learning how to lip-read. Her voice was totally normal because the deafness was of recent onset. Age-related. What a horrible expression that was. Age-related. Deafness and failing sight. Reduced mobility. Most of the teeth capped and crowned if gum disease hadn't ruined them all. Weak bladder control. Pelvic floor muscles. Sans everything. But not quite. Not yet.

She spoke slowly and clearly, enunciating with care.

'How are you, Myf? I've been so busy recently. Didn't you say you were going to see about a new hearing-aid?'

'Yes, I've got it! I'm getting used to it.' She smiled, grateful that Megan had remembered, then, after a pause – 'Shame about Molly!'

'Yes. I'm hoping to go to the funeral. If I can go, maybe we could go together. It'll probably be in Gwaelod-y-Garth. I could give a lift to three people so that we make the best use of my car.'

'Yes, that would be lovely.' She paused, anxious to

convey the right message. 'I don't mean that it's lovely in one way because I'm very sorry that Molly's gone. What I meant was that it would be lovely to have a lift. And some company.'

'Of course.'

Megan could sense Myf's isolation. There were no photographs on the walls, no evidence of other people being part of her life. The letters in the rack all looked official – bills and so on. There was a single hook in the hallway where her coat hung. She seldom had visitors.

'Perhaps I'll change my mind about the cup of tea,' Megan said. 'And what about you? Have you eaten?'

'I'll have a cup of tea with you', she said. 'Would you mind if I eat some toast and jam?'

'Of course not.'

Myf went into the kitchen with the awkwardness of someone who is not used to being watched.

Looking around the room more carefully, Megan did find a photograph. It was small and stood on a little desk. Black and white. Beige frame that didn't really suit it. Probably her parents. Myf never talked about a family. All the wooden furniture was well-polished and nothing was out-of-place. The duty to order probably came from her career in the Civil Service.

Myf came in with a tray on which she'd placed two cups and saucers and two rounds of toast with jam on the side of a small plate. She handed Megan her drink and sat down. 'Excuse me eating in front of you', she apologised.

'Not at all. You just eat your breakfast. Don't worry about me. May I have a look at your photo?' Megan was curious but Myf would be able to eat in peace if she thought she would be stared at.

'Carry on. It's my parents.'

Megan walked over to the desk and lifted the picture up so that she could see it better. Her mother looked rather severe but it wasn't usual to smile in those days. Her father seemed a bit softer even though he too had refused to say 'cheese' to the camera. She reckoned that Myf must be approaching eighty – seventy-five, seventy-six. Something like that. Born in the early thirties. It was then that she noticed a small figure, half-hidden, standing between the two adults. Myf. Myf as a toddler. Strange to believe that she had ever been small and vulnerable and dependent like that. Or maybe it wasn't. Her deafness was making her fragile again.

Megan made an appreciative gesture, replaced the photo and returned to her seat. Myf's toast had been eaten.

'That's you as a child in the photo?'

'Yes.'

'Did you have brothers and sisters, Myf?'

'No, there was just me. Mother had problems having me so . . .'

Megan broke in to avoid her having to explain. 'I thought Harriet could come with us to the funeral. Who else should we invite?'

'I ought to let you know that Harriet and I have had a difference of opinion,' Myf said. 'I think that it's over. Our friendship. I put a letter through her box to settle things but she hasn't replied yet.'

Megan guessed what the problem was and tried to make the situation easier for Myf who knew that she and Harriet were friends. 'It's not easy being deaf, is it?' she volunteered.

'Exactly. I'm trying very hard but Harriet talks so quickly and I think, I think that she dismisses me. She doesn't think that I have any experience of life. I know that her daughter's having a hard time. I try to be sympathetic.'

'We all have different personalities,' Megan said. 'Harriet and I are good friends but, in many ways, we're like chalk and cheese. You're very dependable. Responsible, trustworthy. Those qualities are worth their weight in gold.'

Myf was touched by this and smiled. 'I haven't always been so,' she confessed.

Megan sipped her tea.

'I suppose what upsets me about Harriet is her belief that I've never lived.

Megan took another sip of her tea.

'I left school when I was sixteen. Mother needed help at home and I worked part-time to bring in some extra money.'

'You didn't go straight into the Civil Service then?'

'Not quite. Can I tell you something in confidence?'

'Of course you can.' Megan looked at the earnest face before her and relaxed back in her chair.

'I had a boy-friend. I didn't dare tell Mother and Father. They thought I was too young for that sort of thing. We met up after work. Half an hour here. Half an hour there. Then he got called up for Military Service. He was so upset about it. He wasn't the sort of person to deal with it well. We had an affair – just in the short time he had before leaving. I felt sorry for him. Then he went away.'

'That must have been very hard.'

'Well, it was in a way. But, when I was separated from him, I realised that I shouldn't have let things go so far. I didn't really love him. Not enough to share my life with him. I felt very ashamed of what I had done. And then I knew that I was expecting. The usual thing.

The usual way of knowing.'

Megan nodded so that she didn't have to explain further.

'I was terrified of telling my parents. They would be shocked – I knew that. Then I recalled someone else in the family. She'd had a baby. She and her mother went away for a few weeks and they came back after the baby was born. Her own mother said that she was the baby's mother. I thought that, when they'd got over the shock – my parents – they might be able to do the same thing. Mother would have liked a bigger family but didn't want to risk her health. If it was a boy, I could have given them the son that Father had always wanted . . .'

Poor Myf. She stopped for a moment to blow her nose. She had started crying.

'I'm sorry. I shouldn't be burdening you with all this.'

'I'm privileged that you've chosen to tell me.'

'I kept on putting the day off to tell them. Not today, I thought. Father's had a busy day. Not today. Mother's got the family coming over tomorrow and is busy making food. Not today, not today.'

'What happened then?' Megan asked gently, in little more than a whisper.

'I went to the toilet one day. I had stomach pains. Cramps. And then it happened.'

'You had a miscarriage?'

'I don't know.' Myf 's voice was shaking. 'I don't know whether it was the baby coming away from me. Or maybe it was just me coming on late. I bled a lot.'

'And you told no-one?'

'No. There was nothing to tell. I thought that it was meant to be – that I kept on putting the day off to tell my parents. They were saved from the shame of it.' Then, in a firmer voice, she added. 'Once things had settled down, I decided that I would never get involved again with a man. I went to night-classes, studied . . .'

'What happened to him – the father of the baby?'

'I don't know that there was a baby,' Myf protested defensively. The pain of the experience – of not knowing – was still hurting. 'Not definitely. I wish I'd known. One way or another.' Distaste coloured her words. 'Him? Oh, he came back home. Went out with someone else. I was never able to face him again.' She hesitated. 'Has this shocked you?'

'Oh, Myf, of course it hasn't! It's made me feel closer to you.'

'You won't tell anyone?'

'I promise.'

'Would you mind if I eat the cake later on? I know that it's bad for my digestion but there's a programme on the television tonight I want to watch. I love watching something special with a cup of tea and biscuits usually. I'll feel really pampered if I have a slice of your cake with it.'

A slice of cake. Pampered? Poor Myf had never known what it's like to be pampered. But she shouldn't make assumptions. People were full of surprises. And Harriet's tendency to be dismissive had been the source of this confession. It was unlikely that Myf had known tenderness. There was that soft air about her father, and, in that photograph, the child was leaning more towards her father than her mother. Maybe she had been cherished. For a few years. She suspected that she and Myf were going to watch the same programme later on and she almost suggested that they watch it together. But she had offered a lift to Molly's funeral. She had listened. She had given a generous portion of cake that would last for a couple of days. There were times when she had to think of her own needs and respect them. Life was a constant battle of trying to get the balance right. Too much giving-out without nurturing herself had led to unbearable stress in the past. She would need the evening for herself.

Megan had so many people to catch up with. She could send a card or a letter to some of them but others needed a phone call.

The best time to get Alice was after 8.30 in the evening. She was usually out or busy during the day and she often helped out in the hotel for an hour or two after Bella had gone to bed. She made sure that she had at least half an hour of free time herself. There was nothing worse than ringing someone and then saying that you were on the point of doing something else. Relationships, friendships – needed time to flourish and be maintained.

'Hullo! Alice? '

'Megan! Lovely to hear your voice!' Alice came over as she always did – charming, delightful – an idealist oozing enthusiasm.

'How are you?'

'I'm fine. How are you?' Again, there was sincerity in her voice. She wanted to hear the answer.

'I'm fine. Yes, fine!' Thank you again for my presents.'

'Did you have them already? I thought you might have the Evelyn Underhill, but it was such a lovely edition. Right beside it in the charity shop was the book on the Desert Fathers. Somebody very spiritual must have had a sort-out. I couldn't leave it in the shop. And a friend of mine, well, her aunt died and she had her place to clear. The book on the Uffizzi was a gem. And the reproductions are large. Excellent quality. Well, you can see that for yourself . . .'

Megan smiled. It was all – well, very Alice! 'I have got the Evelyn Underhill book but . . .'

'But you're going to keep the new one and take the old one to the charity shop?'

Dear Alice. How she loved her! Then, keeping the same up-beat tone and trying not to betray any feelings of anxiety, she added, 'How's Bella?'

'Bella's wonderful. Today, she painted the most beautiful picture. Megan, I'll ask her to do one for you tomorrow? Would you like that?'

'Of course I would. I love her pictures.'

'When are you coming up to see us?'

'I'm not sure when exactly. When's a good time for you?'

'Did I tell you that I sold one of my paintings this week? Oh, of course I haven't. I got £250 for it. I was so excited.'

The two women had a good relationship and chatted away. Alice respected Megan and Alice made Megan laugh. She was a free-spirit and had a butterfly mind. She hadn't replied to her question about a suitable time to visit.

When they were on the phone, it had been easy to forget that she and Tom were no longer together. Alice made her forget the pain until she had to mention Tom.

'Tom's got a lap-top for me and wants me to come up and fetch it. There's no rush, of course. I don't think I'm going to be a computer genius.'

'Tom had Bella on Saturday. He looked well. He took her to the park. I think they both enjoyed themselves.'

When she had replaced the receiver, Megan went over to her address book. Alice had changed her mobile number – but not for security reasons.

Tom and Alice Roberts. How proud she had been to

write that down. And how delighted she and Hugo had been to see their happiness. There was a little omission mark in the entry where she had added the name Bella. Tom and Alice and Bella Roberts. Their first married home had been a flat. Prices were so high in London. That address had now been crossed out. She had squeezed Tom's new address onto one side and made a separate entry for Alice, who kept her married name though she used her maiden name – as she always had done – for her art. Poor Bella. Split in two. Still down with her father. There they were – Tom and Bella Roberts. And there she was again – down with Alice.

Alice had gone back to live with her parents in the hotel they owned on the outskirts of Hampstead. They had inherited it and, as a result, were very well-off. They had worked hard, the hotel was efficient, clean and small enough to have a family feel about it.

Money does strange things to people. For Alice and her family, it hadn't made them proud or arrogant or selfish. But, for Alice, it had bought her the freedom to be herself without the necessity of worrying about practicalities. It was good if her painting had been sold but £250 didn't go a long way. Alice had no bills to pay – her contribution was to help out in the hotel. She probably didn't have the skills or the knowledge to take over the hotel when her parents retired, and her brother had shown no interest in the place. Alice didn't worry about such things.

The future would sort itself out because she had never had to face the hard graft of consistency and perseverance that is needed to get by independently. That was what money had done for her, but it had also enabled her to be the delightful woman she was.

It had all seemed ideal at first. Tom was the one with the good job and ambition. Alice was beautiful and funny – a creative wife who enjoyed making unusual food for their guests. No-one had a bad word to say about her. Things had probably become difficult before Bella was born. But they had kept it to themselves. It was the baby who had exaggerated their differences. Although they both adored her, Tom was irritated by Alice's relaxed ways. She had taken a taxi once with the little one on her lap without a car seat. There had been a terrible row.

Then, Alice's aunt, who was Bella's godmother, wondered if there might be a problem. It was then that their different attitudes caused the deep and resentful rifts that eventually led to their separation. Alice had refused to see any difficulties and said that every child was an individual. Tom had read book after book on child development and got hold of self-help groups from the Internet.

Alice had been very supportive when Hugo was ill. They didn't want to break the news of their separation until after Hugo's death.

When Megan had moved from the house to the flat, she had had to get rid of a lot of things. Amongst them were the wedding photographs. She just kept one. The reminder of their happiness on that day was too painful to see. She had a lot of pictures of Tom. And Tom with Bella. Plenty of Alice on her own. And Alice with Bella.

She realised that, although she and Alice had talked in depth about her birthday gifts – she knew Megan's tastes well – they still hadn't discussed her visit.

It was too late to make another phone call so she wrote two short letters on the note-paper she had made from recycled cards. She put them in their envelopes and found the first-class stamps in her purse. Propped up in the hallway, they could be posted when she went out in the morning.

She read the additions she had made to her list during the night.

Phone Sam
Honey

She found it so much easier to sleep if she had written a list of the things to be done on the following day. If she remembered something new during the night, she was usually able to get back to sleep if she added it.

Phone Tom (sort London)
Something for Molly's do
Rice
Cheese
Begin clearing the clutter in spare bedroom
Check Albert (MacMillan nurse 10.30)
Olive oil
Veg for soup – celeriac/butternut squash?
Ring Sam
Honey

Taking another piece of the torn paper she collected from the back of junk mail, she reorganised the list. Rain had been forecast for late afternoon, so it made sense to do the shopping in the morning. She had wanted to get most of the food in the local organic shop but she needed to get something for Molly's tea from Marks and Spencer's – which meant a trip into town. If she bought the stuff from Pulse first, then she'd have to carry it into town, and she didn't like the idea of the cheese being out of the fridge for that long. If she went to M&S first, there was the same problem. What she wanted there were frozen items – vol-au-vents, mini-pizzas – things like that. If she picked them up first, she would have the same problem with the other shopping.

It made sense to get all the items from Marks and Spencer's and then take the bus home straightaway afterwards. She didn't like supporting supermarkets but, along with Waitrose, M&S was fairly ethical. Once she had made the decision, she felt much better and wrote down the items. It was a shame not to get the honey that had been made just a few streets away but she had to compromise.

She wrote the other items down in order of priority. Albert was the first. He was going to see his Macmillan nurse. It might be stressful for him, and she wanted to check that everything had gone well. He'd probably be back for lunch and he tended to have a rest afterwards. Two o'clock seemed a good time to aim for. But then she remembered that he often went to bed and rested a bit longer these days. She wouldn't want to disturb him. Three o'clock would be better. She decided to write him a note and slip it under his door. She'd suggest coming over at three and ask him to slip a note under her door if it wasn't convenient. They saw each other most days now – even if it was only for a few minutes. She had wondered about giving him a spare key to her own flat. Maybe he'd then get one made up for her. It might be necessary. She added 'spare key' to her shopping list. She knew a man who cut keys in the market, and he always did a good job. She'd never had to return a key that was faulty.

If she was going to leave Albert's visit until three in the afternoon, she'd have time to fit other things in beforehand. There was no point in trying Tom until the evening. Perhaps she should try Sam? She and her brother weren't close. But relationships had to be worked at. She decided to send a letter instead with an invitation to come over to the flat and have tea with her one day. He came into Cardiff from time to time. Sam had been very kind when Hugo was ill.

Hugo. He had resisted the Macmillan nurse. Couldn't see the point of speaking to someone who'd tell him what he knew already. And he might know the woman. He'd said that he'd find that embarrassing. She had tried to point out that it was good to have someone who cared. Someone who was a bit detached from the situation emotionally. She'd said that many of his patients knew him. That hadn't got in the way of things. And then he'd said that she didn't understand, and he'd gone into his shell. She'd had to go for counselling herself. Hugo wouldn't talk to her. He didn't want to worry her. But couldn't he see that she was worried anyway? He'd been definite about the treatment he had. There was nothing to discuss. There are some things that you can't protect your partner from. In the end, he had had to accept help and, somehow, in those last few weeks, they had become closer than they had ever been.

She looked at the list again. Clearing of the clutter. She had quite a collection of unwanted gifts that she intended taking to charity shops. Then there was all of Cicely's stuff. She had brought away the Down Manor boxes along with her address-book and a stack of diaries. Bill Price said that he didn't want to pry into something so private. But what was *she* meant to do with them? She'd also brought home the framed photograph of a Down Manor class that had hung on the wall. It was the one that she had seen that day and Ronnie thought that she might like it. He, himself, had already taken all the other photos in which he featured. She'd keep the photograph but not in its frame. When she'd left her large house, this photograph had been one of the many that she had recycled. Because of Ronnie, she'd keep this one. She thought the frame might suit the Berthe Morisot print.

Maybe, after the shopping, she'd be too tired to begin the clearing before seeing Albert but, nevertheless, she wrote 'Clearing up?' above 'Albert.'

Molly had a wonderful send-off. The bilingual service was inspiring and the chapel had been full. The Minister had known Molly well and spoke about her with great affection. One of the grandchildren had read *Y Border Bach* by Waldo Williams and anyone who understood the Welsh was moved to tears.

She drove Myf, Harriet and Sally back to the sheltered housing complex. The family had decided to have the tea in Molly's flat. Megan had put in her contribution earlier and, predictably, when they went in, there was food everywhere. An old-fashioned Welsh welcome. 'Better to have too much than too little'. 'They'll want to eat afterwards'. There were stacks of sandwiches, but people tended to go for the sweet and savoury snacks, and she was pleased to see her mini pizzas on a couple of paper plates.

She went up to the daughter she knew best and kissed her. 'Lovely service!'

'Yes, it was, wasn't it?' She had been composed but the words of comfort brought the tears back. She controlled them and added – 'Please have a cup of tea –

or coffee. And thank you so much for the food. We've overdone it a bit but it's better to have too much than too little. I wonder if, afterwards, you'd mind taking what's left and sharing it with the other residents? Mam was so happy here. Sion?' She was calling her son. 'Get this lady a cup of tea – or did you say coffee?'

She went over to the work-surface in the kitchen where Sion was doing a valiant job. 'Tea?' he asked. 'Or coffee?'

'Don't worry about me,' she said. 'I'm not very thirsty now. Maybe later on.'

She circulated a bit, speaking to the family, friends and other residents. She hadn't realised that Molly's niece taught at St. Anne's. She was younger than Megan, but they had crossed paths for a few years before she took early retirement. They were busy exchanging contacts and memories then they parted company. She'd read the body language. The side-ward look, the furrowed forehead, the concentration going. Hardly discernable. But there. It was time to let them be on their own.

'We must catch up some time,' she said. 'I must let you go. You know where to find me.' There were lots of kisses, hugs, tears and laughter.

There was something wonderful about a large extended family that is happy. They were all ages. Different personalities. They undoubtedly had their arguments. But they were as one. United. Whole. It was hard to put her finger on it. But it was enviable, yes, even in bereavement. It left a searing, yearning hole in the heart of others. The onlookers. Comparisons were compulsive. And destructive.

She saw Harriet talking away. She was happy enough now – glad of the company – but, later, it would hit her. She'd come out with the wretched comparisons. Had she done something wrong? Why had Molly got it so right? Myf was talking to one of the residents. She didn't have the confidence to go up to the family although she had shaken hands with the daughter. Megan had seen it and was pleased. Albert had come in to pay his respects to the family – he had refused her offer to take him to the funeral – and their eyes met briefly. Albert. What was going through his mind? He still hadn't told his sons. Albert – who'd never been happy with his wife but just put on a good face. He had his own comparisons too – if he could bear to face them.

The crowd was thinning out as she took her leave. The family had business to attend do. They were going to make a start on sorting out Molly's affairs.

Chapter Eight

"What, you mean she's left the house to them?"

'So it seems. The son's the executor of the Will. The relatives were coming to pick up some of the furniture and the jewellery. *Finito.*'

'Why didn't they move in there themselves? From what you say, it sounds a lovely bungalow. I went into one of them years back now. Someone from St. Anne's. Her car was in the garage and she needed a lift home. That was Sycamore something . . .'

'The reason they didn't move in was that they fell out with the neighbours – and one in particular.'

Megan was aware of a slight hush in the café around the table where she and Annie were talking. They drew their heads closer together so that they could whisper. She continued with the story of the nameplate.

Annie began to laugh and she made Megan laugh too. Annie's humour was such a gift. This was no ugly nod-wink-nudge-know-what-I-mean, sort of laugh. Neither did it have the brittleness of the cynic. Or the tainted edge that comes with cruel humour. Annie's laughter didn't hurt anyone. And it was very attractive. People envied it – and they were watching.

'You lead such an interesting life! I don't know! I'm the one who goes out looking for a bit of excitement and you're the one . . . No-one would believe it. If it were in a 'soap', no-one would believe it. Storyline too far-fetched!'

Megan smiled fondly at her friend. She paused for a moment then added cautiously, quietly. 'There's a new man in my life, Annie.'

'A new man? This gets better and better!' Annie had been searching for years and, for a moment, Megan saw a reluctant half-smile of envy. Then, kindly, she let go of it and added 'I'm so pleased for you. Tell me all about him!'

'He's someone I've known for years. More of an acquaintance until recently. He lives in one of the flats.'

'That's very convenient. Wish I had your luck.'

Megan said slowly 'There's a complication.'

'He's married?' She drew her head closer to Megan again.

'No. He has cancer. Metastases. Secondaries. Nothing they can do.'

Annie's face puckered in disbelief. 'Did you know about this when you started?'

'In a way, it's because of it.'

'*Because* of it?'

Megan tried to explain but the words didn't come out easily. She began to stutter.

Annie cradled her hands round Megan's. She was concerned. 'But why put yourself through the pain?' she asked. 'You've been through it all with Hugo. You're only just beginning to pick up the pieces. Why put yourself through it again?'

Megan twirled her wedding-ring round with the thumb and index finger of her right hand. 'Because I love him.'

'Surely he's in no state for . . ?'

'It's not like that. It's the company. But *more*. Gentleness. Tenderness. The body begins to break down. Little intimacies.'

'Megan, you can't . . .' Annie stopped short. 'Sorry. I don't mean to be telling you what to do. You – of all people. But I'm worried about you. It doesn't make sense. Why can't you keep him at a bit of a distance? Where's his family? Does he have a family?'

Megan could feel nothing but gratitude for Annie's concern. She had asked herself the same questions. But she couldn't go back. Not now. She couldn't explain why. *'Le cœur a ses raisons que la raison ne connaît point.'* she said firmly but softly. 'Pascal. 'The heart has its reasons that reason knows nothing about.'

Chapter Nine

She sat on a low chair in the spare bedroom and sighed at the clutter before her. She had taken a quick glance at the contents of the boxes and worked out the best way of dealing with them. First, there were the diaries. These took up a lot of space as Cicely had written them over several decades. There were over thirty of them though they were not big. Diaries were so personal that it seemed an intrusion to look at them at all. She needed to establish whether or not they had any historical value. Or any value to the family she *did* have. In order to do this, she would need to start at the beginning and dip into them over the years. The first one was dated 1970. What had happened in 1970 to make her start them then? Had she written earlier ones and destroyed them? Ones that dealt with romance?

The 1970 diary was a smallish desk-diary in green. It looked strangely old-fashioned – not because of its age or the slightly faded cover. Imperial measurements, stronger margins in red, firm hard-backed cover. It didn't take her long to realise that the diaries were trivial. Cicely had passed New Year's Day alone – though her niece, Jenny, had visited her on the 2nd. Jenny had been the one who was closest to her aunt. Appropriate then that she featured on the very first page. It had been a pleasant afternoon – the 2nd of January. They had talked about old times – Jenny's mother had been Cicely's sister. Jenny lived in Exeter – she had studied at the University and never left. They had eaten together in Cicely's house and shared a glass of champagne to welcome in the New Year. The only other entry for that day had been – 'Cold day, biting wind.' She had flicked the pages over to mid-January when school had started. Again, there was nothing of any significance to other people. She noted what happened in school. Made comments about the staff and pupils. 'Twelve pupils away today with 'flu. Hope none of the staff go down with it' – then, two days later – 'Helen Shuring's gone down with the 'flu. Short-staffed. Top Infants.'

She heaved some of the diaries out and sorted through the others in the box until she found the most recent. There was a neat, thinner, diary for 2003 but she had only written on a few pages. In a slightly unsteady hand. 'Bill came today' and 'Ronnie dug the garden for me.' Out of curiosity, she found the 2002 diary. This had been filled in on most days but, again, the contents showed nothing out of the ordinary. Bill and Ronnie were mentioned frequently. On July 23rd, she had put – 'Don't know what I'd do without Bill and Ronnie. Poor Ronnie! I believe in him.'

At least these entries proved that the two men really had been genuinely helpful. That put her mind at rest. Should she send the diaries to Jenny? Or offer them to her? But, to do that, she felt that she'd need to go right through them to check that there had been no unfavourable comments. With the tension in the family, it was probably better to leave well alone.

When does conscientiousness become curiosity? And when does curiosity become voyeurism? She sent up a little arrow prayer. Like a missile. For discernment.

She had taught at Down Manor for nine years and finished before Susan was born. Most of this time was uncovered by these diaries. But she found herself turning to the end of the year 1970. And she felt a slight chill going through her entire body. This was where their lives had met so closely when she was unwell. She found it compulsive reading. Yes, she remembered the time when they had had a burst pipe and lost a lot of the children's work. She recalled the young woman who had come straight out of college. She'd had a disastrous romantic relationship during her first term – wouldn't listen to anybody and left without notice. No-one ever saw or heard from her again. And the children's names. They came back. The clever ones, the difficult ones, the ones with demanding parents. And the ordinary ones. Cicely had been very good with the children who didn't excel. She had been a great encourager. Children like Ronnie Price. There would be many adults around who owed a lot to Miss Stafford.

She saw the first entry in which she, herself, was mentioned. 'Megan's struggling on with a bad cold.' It wasn't a very impressive start. Later in the term – 'Went over to have dinner with Megan and her husband, Hugo, after school. What a charming man! We had a chicken korma (Megan checked that I liked it beforehand.) Such a lovely couple! I'm so lucky to have her – she's one of my best teachers.'

There were a few more comments and it touched her to see the older woman's confidence in her. And she needed that assurance before daring to turn to the November.

The concerns had begun. 'Megan seems 'not herself' today. Perhaps it's just a bad day.' then 'I'm getting very concerned about Megan. Her work's not up to its usual standard. Should I say something? The children are playing her up. This can't go on.'

Megan remembered it to the very day. The day when she felt she had lost control. But she was taken aback by the next reference the following week. 'I've tried to talk to Megan but she says there's nothing wrong. I had to make the decision.' The decision? Megan wasn't aware of any decision having been made. On the following day – 'I kept my appointment to see Dr. Hugo Roberts just after lunch. I told him exactly what I thought. I explained how much I appreciate Megan. I don't want to lose her. He told me in confidence that Megan has been depressed for some time. I asked him what I could do about it. I have the children to think about. He told me that I don't need to do anything. She'd just found out that she's expecting a baby.'

Megan felt her face flushed and hot. A secret between Cicely and Hugo! One that he'd never shared with her. The diary continued to reveal the plan. Hugo said that she had been depressed before she knew about the pregnancy. He told her that it had happened before. Cicely had said that she couldn't take the responsibility of having her in the classroom. The children were running riot.

She remembered it well – but as isolated images without sequence. She had gone home one day after school and burst into tears. Violent, desperate tears. She knew that she was doing a bad job. Hugo had told her not to take any medication because of the pregnancy – for which she had no enthusiasm. She had even mentioned having a termination. She worried that her mood would have a bad influence on the baby. And, somewhere in the middle of the muddle, Hugo had said to her 'It's all very well for you to have the check-ups at the clinic, but I want to take a look at you myself.' And she had gone along with it! He said that her blood pressure was sky-high, and she should give in her notice straightaway. She was at risk of developing pre-eclampsia. She'd cried and said that she couldn't let

Cicely down and he'd said that he would deal with it. Normally, she'd have been more . . . well, more assertive, alert. But she'd been in such a dark place that all she felt was relief.

'Thank God that Hugo's sorted things out' read the diary. 'I shall miss Megan so much. I'll keep in touch and no-one will ever know. How awful mental illness is. I hope that it won't affect the baby.'

She could hardly believe that she'd never guessed. Had any of her other readings at the clinic been high? She couldn't really remember. For a moment, she felt resentment. Then she realised that they'd done the right thing. What else could they have done? They had saved her from humiliation. Cicely had given her a good reference when she went on to St. Anne's. Tom had started school and Hugo had said 'Get a reference from Cicely Stafford. She'll be only too happy to help out.' And so she had been. A glowing testimonial. Their kindness suddenly overwhelmed her. They had really, really cared. And she'd not been able to say thank-you. Face-to-face.

It was in the genes, of course. The depression. She didn't need Hugo to tell her that. Her poor mother! In that beautiful, brutal, Valleys town with the tall-spired church. It stood like the body of a spider – villages like legs straddling the hills. Gossip soon spread. Everybody knew that Mary Probert had taken to her bed. 'Think of her husband coming home from work. And no tea ready. As for the children! Well, the three of them seemed to be bringing themselves up. Those wagging tongues didn't understand the illness. Put it down to laziness. But if she were lazy, why was she so willing to do anything for everybody the rest of the time?

The children! Megan, James and Sam. Sam had

always been a bit of a loner. Didn't have mood swings –
as far as anyone knew – but he kept to himself. James?
Dear James. Even now, she could hardly bear to think
of James . . . She'd made a point of going home often
after James . . . Made sure that the neighbours knew.
She had nothing to boast of – only small people boast.
But it was important for her mother – and her father –
to say that Megan was doing well. College. Teaching.
Then going out with a doctor. Mary Probert must have
done something right by the children. Yes, it was in the
genes.

She prayed for the gift of discernment. And suddenly,
it came to her. There was only one thing to do with
these diaries. If Cicely had meant them to be kept and
used, she'd have written them in more detail. With
literary correctness. No, these were the jottings of a
lonely woman. At the end of the day, she had no-one to
talk to about its simple, everyday events. 'Had a rough
day today. Children been noisy' 'They couldn't go out to
play because of the rain.' 'I'm dreading the HMI's visit
next week.' These diaries had been her friend, her
spouse. Cicely had no more need of them. Neither did
she.

Megan took the recycling bags out from under the
sink in the kitchen. Systematically, manually, she
shredded them to pieces. And her mood swung as she
did it. She felt betrayed. She had been manipulated.
How dare they? And yet it was the kindest thing. But
she had been left out of it. The pregnancy had been so
hard. She had felt nothing when Susan was born. Just
the relief that she could take some medication at last.
She'd had a short course of ECT – and nobody knew.
She'd tried, ever since, to compensate – to forge a close
bond between herself and Susan. It had worked well

enough. She stopped shredding for a moment, lost in a sadness that she couldn't identify. And then she laughed without knowing why.

Thirty-three diaries filled several bags. She knotted them at the top. Tying them up was like a symbol of . . . a symbol of a conclusion. Silently, she murmured the words – 'Thank you Cicely. Thank you for everything. God bless you.'

Chapter Ten

Megan finished her tea and sat down. There was another half an hour or so to go before she'd call for Albert. The service in Ebenezer began at 6 p.m. The original plan the previous week had been to go to St. Michael's in the morning and follow it with a pub lunch. Then, after a rest in the afternoon, they had agreed to go to Ebenezer in the evening. They had gone to St. Michael's in the morning as planned, but, then, Albert felt sick in the middle of the lunch so he went back home to bed. He was still tired in the evening when Megan called in to see him so she had just kept him company.

As she sipped her peppermint tea, she reflected on the earlier visit. It had been interesting, and she certainly thought that Albert had been touched. He said that, when the Priest said – 'And, on the night that He was betrayed, He took bread', there was a lump in his throat. But had he just been identifying with his own situation? Was he just picking up some of his own pain? He had admitted as much when he said – 'My body is breaking down too.'

The biggest surprise to her had been his reaction to the two children sitting close to them. The girl was about 7 – maybe 8 – and her brother was a few years younger. They were with their father. Was he divorced, Megan wondered? Or did he have a wife who was happy for them to be out of the house for an hour or two? Whatever the situation was, the two children began to play their father up. They had been out for most of the service in Sunday School and trouped in with the rest just before communion. Their father handed them their bags filled with activities and the girl had chosen her crayons to colour in pictures of Dora the Explorer. The boy had copied his sister and began colouring in a little book with drawings of Tractor Tom. At first, they had been no trouble at all but then the boy lost his concentration and hurled a blue crayon at his sister like a missile. The father frowned at them and looked disapproving, hoping that that would be enough. They toed the line for a few moments then the girl flung the blue crayon back. The boy took the red crayon next and threw it across.

That was the problem with Family Services. Of course, the children had to be encouraged but it was hard to focus on spiritual matters when confronted with a war of crayons. Megan herself had been a little irritated and sorry for the father who didn't really know how to deal with the situation. She looked sidewards at Albert and, to her surprise she noticed that he seemed to be enjoying their little game. The girl had already acquired feminine gifts. Flirting for attention. She made a gesture of apology to her father – but noticed the amusement on Albert's face. She carried on playing to her audience. The boy understood little of the underlying games she was playing and just ended up tipping the entire box of crayons onto the floor. At this point, the father had lifted the boy up and took him to the back of the church to try to calm him down. The girl remained in her seat and smiled at Albert. He reciprocated with a little grin.

Albert didn't take Communion but, after the service, the priest and congregation had made them very welcome. They refused the cup of tea but stayed behind for five minutes or so. Megan was not a very regular attender, but most people knew her and they were kind. She had introduced Albert as a 'friend'. This was the first time that they had gone out together socially and she knew that people would talk. 'So nice to see Megan Roberts with a new partner.' 'Good for her.' 'Isn't that Albert Evans, the Pharmacist?'

Megan had wanted to ask him about the children – he had grandchildren about the same age. But then he felt unwell and she had let it go. In the evening, when she sat with him, he had dozed off in her arms. She had taken another look at the photographs that hung on the wall. There was a largish one in a silver-plated frame. This was Duncan, their older son. It was a formal photograph. He was standing with his wife and two children sat in front of them – a girl and a boy. They were smiling but it was a posed picture. All four of them wore spotless clothes. The little girl had short white socks that turned over to reveal a row of pink bows made from ribbon. She wore white sandals. The little boy was wearing blue – pale blue shirt, darker blue trousers – not jeans – and a navy tie. He too had white shoes. White shoes for a boy? It was all too perfect – the sort of picture that eminent people liked to put on the front of their Christmas cards. Albert's son resembled his father – but he was far darker.

The other son, Charles, featured in a different frame. He seemed to take after his mother in looks. The photograph of him on his own was smaller and he stared out at the lens broodily. He was very handsome with impressive brown eyes. Although he looked more like his mother, there was a sensitivity in his mouth that he had inherited from Albert. She couldn't see the photo of Albert with Doreen clearly without disturbing him, so she had stayed with her thoughts. She stroked his arm and, although he was still sleeping, she sensed that it was giving him some comfort. And it had pleased her to be doing it. More than words could tell.

Albert had not had a good week, but he had insisted that they should make up for lost time and go to Ebenezer together that night. She had told him that it would be quiet and reflective. And so it proved to be.

The two of them sat together towards the back of the chapel. They both bowed their heads in prayer when they went in. Then they found the first hymn in their books.

All traditions have their attractions. The prayers in Ebenezer were always beautiful – even if they were only taken on board as words talking to nobody. They were beautiful. They touched the heart.

'Lord, we ask You to be with all those who are lonely tonight, facing illness, afraid.' The Minister was saying – almost singing the words. Softly. 'Those who are ready to come home to You. Comfort them all, Lord. Be the lamp that guides them. Remind them that they are not alone with You by their side. Let those who are weary and burdened with cares, come to You. Hand it all over to You at the foot of your Cross. For You have been there before them. And by Your wounds, they are healed . . .'

Megan didn't look at him but she could tell that Albert was crying. Not loudly. Hardly discernible to anyone but herself. His body was shaking beside her. He blew his nose gently, conscious of the sound interrupting the prayers. He put his handkerchief back in his pocket and, when his hand was back at his side, she gently took hold of it. His hand shook very slightly. Without looking at each other, he moved his hands so that they encompassed hers.

They remained like that throughout the service. Somehow, through that contact, they both knew that the right thing to do was to slip out of the chapel. Just as the last words of the last verse of the last hymn were being sung.

They talked very little on the way back. Albert had struggled with his breathing a few times and they were relieved to be back in her flat. Albert sat on the armchair with the brass buttons as she made a cup of herbal tea. She moved a little table so that they could both put their cups on it. Bella had painted a design on the little saucer to take the teabags. For a moment, her mood sunk as she remembered her grandchild. Beautiful Bella. She caressed her cup, and its warm contents soothed her.

'I enjoyed the Service,' she said. 'What about you, my love?' She looked across at him, smiling.

He frowned as he struggled to find the right words. 'Something happened!' he said. 'During the prayers. I don't know what it was.'

'I thought it had. You don't need to explain.' But she hoped he would try to tell her.

Albert was still puzzled. 'When he said about the handing over of burdens, well, I think that's what I did. I just said to myself – maybe to God – I'm dying. Then I felt that I wasn't carrying it all around with me. Does that make sense?'

The delight in her smile gave him the answer.

'Is that what it is?' he asked, confused.

'What do you mean?'

'Is that what it's all about? Faith. Believing. It's that simple?'

'Yes, I think it is. People can get so intellectual about it all. Try to analyse things. You've spent your life measuring, dispensing. It's harder for you to accept.'

He wanted to go over to sit with her but the earlier

rejection all those months ago had left its mark.

'Come and sit here!' Megan offered. And she patted the cushion on the seat beside her.

She was just about to run the bath when the phone rang. She could always let it go and check the message later. But intuition told her to answer it. She wrapped her dressing gown around herself and managed to pick the receiver up in time.

'Mum, is this convenient?'

Megan had guessed that it would be Tom. She'd been waiting for two days for him to call back. This was about the time when he often began to switch off from work. 'Yes, it's fine.' She moved the stool so that she could sit down. The hall was rather soul-less. 'How are you?'

'I'm sorry I didn't get back to you earlier'. She could hear the sincerity in his voice. The earnestness. He was a good boy. A good man. 'I've been so busy at work. I haven't had a minute to myself.'

'But you are eating?' There was something poignant about a man looking after himself. Take-aways. Ready meals. Eating out. Skipping breakfast. Skipping lunch. Chocolate bars.

'Just had a take-away!' he said cheerfully. 'A Pizza Marguerita. Delicious. As good as Mamma's.'

She smiled softly and imagined how he might look at that very minute. Had he changed out of his working-suit? Probably. He had a habit of getting into his dressing-gown after a shower now that he was living alone. 'I'm trying to plan a visit,' she began. 'Alice said that I could stay at the hotel. The usual thing. Nice room. Discount. No date yet. I thought I could combine things. I'd get a chance to see Bella and Alice and then in the evening, maybe I could come over to you and catch up. I could take the laptop back with me. Perhaps you'd give me a lesson or two. You know how bad I am with these things.' She stopped, aware of the silence at the other end. 'Tom? Are you still there?'

His tone had changed. His voice was tense and strident. On edge. 'I'd rather you didn't get involved at the moment,' he said.

'Involved? Involved with what? Involved with who?'

'With Bella.'

'With Bella?' She felt crushed, faint – glad that she was sitting down. 'Tom, what's the matter? Has something happened?'

'Please try to understand, Mum.' He was softer now, anxious to explain. 'I took Bella out last Saturday. We went to the park. I've been there with her so many times now. But on Saturday, it was a nightmare.'

Alice had said that he looked well at the week-end. She said that they'd had a good time together – Tom and Bella. But she wasn't going to mention that now. He needed to tell her what had happened in his own words.

'Was it something specific?' she prompted.

He sighed. 'Oh, it started off well enough. I picked Bella up at 10 – on the dot. I went through the day with her – you know how she needs to have her sense of order. Walk until 11, feed the ducks, go on the swings – she loves the swings. She has her favourite one. On the end of the row. It's blue. The seats have all got different colours – they're plastic – and Bella has to have the blue one. Lunch was going to be at mid-day then we planned to walk around the lake before I took her back home at 3.'

'It didn't work out like that?' The question came to

show that she was still listening and sympathetic.

'No. We were feeding the ducks when an old woman fell over. I went over to see if she was alright and she wasn't responding. I called an ambulance. There were a few of us gathered round by that time but I felt I should wait until the ambulance arrived. I was the one who saw her fall. I think she might have had some sort of fit. But not a *grand mal*. I was the best person to speak to the crew.'

'Of course you were.' She knew already what was coming. The incident would have upset Bella and disturbed her system of rituals.

'Well, I kept a check on Bella all the time, of course. She seemed alright at first. Then she sat on the ground and began rocking herself just before the ambulance arrived. I knew I'd only be another couple of minutes. Anyway, I explained to them what had happened. Then I left them to it and went over to Bella. The people who'd gathered round started looking at us. I told Bella that we were going on to the swings – as planned. But she was having none of it. She always wants to go right around the railings to feed the ducks so that they all get fed. I said it wouldn't matter for once. Then she blew it. Out of control. Screaming, shouting, hysterics . . .' His voice wavered and, for a moment, she thought that he was going to cry. 'I felt so awful' he admitted. 'When it happens in a public place like that, it's so, well, humiliating.'

'I'm sorry, Tom. Really sorry.'

'The only way I could get her to calm down was to go back to feed the ducks and start all over again. And that made us late for the swings. We had to wait for the blue one because another child was using it and, oh, I just don't know what to do.' He sounded defeated. She wished that she could reach out and console him.

'What do you mean?' she asked gently. You handled it very well. We all know how Bella can be . . .'

'But *they* don't. The onlookers.'

'Don't pay any attention to them.'

'I don't know if I want to do this anymore, Mum.'

'Don't want to do what?'

'Spend my Saturdays like this. I've thought about it. Agonised over it. I love Bella dearly. But I don't think I'm helping her. And if we get a wet week-end . . .'

'Isn't there some way around it? Could she go over to your place?'

'It's too hard. Alice, well, Alice seems to be in denial about the whole thing. She thinks everything's fine. Just thinks that Bella is highly-strung. She puts it down to an artistic temperament. Like her. Goes on about the things that Bella's good at. It's so infuriating, Mum. Bella's a high-achiever – way up on the spectrum. With the right help, she could make some sort of a normal life for herself. I've done so much research. On the Internet. Self-help groups. But Alice just wants to let things be. Sometimes, I don't want to know anymore – about either of them.'

She let him talk. She murmured the odd word now and again to let him know that she was still there and listening. He needed this confession. There were pieces of paper and pens by the phone and she started drawing. Doodling. Big, angry circles. She pressed so hard that she tore the piece of paper. She took it in her hand and scrunched it up. Then she let it fall to the floor and stamped on it quietly with her bare feet. She couldn't let Tom guess what her own feelings were. Aggression. Frustration. Anger. And a sense of loss.

She agreed to keep the visit on hold until things had

settled down. There wasn't much else she could do. And then he'd offered to send the lap top down to her. She'd said that it would wait.

When she had put the receiver down, she felt a hollow pain that was almost unbearable.

Half-heartedly, she ran the water for her bath and had an idea as the scented steam began to relax her. Badedas. Horse-chestnut. She had been looking at the Observer's Book of Trees again. Bella loved scrapbooks. She could make her one with bits of bark and leaves – anything she could lay her hands on. And she would label every page. 'Here is a leaf from an oak tree near Grandma's home.' She'd make stories out of them for each page. She knew that Bella would love it. It would please Alice too. As for Tom, she just needed to be patient. He was going to ring her when he got the laptop. 'A big noise in the city' – that's how Susan described her brother. Megan was reduced to tears. Because that was what she thought he would be doing. Right then. After the call. Alone.

'Is this any good?' Harriet rushed over to Megan with a stick in her hand. 'It's a nice piece of bark and you could do a cross-section to show the rings.'

The two women examined the stick with excitement.

'Yes. That's ideal. What a good idea! Don't know how I'll cut a cross-section though.'

'It's not thick. A pair of secateurs will do it.'

'I've given mine away.'

'I've kept mine. Don't know why. Just couldn't let them go. They remind me of all the gardening I used to do. Funny what we keep, isn't it?'

There had been very heavy winds the night before which had battered the trees in the park. The two women were clutching on to their finds like children on a treasure hunt. The meal at Cibo's had given them a chance to talk and it helped to heal the resentment that Harriet had been nursing. They both agreed that they needed more exercise so they were aiming for a couple of walks a week. Nothing strenuous. Twenty minutes or so.

They sat down on a slightly damp bench before going back. Megan had a little foldable bag in her handbag which, when separated from its holder, provided them with mini-groundsheets.

Megan had told Harriet about the problem with Bella. She had chosen her words carefully so that her friend could sympathise – but not intrude. And Harriet had been as enthusiastic as she was herself about making the scrapbook. They took a closer look at their collection. Harriet had picked up a small pinecone that had fallen to the ground. Her green jogging-suit – bought the year before when she had originally planned to get fit – still had the creases made from the way it had been folded in the shop. Now it was stained with resin and mud.

'You could do another one in the spring,' Harriet said. 'So that she sees the difference in the seasons. And another for the summer.'

Megan smiled at her friend. She really was a good sort. She was exhausted by the continual demands from her own daughter. But, if she didn't listen, she might take it out on the children. So every telephone call ended with her daughter feeling lighter. Harriet just carried the heaviness of it all. She needed friends.

'I've really enjoyed this walk!' she said and then, lovingly – 'I'm so glad that things are right between us again. I value your friendship. More than you know.

And I had no right to pitch in about your friendship with Albert . . . To be honest, I didn't realise how lonely I've been recently. Myf and I have had a long chat too – she wrote me a note. I felt ashamed of myself. Invited her in for a cup of tea . . .'

'There's a lot to Myf!' Megan said, glad that the two were reconciled.

'Yes, I admit that I'd completely underestimated her.' Harriet paused for a moment and then added. 'I'm sure that Myf's told you about . . .' She turned her head sideways to look her friend in the face. Megan's smile and nod implied that she was safe to talk about the miscarriage – or the delayed period.

'To have lost a baby like that. And not to have told anybody. Then, from one rat to another . . .' Harriet was a very emotional woman and she was vehemently championing Myf's cause.

It was strange how people needed to test out their innermost secrets on somebody. And, if they were met with acceptance and kindness, this was often a spur to share further revelations. Layers of onion skin peeled open with tears until the heart was exposed. Secrets kept inside the soul for years – decades – suddenly were let loose and liberated.

'That was a terrible way to treat a pupil – even if she was eighteen.'

Natural curiosity made Megan want to know about this further secret but she felt duty-bound to her own conscience. She had to be honest. 'Myf hasn't told me about that,' she stated simply.

Harriet's face flushed a little. 'Maybe I shouldn't have mentioned it then,' she said hastily. 'I just assumed she would have told you. But you know what Myf's like with secrets. Instilled in her from the Civil Service, I suppose.'

'You don't have to tell me.'

'Well, I've more or less told you already. And I trust you. One hundred per cent.'

Exchanging confidences was very intimate and satisfying. Megan reasoned with herself. Harriet probably needed to tell it. And it would help her understand Myf better.

'Well, after that other chap let her down – the father of the baby – she was determined to get an education. She must have told you that.'

Megan nodded.

'Well, she went to these night-classes. How she did it, I don't know. She was working in a shop in the day and helping her parents out at home. Her father was ill at the time . . . Anyway, this one tutor took a shine to her. History 'A' level.'

Megan looked down at one of the sticks and began peeling off a bit of the bark. If she looked across at Harriet and faced her, she'd feel nothing better than a gossip. Savouring its juice.

'Of course, she was the ideal student. Well-motivated. Hard-working. They chatted after the classes. Then he invited her to a meal. To talk history. Extra personal coaching. She was flattered, of course.'

The bark had now been peeled off but there was a tough bit that insisted on staying put. Megan twisted it back and forwards.

'Needless to say, he eventually got her into bed. She'd said no – then he talked of marriage. She said she needed to take precautions and he had a French letter. At the ready. Surprise, surprise! She said she'd been hurt before and he promised he'd never do that to her. Men!'

Miss Myfanwy Squires. Spinster. How the term must have hurt her. Never a wife. Never a mother. Whatever had gone wrong – and Megan was fairly sure that she knew what would follow – had probably bruised her for life. Changed her personality. Once bitten, twice bitten. Shied off for ever.

'She was in town one Saturday when she saw him. With his wife. And a baby.' Harriet's voice was hot with indignation, but she hesitated for a moment as someone was passing with their dog. 'Well, she had it out with him. He pleaded with her. Mainly not to tell . . .'

'Did she get her History 'A' level in the end?' Megan asked, wanting to avoid a conversation that fed on the situation.

'Passed with flying colours.'

Chapter Eleven

A fine day was predicted and Megan went down to the laundry-room early. There was usually a queue by mid-morning and she wanted to get her washing out on the rotary line before anyone else. She lifted the bundle out of the machine and into her laundry basket. It smelt wonderful – a lovely fresh, citrus fragrance that came from her favourite eco-friendly washing fluid.

She had persuaded Albert to let her wash his clothes with hers. As she explained, it took her a long time to get enough of her own stuff to fill the drum. He was, in fact, doing her a favour. Four shirts, two pairs of trousers and several pairs of socks and underpants were ready to be hung out with her own clothes, a sheet and a few towels. She washed her own underwear by hand. She reckoned that the combination of an autumn sun and a moderate easterly wind should get a good result. She pegged the items out. There was a certain satisfaction in seeing a menial task through. Dirty clothes washed, dried in the fresh air, soon to be ironed. She hung out Albert's socks and underpants first and then began to peg the shirts. Alongside the fourth and final shirt, she hung her own blouse. She felt strangely moved to see the two garments hanging together. Freed from their bodies. Blowing together vigorously. Intimate.

'Meg!' She frowned and wondered if she had imagined the call. No-one outside her immediate family called her Meg.

'Meg!' She turned around and saw Sam approaching her.

'What are you doing here?' she asked, mystified, worried that he might be bearing bad news of some sort.

They had never been in the habit of kissing each other and, when she saw him smiling, she just welcomed him with her own smile.

'Thanks for your letter.' He stood there awkwardly beside the rotary-line. 'I thought I would just drop by. Try to arrange for you to come over for a meal.'

'Look, I'll only be a minute hanging this stuff out. Come in and have a cup of tea? Is Jack with you?'

'He's gone for a smoke.'

'I thought he'd given it up.'

'He had – but you know what it's like. You get a bad patch and you're back on it. How are the children?'

'Fine.'

'I never see them.'

'I don't see a lot of them myself. I must let you have some photos.'

'That would be nice.'

She looked at her brother with affection when she had finished hanging the washing out.

'Shall we wait for Jack to come back?' she asked. 'I can't invite you in and leave him outside.'

'No, we won't come in. Not today.'

She walked with him to the car park reserved for the residents. Jack was only a few yards away and she waved at him. She beckoned for him to come over and he pointed to his cigarette. He had a bit of smoking left before he'd join them.

'You're right. We must make the effort,' Sam said. 'There's only the two of us now.'

His hair was completely white though it was partially concealed by his flat cap. His eyes were kind though exposure to the elements had aged his face. Well-established wrinkles ran across it like furrows. The sunshine had exaggerated them. His skin was not good.

It never had been. A rough redness coloured his cheeks and most of his nose and chin. Country air had accentuated it, but the main cause was acne rosacea.

'You didn't come all the way to Cardiff just to stand outside and have a five minute chat?' she asked, bemused.

'No, we're looking into the possibility of having a stall at the Riverside Farmers' Market. We've been checking it out.'

'To sell jam?'

'Yes – and the chutneys. Maybe more.'

'That sounds a good idea. It won't be too much for you?'

'Shouldn't be. Jack and I are just checking it out. We've not committed ourselves to anything. Not for the moment.'

Jack had stubbed out his cigarette and walked towards them. The three of them stood by Jack's Land-Rover, out of the wind.

'Are you sure you won't come in?' Megan repeated. 'I won't keep you if you need to get on.'

'No, we won't come in.'

'When could you come then?'

'For the meal?'

'Yes. Jack's a good cook.'

'Yes, I remember. The day of Hugo's funeral . . .' Jack had provided an array of food – she had no idea that he was so gifted.

'How are you, Megan?' Jack asked. 'We'd love you to come over. Do you eat meat?'

'A little.'

'Would you prefer fish – or I could do a vegetarian meal? Just say.'

'Fish would be lovely. But not shellfish. It doesn't

agree with me, I'm afraid.'

'We'll make it fish then,' said Sam, looking across at Jack. 'I've brought my diary. Not that there's a lot in it.' This was Sam's humour and Megan smiled.

'Let's fill it up a bit then,' she said affably. 'Are we talking about an evening – or lunch-time?'

'Evening would be best for us.'

'Fine.' Megan tried to remember her commitments. Most of them were flexible anyway. 'A week next Thursday?'

Jack looked anxiously across at Sam.

'A week on Thursday, Jack's playing at the Club.'

'Well, you suggest a good evening!' said Megan.

'We could do a week on Wednesday.'

'A week on Wednesday it is then. What time would you like me to arrive at the farm?'

'Seven? Seven thirty? We usually eat about that time ourselves.'

'I look forward to seeing you both then.'

As soon as the arrangement had been made, the two men seemed relieved to climb back into the Land Rover. Jack was at the wheel. He was a few years younger than Sam and it had always showed. But now she noticed that he was a little bent and walking with a slight limp. Suddenly, he seemed like an old man. Which, she supposed, he was.

She stood on the concrete paving and waved. Sam lowered the window to wave back and they were gone.

She took the empty laundry basket back to her flat and made herself a cup of tea.

She had already had breakfast while the clothes were washing but she felt like another cup of tea. Green tea.

She tried to make sense of the meeting. She and Sam didn't see each other often. It was little more than

Christmas and birthday presents. There were phone calls – especially if one of them was ill. But they had grown apart. In an amicable sort of way. It was just that their lives were so different. The children had enjoyed going to the farm when they were small but that was over twenty years ago.

They had never been close – she and Sam. Even all those years back. She had been the youngest of the three and yet she had been the one who had to deal with things. Because she was a girl. When their mother was well, there had been few demands made of her. Indeed, efforts were made to compensate her. She was given treats that were denied to the other two. Money for the cinema. Things like that. The boys hadn't seemed to resent it. If they did, they had kept it to themselves. When the illness returned, everything changed. Megan did the cooking and the cleaning. She made Sam and James responsible for tidying the bedroom that they shared. But, apart from that, the boys were let off lightly.

Things would have been different today, she thought. Their mother would have had a proper diagnosis and treatment. She wouldn't have had to endure the criticism. The stigma. Some neighbours had refused to speak to her altogether. No, these days, the family would have had help. And maybe someone would have picked up the underlying problem with James.

Sam had always been quiet, but he became surly in adolescence. Their father had tried his best to understand him, but he had enough to worry about with his job. Mining was tough. Things got worse after an attempt at matchmaking. Their mother and her friend had tried to kindle a relationship. When Sam discovered what they had tried to do, he'd become aggressive and moody. Closed in on himself.

The difficulties with Sam were balanced by their pride in James. James – the oldest – had never been any trouble. He always had his head in a book and was deeply immersed in the work of the French existentialists by the time he was seventeen. No-one was surprised when he won a place at university – the first in the family. They said he had a brilliant future ahead of him – a post in academia was in the offing.

No-one in the family knew that he was taking drugs. It's easy to be wise after the event. He hadn't been home for a while but they knew that he had his final exams ahead of him. He was bound to be busy studying. They couldn't get hold of him. The letters stopped. He was sharing a house with three other students. 'Sorry, he's not here' – they used to say or – 'I'll leave a message on his door.' But students were like that, weren't they?

Brilliant James. Barbiturates were found by his bed. There were three empty bottles of vodka in his flat. Apparently, he was worried about a viva. He hadn't left a note.

She sipped some of her tea and went to the cupboard to fetch an oat biscuit.

She had been devastated, of course, but a lot of her feelings were suppressed as she'd had to struggle to restore some balance at home. Their mother had predictably gone into a reactive depression. Sam blamed himself. They had shared a bedroom – he should have known that there was something wrong! When they cleared his things out, Sam had found some cannabis wrapped in foil concealed under the lining of one of the drawers – a drawer that they had shared. The drawer where they used to put their clean underwear – Sam's on the right, James' on the left.

Sam never quite forgave himself for several reasons. Apart from thinking that he should have noticed that something was wrong, Sam had always harboured resentment of James when he was alive. James had sailed through life and was good-looking. Sam's face had been so badly affected by acne in his teenage years that it was difficult to see beyond it. Yes, Sam's grief had been complicated. Not that he ever talked about it.

She held her hand under her mouth to catch the crumbs from the biscuit. She was tempted to take another but didn't have the energy to go back to the cupboard. The unexpected meeting had completely unnerved her.

She was so grateful that Jack had come into Sam's life.

'There are only the two of us now'. That's what Sam had just said. Was this a cry for help? He and Jack were so settled. It was true that Jack had aged. Was he worried about the prospect of being alone one day? But, no, they had talked about setting up a stall at the Farmers' Market. Was there a financial problem? Surely not! They had bought the farm outright years ago. They had managers for the farm now, but it had been a bad year. Foot-and-mouth – again. Bluetongue.

She went over to her diary and marked the date down. Sam and Jack's. Seven p.m. It was so long since she'd been there that she'd have to check the route again. Once she was off the main road, there was a whole series of narrow lanes and no street lighting.

She took her empty cup back into the kitchen and swept the crumbs out of her hand. She would have given them to the birds but they were discouraged from doing that in case of rats. Out of the corner of her eye, she saw the clothes on the line. The arms of one of

Albert's shirts had become tangled into the sleeve of her blouse.

She didn't know what to do with herself. The weather changed so she brought the clothes in and put them on the radiators. She turned the radio on and then switched it off. She was making a point of just listening to programmes that genuinely interested her. She looked at her CDs but couldn't decide what to listen to.

Albert was going to a class to learn deep-breathing techniques. She didn't feel like calling in on any of the other residents. She didn't want to meet anyone – not even Annie.

She knew that she had to do something, so she turned her attention to the affairs of Cicely Stafford.

She would keep her address book for the time being. At a later date, she'd go through it systematically to see if there were common colleagues, friends. But she wouldn't do it then. There was something almost sacred about an address book.

The Down Manor files were extensive. She had to get rid of them somehow. They were taking up too much room. Reports, plans, newspaper cuttings, schedules, time-tables . . . Was there anyone who might value them? Bill and Ronnie Price obviously didn't want them. There was no-one in her family who'd take an interest. What about the school itself?

She sighed. Did Cicely know what had happened? That they'd had to merge with another school when it fell into financial difficulties. St. Gwynno's with Down Manor. She hoped not. Bill and Ronnie would have protected her from it surely? The dementia had saved her from breaking her heart.

No. The new school wasn't interested in her scrupulously kept records. She intended to shred it all.

But she couldn't make herself do it. After all the effort that had gone into their making, it had to be done when she was feeling more positive.

A thought occurred to her. How had Bill Price been able to afford to put Ronnie through Down Manor? Admittedly, it wasn't expensive – as private schools go. He had been a painter and decorator. Not big money. His wife had left him when Ronnie was a very small boy. It was difficult to remember so far back, but she couldn't recall a mother ever having come to have a talk with her about his progress.

The pain and problems of this world weighed her down and she went to rest on her bed. She had put Albert's underwear on the radiator in her bedroom. She hadn't consciously thought about it. Her subconscious motive had probably been to conceal it in case anyone called. Or maybe . . ? Seeing them dangling there confused her. There was a deep yearning to have him with her. At the same time, there was a loneliness that gnawed at her heart. She felt the feelings that would have led to tears if she were not on medication. And then she fell asleep.

Love, true love, does not possess. There are all the conditions that people impose on each other if possessiveness dominates. *'If you really care, you'll do this – you won't do that. Do it for me.'* There is no need for manipulation in true love. Just acceptance. A little persuasion at times – but nothing forced. She knew that she had to allow Albert space. He'd said that he'd call in after the deep breathing session. Maybe he'd decided to have some lunch out. Maybe he'd met a friend. He hadn't mentioned it but she had to let him be free. She didn't own him. Neither did she have the right to cluck over him like a broody hen all the time.

She realised that she would need to keep other activities going. After Hugo's death, it had taken her a long time to build up a new life for herself. There were still some old friends whom she saw. But it was different being the third person. A couple and a widow. The balance changed. Sometimes it worked and sometimes it didn't. She had made new friends and she would soon need them.

She had thought about going to an Italian class at an Adult Centre in a local school, but she'd left it too late. Maybe, if she borrowed a book from the library, she could start herself on the language and begin the following September at Stage 2. She decided to walk past the Centre, call in and drop a note to the teacher, asking what book they were studying. It would be a solitary pursuit for the time being, but it was better than doing nothing at all. If all went well, she could move on to make it happen in September. The language was so beautiful and maybe she'd learn enough to go to Italy and hold her own. Venice. Florence. Rome.

She'd never looked into it, but there were holidays organised for people who were on their own. Maybe, in a year or two ...

Call at the Adult Centre in Severn Road, she wrote on her list, followed by *Order book from Library.*

A structured list helped her to focus on things.

She was also running short of fruit. Apples were still in season and plentiful – British ones. She might make an apple tart. The trouble with making things like tarts was that a person on their own could never eat it all.

Albert? But, no, Albert was on a strict diet. However, as he was eating a lot of fresh fruit, she might be able to pick something up for him.

She needed to call into Boots too – she was running out of her foundation cream. Although she had a spare jar in the bedroom, she would soon be using it. She felt more secure having an additional one stocked away. In case she had a bad patch and couldn't get out. In case they discontinued the line. It was infuriating to find something that suited and then to be faced with having to start searching again. She could buy some more tights in Boots at the same time.

That only left the charity shops. She wasn't actively looking for something to buy (apart from a picture frame), but she needed to get rid of quite a lot of stuff. She felt happy enough about leaving general things in local charity shops – things that could not be easily identified. She had three scarves – one was from Accessorize, another from Marks and Spencer's. She could hand those over easily without worrying, but the third scarf had a very distinctive pattern and a designer label. She'd have to take that to another town another time. There were several hard-backed books, three paper-backs and two address books. Annie's address would also have to go to another town – it was so distinctive. She'd keep the spare diary for rough paper to make her lists. Soap was easy to dispose of – she'd keep the ones that the children had given her and give the rest to the woman in the complex who held coffee mornings for Mind.

She brought an old evening dress out of her wardrobe. She had kept it in case she needed it, but there was little chance of her going anywhere where she might wear it. It was beautiful and she stroked it with affection before she folded it. Dinners and balls with Hugo – not that she had especially enjoyed these occasions. But there was usually cheerful company, and it reminded her of the good times. Hugo had been proud of her when she looked smart. 'You're a good-looking woman, Megan,' he used to say. 'In fact, you're gorgeous!' She had remembered the words exactly because he wasn't usually an effusive man. There were also two pairs of shoes – high-heels – which she would never put on again. She'd kept them for the same reason as the dress, but, with her arthritic knees and advice from her osteopath, she knew that they belonged to the past.

There was far too much for her to carry, so she placed all the items in her elegant shopping trolley. She put the shoes and the books at the bottom, then some toiletries and, using one of the few plastic bags she had, she folded the dress. She nearly took it back, but common sense told her to pass it on.

There was plenty of room in the trolley. Vegetables got heavy when she carried them. The heavier fruit too. She'd be able to get a couple of pounds of firm apples – she had decided against making a tart. There might be a water-melon for Albert. Yes, she knew that it would have been imported from the other side of the world – or maybe Spain – using masses of carbon emissions. The people who grew them were probably badly paid. But she did the best she could and Albert wouldn't see another summer. Strawberries. The next crop from Herefordshire, bursting with goodness, generously piled into a paper punnet, stained by their juice, would be something that he'd miss out on.

As she made her way home, she was pleased with herself. She had met the Italian teacher at the Centre.

She knew the name of the book they were using and had even suggested that she should come along to the class when she was ready. 'You'll soon catch up!' she said when Megan explained that she had a lot on at the moment. The tutor had taken Megan's details and said that she'd be in touch. She wasn't Italian but she had an Italian surname – Corelli. Married to an Italian maybe? Yes, Megan was pleased with her trip. She had half-committed herself and, as she had the title of the book, she was able to borrow it from the library. If it was good, she would buy it.

When she went into the Charity shop with her goods and handed them over, she saw a woman eyeing the evening dress. It would sell. So would the shoes which had hardly been worn. The scarves should go too. It was usually the books that stayed on the shelves. And they took up so much room. From time to time, they had a 3-books-for-a-pound week. All her books were in good condition. The art book would be a bargain for someone. She had read the John Humphreys book *'In God, do we doubt'* and she had enjoyed it. But she wouldn't read it again.

She had turned to the corner where the picture-frames were in the charity shop. She had put her Berthe Morisot print in a plastic folder in a zipped section of the trolley, and she took it out because there were two frames which might have been right. But, with the print beside them, they were both unsuitable. The cream surround in the first one was too over-powering for the print and the inset cardboard frame within the second one was a bit too big. At one time, she had mounted her own.

Back in the flat, she did some clearing up and dusted

the furniture before putting the hoover over the carpets. It was not heavy work but she realised what a good move it had been to come to the flat. She could never have done a good job of things back in their lovely old house.

She drew the curtains and took the clothes off the radiators. Apart from the towels, which were still slightly damp in a patch that had not been directly in contact with the heat, they were all dry. She considered doing the ironing but decided against it. It was something she could do later. She found ironing quite relaxing and, with some music, or perhaps the radio, it would act as a gentle evening activity. It relaxed her and helped her to slow down before sleep.

She had some bulgar wheat salad in the fridge and put a Glamorgan sausage in the microwave. There was some green salad left too and she tossed in a few walnut pieces. She hadn't managed to get a watermelon for Albert, but she'd bought two punnets of strawberries. She looked at them and smiled to herself.

She took the tray of the main course, dessert and a cup of chamomile tea into the living-room. She didn't like the idea of eating in front of the television, but she had got into the habit of watching the early evening news as she ate. The news was, as usual, very depressing and a variation on the items she had heard in the morning on Radio 4.

She finished her tea and turned the set off. It looked as if the world might be tottering towards a major economic depression, and she wondered how everybody would cope. It wouldn't be too bad for her – she remembered the rationing after the war when she had paid for her flat and had some savings. But the youngsters – those who'd committed themselves to exorbitant mortgages? They'd never known shortages. The world around them had been openly available on plastic for years. And now the tide was going to turn . . .

She glanced at the Italian book from the library. Although she had forgotten a lot of her French – she had done it to 'A' level – she recognised the similarities in the languages. This was definitely something that she was going to pursue.

She looked at her watch. She was now worried about Albert. This was no longer to do with 'letting him be'. This was genuine concern. She put the book aside and lifted the receiver on the phone. There was no answer. He might be in the toilet – he might have dropped off to sleep. She didn't want to convey any feelings of anxiety. She went into the kitchen for the strawberries and went over to his door. She knocked gently. There was no reply. She began banging, calling out. There was still no reply. This was the time for her to use the spare key that he had had made for her. She slipped back to her flat to get the key and left the strawberries on the table in the hall beside her phone.

She could hear her heart pounding as she tried to turn the key in the door. In her anxiety, she missed the keyhole and heard the key scraping around the metal disc. 'Calm down!' she told herself and forced herself to take deeper breaths. 'You must be prepared for whatever you find. Put the key in the hole and turn it.' She did exactly that and then she pushed the door open.

'Albert?' she called out. 'Albert, are you alright?'

He was sitting in the armchair with his back to her. She could see the top of his head, his arms resting on the chair and his feet. He was wearing socks but had taken off his shoes.

'Albert!' she called again – but more gently this time.

She moved over to the chair and stood alongside him. His eyes were open, but they were not focusing on anything. He had made no attempt to respond to her voice. She resisted the temptation to go up to him and put her arms around him. Instead, she drew up a cushioned stool in front of him – but a few yards away. She needed to be patient and wait until the time when he was ready to make eye-contact.

'Albert!' she said in little more than a whisper. 'Can you tell me what's wrong?'

He still stared ahead and beyond her with dull, glazed eyes.

'Take your time.'

She began to panic and wondered if she should call the doctor but was determined to keep sounding calm for him. Her patience was rewarded.

'I can't do this to you,' he said, still gazing ahead.

'What can't you do?'

'I can't let you suffer like this.'

'Suffer?'

For a moment, he looked at her directly then he averted his eyes again.

'It's not fair. We've had no time for enjoyment. I'll be leaving you with a legacy of pain. No happy memories.'

'I already have enough happy memories. And I was the one who encouraged this. Do you remember when I' – she let her voice drop to a whisper. Albert turned to look at her directly.

'Are you sure?'

'Of course I'm sure.'

She moved the stool a little closer.

'I'm as sure as I could possibly be. Honestly. Cross my heart.' She smiled at him softly and made the gesture of a child's promise.

He gave a tired smile. 'Dear Megan. My love, my love.'

'Did anything happen to start you thinking like this?' she asked. 'Did you have a bad time at the deep-breathing and meditation class?'

'I didn't go.'

'You didn't go?' She knew that he had been looking forward to this. A positive thing to do, he'd said.

'I was too breathless.' He looked across at her and gave a weak laugh. 'Too breathless to go to the deep breathing session. It's a classic, isn't it?'

'But you're better now?'

'Yes, I used the nebuliser.'

'You can go next week!' she added. 'I'll take you there in the car if you want.'

'I've blown it.'

'How's that?'

'Oh, after I'd been on the nebuliser, I rang the woman up to apologise. She was very charming – trained to be so – but she said that she'd have to make a charge.' He hesitated, uncertain as to whether or not he should continue.

'It's annoying to have to pay when you've had no benefit.' She was keen to keep the conversation going.

'It wasn't really that. I don't think so. I did an appalling thing. You'll be shocked!' I just, well, I resented the fact that she was fit and had a life ahead of her. She said 'Shall I book you in for next week?' – and I said no. I said that I'd be in touch.' He looked at her appealingly now. 'I heard her confidence break – just a bit. I heard it in her voice – and I was glad.'

She knew how hard it had been for him to admit to such feelings – feelings which we all have but usually refuse to acknowledge. She moved the stool again so that it was very close to him. And, as she sat on it, she took his hands.

'Albert, these feelings are normal. We all get them at some time or another.'

He let her stroke the backs of his hands, but he went back to staring ahead. 'And I shouldn't have said those things about Doreen. She wasn't a bad woman.'

From the way he spoke she realised that he had probably spent hours going over and over these things in his mind. He needed to let them out.

'She was a good woman. She helped me become a successful pharmacist – I had no confidence when I was younger. I needed her. It's just that she, well, sometimes I'd come home from work and I'd forget to take my shoes off and she said 'Shoes, Albert!' As if I were a child. She'd say that before saying hello, asking how my day had been. I tried, once, to tackle her on this but she said she couldn't have one rule for the boys and another for me. She said that it was hard to keep the carpets clean – all that sort of thing. She wasn't a bad woman. And I've been talking about her. And she's gone and not able to defend herself . . .'

He hung his head. She continued stroking the back of his hands which were locked tightly together. Clenched. Gently but firmly, she massaged the tense muscles. Then she prised his hands apart by gradually pummelling in her index fingers.

'Most marriages are muddled compromises,' she assured him. 'And that's alright. You've not built up a bad picture of Doreen to me. A woman who was strong and determined maybe – but not bad.'

'I just thought today, what's the point?'

So, he had visited that dark place already. 'Have you eaten?' she asked.

'A couple of slices of bread at lunch. An apple. Some herbal tea. I had to force myself to eat. I was just thinking of the uselessness of putting more fuel into this wasting body... Why not just ...'

It was painful for her to hear this but her voice remained calm – though firmer than it had been. 'You need something to eat, Albert. And something to drink. Can I put something together for you?'

'I'm running low on things.'

He had refused her offer to do some of his shopping. 'Will you come over to my flat?' She remembered the strawberries.

'I've bought some strawberries. We could eat them together.'

'You've bought strawberries for me?'

She laughed. 'Yes – for you. But, also, for me.'

'But strawberries are out of season!' he said. 'I thought you didn't believe in ...'

She stood up and bent down to kiss the back of his neck. 'I bought them out of love. Love for you. It got the better of my principles.'

It took a few days for Albert's mood to lift. During this time, she knew that he was facing the toughest of internal struggles. A path both bitter and lonely. After the diagnosis, he had had bad days and miserable moments. But he'd also been positive as he sorted out the alternative therapies. His brain had accepted the palliative care that he had often talked about to others. His emotions had now caught up with him. Letting go was hard. How long would he have? Could he face his grandchildren again – knowing that he would never see them grow up? And what about his sons? Friends, colleagues. And her. Megan. To have to say good-bye when he had only just learnt how to say hello.

Little by little, he had become more cheerful. She told him that he was bound to have difficult patches as well as lighter days. He knew that too, of course, but it did no harm to be reminded and to know that he had someone to accompany him on his journey.

She'd noticed that he had several board games in his flat – Scrabble, Monopoly, Dominoes. It was strange what people chose to hang on to. For her, it had been the evening dress and the shoes. For him, it was the hope that he would have someone to play a board game with.

She suggested that he might like to bring one over to her home – he valued getting out of his own flat, especially as he was spending a lot of time sleeping there during the day. So, he came with the Scrabble board, and they had set it up with the letters hidden from each other, even though they didn't bother to note down the score. It was a pleasant enough game, and they found themselves in the usual predicament at the end with an assembly of awkward letters.

'I can't go,' he said.

Megan shrugged. 'Make something up!'

'Make something up?' he asked, smiling.

'Yes. Why not?'

He thought for a moment and placed the word 'qenj' on the board.

'Meaning?' Megan asked.

'As in 'She drank the lemonade to 'qenj' her thirst.'

'Well done! My turn now!'

She frowned briefly – she had a Z, a P, an I and an N – then placed her word down triumphantly. 'Jipnz' she said.

'Meaning?'

'Text message – the 'Jpinz' beat the English'

They both laughed as she tipped the wooden squares back into the box, replaced the two mini shelves that had held them and folded the board on top. She handed him the box. Simple things like this reminded her of their ease with each other.

They sat together on the settee afterwards – as they did so often now – and just enjoyed each other's company. Little things. Simple things. A word here and there. Comfortable silences. A kiss, a caress. A cup of tea. A glass of wine. Dozing off. Some music. A programme on the radio. Giggling when his stomach rumbled. Thoughts uttered like meditation into the air without needing a response. Stroking each other. Accepting each other as they were.

Albert was worried about meeting up with an old friend and former colleague. He'd tried to put him off, but he'd insisted. He lived in Caerphilly, but his dentist was still in Cardiff. He was going to have a crown fitted.

'Shall I tell him?' Albert murmured.

He was lying across the settee with his head in her lap. She had told him how much she liked the smell of his after-shave. Sandalwood. Or cedarwood. Or both. She stroked his stubble and bent down to kiss his lips.

'If he's a good friend, it'll probably do no harm,' she said. And she thought – 'He'll know. My sweetheart, he'll know.'

Harriet knocked on the door with an assortment of things for Bella's scrapbook. She'd found a lovely feather and a few skeleton leaves that had kept their veins.

Megan invited her in and showed her what she'd done to the scrapbook already. She had prepared it and

Harriet said that she was going to make one for each of her own grandchildren.

'They're so overwhelmed with all these league tables and things,' she said. 'Something like this is a real treasure. Even for . . .' She stopped suddenly and her face flushed.

'It's alright!' Megan assured her. 'I know what you were going to say. Even for normal children. Thank you for being sensitive, Harriet. It doesn't matter. What is normal anyway?'

Harriet put her little collection down on the work-surface in the kitchen on a piece of paper and changed the subject.

Megan's relationship with Albert was now evident to all. One of the residents had been in the corridor when she'd opened his door with her own key. News had got round that they'd been to St. Michael's together. The daughter of another resident was one of the churchwardens. Yes, they had all seen the comings and goings. Harriet and Myf had both backed off a little. Knocking politely. Asking – 'Is this a good time?' or 'I hope I'm not interrupting.'

'Albert's ill, isn't he?' Harriet asked impetuously in a high-pitched voice.

Megan didn't know how to respond. He didn't look well now but she was still sworn to secrecy. 'I can't talk about it, Harriet,' she said gently. 'Not at the moment.'

In a way, she had supplied Harriet with the answer.

'I'm always here if you need me,' she said.

'Thank you.' She smiled at her friend. 'Friendship's so important, isn't it? Tell me, how are things with Sheila?'

Chapter Twelve

Megan had planned her day. She had been so impressed with the Italian book she'd borrowed from the library that she decided to buy it along with the CD. It was important to hear a language being pronounced properly at the beginning. Bad habits would be difficult to break.

If she caught a bus into the station early in the morning, she could take another bus into a nearby town and deposit the identifiable items in a charity shop. That would give her plenty of time to get back and call into town to pick up the book. Waterstone's had a copy. She had checked.

Some people thought it wrong to move unwanted gifts on. But the wealthier countries were heaving with their own excesses. She sometimes received more on a single birthday than she had had throughout her early childhood. Then, a gift had almost always been something that she couldn't normally afford. It was a treat. She remembered when she had been given her first book-token. There had been great excitement in buying the book on the Renaissance that had recently been published. She had covered the paper cover with old wallpaper to protect it. And she still had it. Now she was inundated with things she didn't want.

She had mentioned a few years earlier that half the people in her address book were now dead. It had been an exaggeration, of course, but it had prompted a flurry of new ones sent to her as gifts. Even from people who usually gave just a card. They were becoming cheaper all the time – hardly cost more than a card. No-one under the age of forty had one. Their numbers were all stored in the memory of their mobile phones. Addresses were locked in computers.

Annie's address book with the luscious Renoir girls on the cover was a good quality one. She had forgotten to take the receipt out. It was an exclusive London Museum item. There was probably no-one on this side of Offa's Dyke who had one. Then there were the other things, the designer scarf, the tankard that had been personalised with her initials. It was a nice piece of pewter, and someone might buy it just for the metal. She couldn't hurt anyone by putting their gifts in a local shop. Most of them – the women, at least, browsed in the charity shops.

She decided not to go too far because she had to go into Waterstone's later. Pontypridd – usually known as just Ponty – seemed a good compromise. She didn't know anyone who lived in Pontypridd, but it was only a short bus ride away. An anonymous place to leave her things.

The bus stopped in a main shopping street and she stepped down, thanking the driver who spoke with an Eastern European accent. Polish maybe? Or Slovakian?

Apart from the need to find a charity shop away from home, she was pleased that she had taken them there. There was something so defeated about The Valleys. Somewhere – after Tongwynlais – the world was greyer. Her gifts might brighten up someone's life. She imagined someone smiling at the lovely address-book or taking a pride in the pewter.

She walked into the first charity shop she saw. 'I've just brought these things in for you,' she said kindly, trying not to sound like Lady Bountiful. Her accent had changed after all the years away.

'Oh, thank you.' The young woman volunteer put them down to the side and served a customer. Someone was buying some children's games and a CD rack.

Megan looked around the shop and then she saw it. At last, she had found a picture frame to suit the Berthe Morisot print. She didn't have it with her, but she had written the dimensions down. She hesitated for a moment – she needed to make sure that it was exactly right. It would be awkward carrying it back, but it wasn't too big and now that she had dispatched the other things . . .

Feeling very pleased with herself, she went up to the volunteer and said brightly, 'I expect you see this all the time? I'm not going home empty-handed!'

It was then that she noticed that the woman was crying. She looked around her to see if she could work out the cause of the unhappiness. But the shop was now empty.

'Are you alright?' she asked kindly.

The woman bit her lip. She was in her late twenties or early thirties, a pretty girl, though rather overweight. Megan thought that she might be pregnant but it was hard to tell with someone of her physique. She was aware that she was staring, and she repeated her question. 'Are you alright?'

The woman tapped her fingers nervously on the little counter. Then she said, 'You're Mrs. Roberts, aren't you? Mrs. Megan Roberts?'

'Yes, I am.' Megan tried to recall the face and looked for clues. She was wearing a ring, but maybe it was one of those friendship rings – silver studded with jade stones. It was on the third finger of her left hand. She had more of a Cardiff accent than a Valleys one. Could it be a Down Manor connection?

'Were you at Down Manor?' she asked but, even as she asked, she realised that the woman was far too young. 'St. Anne's!' she said with more confidence. It was a safer bet.

The woman shook her head and bit her lip again. It was dry and cracked and began to bleed a little. She sucked the blood away.

'Do you want to buy the frame?' she asked weakly.

'Yes, please. But can you help me out a bit? It's not easy to remember everyone.'

'I should never have mentioned it.' The volunteer sat down. Megan felt unsettled.

Why was she reluctant to introduce herself? Did she have something to hide – something in her past that she regretted – something in which she herself had been involved? If there was something... She couldn't let it go now. It would trouble her.

Megan's voice was strained. 'Are you going to tell me who you are? I don't understand what's going on.'

A couple of women had come into the shop and looked at the ladies' tops.

'Fancy this for your 'do'?' said one to the other.

'What size is it?'

'14.'

'Too small. Like this on me?' She held a top in front of herself provocatively – orange with flecks of sparkling silver and a deeply scooped neck. The sort of cut that would attract a man's attention. A lot of cleavage – especially in a size 16.

'Can I try this on, dear?'

Without waiting for an answer, the woman went into the makeshift changing-room. It had a strand of cow-bells across the curtain to ensure that no-one stole.

She came out and showed it to her friend. 'That'll wow old Jonesey!' she was told. 'Yeh. Get it!'

When she had put her own jumper back on – she

didn't bother with the changing-room to do this – she went over to the counter with the top. 'Is that £2.50?' she asked cheekily, pointing to the label. 'I could buy this new at Ethel Austin's for that.'

'It is £2.50' the volunteer replied firmly. 'We check all our clothes. It doesn't have a flaw. You'll be helping the Red Cross.'

'I need the bleeding Red Cross myself!' the woman chirped in aggressively – spurred on by her friend. 'Bleeding Red Cross – get it?'

Megan found herself sympathising with the volunteer and was concerned for her safety – this woman who knew her from somewhere – this woman who was so troubled about something. She made a sign to let her know that she was going to stay in the shop.

The woman who wanted to buy the orange top with flecks of sparkling silver and a deeply scooped neck searched in her purse. 'I've only got £2,' she said in a surly tone. 'My money doesn't come in till Monday.'

To her surprise, Megan found herself saying firmly but without a trace of anger – 'That's your problem, not ours.'

The two shoppers stared at Megan, completely taken aback. 'I'll lend you 50p,' the second one said. The exchange was made, and the women left the shop.

'Thank you for that!' the volunteer said. 'Thank you very much. I was quite scared. You see, I'm expecting. I had a miscarriage last year and I'm trying to be careful.'

Megan smiled. 'That's alright. But now will you tell me your name?'

She hung her head in shame. 'It's Gracie Millstone.'

Megan's head began spinning. Millstone. She could never forget the name. Millstone. It must be the same family. It wasn't a common name. Why was she so nervous about telling her who she was if there wasn't a connection?

'Are you a relative of Frank Millstone?' she asked. She still had the frame in her hands, but her mind was far from Berthe Morisot now.

'Frank Millstone was my father.' She still hung her head but lifted her eyes for a moment to check the reaction. 'I'm sorry. I should have let it go.'

Forgiveness is a gift. It brings healing. But it can't be forced. Sometimes, it has to come in stages. It can't be honest until the feelings that caused the original hurt have been explored and dealt with. Megan felt a surge of anger rising inside her. But misdirected anger was the source of so many problems. Individually – and collectively. She wasn't angry with Gracie. But she was angry with her father – and her mother. And she realised that the anger had never surfaced before as strongly as it was at that very moment.

It was Frank Millstone's stupidity and his wife's subsequent ruthless action that had led to the first complaint being made. They had blamed Hugo.

She stepped out of the taxi and paid the driver. There was an assortment of change in her purse, and she peered inside to see if there was enough for a tip. There probably was but the light wasn't good, so she gave him one of the pound coins that she kept in a separate compartment.

She put her bags on the ground as she opened the front door to the complex. She had intended taking the bus home but, after her visit to Pontypridd and the trip into town to pick up the Italian book and some coach-tour brochures, she was exhausted. Her knees were painful and there was a dull ache in the small of her back.

The frame for her Berthe Morisot would always remind her of the Millstones now. But that was life. There was no such thing as pure joy. Not in this world anyhow. Sometimes, she glimpsed it – ecstasy – when she was lost in meditation – a foretaste of the promise of Heaven. Tiny drops of nectar to sweeten the hurts.

Life on earth would always be flawed. The Berthe Morisot print had seemed perfect at first. She loved the painting, and the reproduction was good. It had been sent by a dear friend, but she'd spent a long time trying to find the right frame. And, when she did . . . She would use the frame – she was determined about that. She would see it every time she opened her door, and she would take delight in it – but not yet.

Still wearing her coat, she sat down on the armchair with the brass buttons. She found herself fingering them – the round, shiny smooth part and the sharp little gap between their edge and the leather. Hugo had sat here when he came home that day. He had done exactly the same thing. And she had suppressed her horror. So that Hugo was free to speak.

The formal complaint had arrived in the morning post – addressed to the surgery. Before he had had a chance to read it properly, the receptionist had put him through to a persistent 'drugs representative'. They hadn't realised that the man was a journalist. By lunchtime, it was in The Echo and on the placards. 'A Millstone Round Dr. Roberts' Neck.' It hadn't needed a great deal of imagination to capitalise on the name. He had been so shocked that he came home after morning surgery. He couldn't face house calls.

She'd been cleaning the bathroom when he arrived home.

'Is that you, Hugo?' she had shouted down. 'Come home for a bite to eat?'

He hadn't replied so she washed her hands and went downstairs. He was sitting in the armchair – ashen, eyes staring ahead, uncomprehending.

'What on earth's the matter?' she had asked, going up to him. He had brushed her aside.

'Frank Millstone's wife has made a formal complaint about me,' he said blankly. 'I've had the press onto me. It'll be in the papers. I'm finished.'

She had sat on the settee and pressed her fists against the leather so that the imprint could be seen when she took them away. She was sitting at such an angle that Hugo couldn't see her doing that. It had probably enabled her to listen without interrupting. As soon as she saw that she had made an imprint, she moved her fists a little further on. She stared at the marks and, when they puffed back into place, she moved her fists again.

Frank Millstone and his wife were difficult patients. They always had been. On the fateful day, he had come into the surgery with a classic case of 'flu. Hugo had checked him out and told him to go home to bed, take paracetamol and drink plenty of fluids. He had also told him to be in touch if he became worse or showed no sign of improvement after 48 hours. Millstone got aggressive then and said – 'So you're not going to give me anything for this, are you? Do you know how bad I feel?'

Hugo had explained that influenza was miserable, but he repeated his advice. 'A couple of days in bed, Mr. Millstone, and you'll be back on form.'

When he contracted pneumonia four days later, he became dehydrated and died of a heart attack.

His wife contacted the papers straightaway with her

story. Her picture was on the front page. With bags under her eyes and wearing a suitably bereft expression, she was pictured with a photograph of Frank in her hand. Megan could memorise the headlines from those few weeks. 'Doctor refuses to treat dying man' was one. And 'You'll be back on form in two days' – doctor says of man who died.'

Suing doctors had not been a regular habit then. It had not been taken on as an alternative way of getting rich. People still accepted that life is imperfect. People are fallible and usually do their best.

The other members of the practice had spoken up in Hugo's defence immediately and the professional bodies had been totally supportive.

A month later, one of Millstone's friends – who had asked to be anonymous – told the Echo that Frank had gone to the 'Bird In The Hand' after he'd seen Hugo. He'd drunk four pints of beer and swallowed a paracetamol with each one. 'I'll show him!' he'd boasted to his friends. 'Not giving me proper tablets.' His wife had had to pick him up as the combination of a fever and the beer had made him incapable of walking home. After that revelation, more people had come forward with information. Frank Millstone had gone out the following day – to cheer himself up. They had refused to serve him at the Bird in the Hand so he'd gone to the Blue Boar. By the following day, he was so ill that he refused food and drink. Another anonymous informant had said that Frank bullied his wife – he had a dreadful temper. She had tried to get him to see a doctor, but he had threatened her. She hadn't persevered because he was in the habit of hitting her.

By that time, of course, the damage had been done to Hugo. He had resorted to anti-depressants and taken up smoking again. Every day, he had returned home with a haunted look. He wanted to retire, but she had told him that it would give out the wrong message. 'You're a fine doctor!' she had said. 'Don't give in!' She had had to force him out in the mornings like a reluctant child.

She'd listened to him for days – for weeks – for months. Sometimes his mood lifted, but then he went down again. She hadn't let him know about the tranquilisers that she'd been prescribed herself on top of the anti-depressants. She didn't want him to worry about her. He had always helped her through when she had been ill.

She never knew what the days would bring then. Patients showed their appreciation and he'd broken down once – in the armchair with the brass buttons – after an elderly woman had brought him some flowers. 'I know it's not usual to give flowers to a man,' she had said. 'But I wanted to do it. No-one could have a better doctor.'

She had listened so long that her own feelings had melted away. Disappeared. But now, on that same armchair, she felt the full force of her anger. How dare someone destroy Hugo! And, in trying to destroy him, they had diminished her and the children.

She reached for the beige cushion that was at the other end of the settee and sat back on the armchair with it in her hands. She pummelled it violently and, to her surprise, tears came. They fell on the beige cushion and she felt proud of the small dark smudges they made.

Chapter Thirteen

Megan was looking through the coach trip brochures
when Myf knocked. She put them aside and answered
the door.

'Have I called at an inconvenient time?' Myf asked.

'Not at all! Come in!'

Myf was holding a bunch of flowers. 'Here! These are
for you!' she said.

'For me?' Megan was genuinely surprised. 'It's not my
birthday . . .'

She extended her hand to invite Myf in to sit down as
she took them. Chrysanthemums. Yellow and white.
She didn't arrange them but poured a little water into a
bowl and left them there. 'I'll arrange them later!' she
said, going up to Myf and kissing her on the cheek.

'It's just that, well, I saw you getting out of the taxi
the other day. You looked so tired. As if you had
something on your mind. I know that it's none of my
business but Mr. Evans – Albert – doesn't look well. I
know how close you've become. And I'm sorry. Sorry
that he's ill, I mean . . .'

'Thank you.' There was a short silence – an awkward
one – and Megan broke it.

'How are you getting on with your new hearing-aid?'

'Oh, alright. But I suppose I expected that it would be
perfect.'

'Does it help at all?'

'Yes. It's better than the last one.' Myf was trying to
search for the right words to say something that really
mattered to her so Megan just let her be. 'I was really
grateful for that chat we had the other week,' she said.
'I've never talked about it before, and it did me good. I
thought that you'd be shocked. I felt reassured. I told

Harriet about it all afterwards. And we've become good friends. We put little rings around the programmes we want to watch and, when we both want to see the same thing, we've started to take it in turns. My flat for a programme and a cup of tea. Then Harriet's. We thought that we'd do it once a week. If we did it too often . . . well, it wouldn't work.'

'Thank you so much for the flowers!'

When she had seen Myf out, she went into the kitchen, found a vase and began at arrange the chrysanthemums. And she began to cry. Again.

She put the vase on the side-table in the corner of the living-room. The flowers wouldn't last long in the kitchen.

There was something comforting about seeing them. They were robust, long-lasting. Chrysanthemums had always been around. As a child, visitors had bought 'a bunch of chrysanths to the house. As a young teacher, children had brought them to her at the end of term in little pots. After Tom's birth, she had been inundated with chrysanthemums.

She found it hard to understand her tears. In part, it had been the kindness of Myf's gesture. Its unexpectedness, her innocence. But it was more than that. They had reminded her of Tom and his current unhappiness. Surely Alice would understand that it was important for Bella to see her father? Megan never let it show that she had always been closer to her son than to Susan. She hoped that it had not been picked up. Parents make so many mistakes.

The encounter with Gracie Millstone had disturbed her too. She wanted to be able to tell someone about it. She might, in due course, tell Tom and Susan – but not until she had resolved it herself. Even if Hugo had still been alive, she wouldn't have risked exposing him to the situation. She wouldn't have shared it with him even if she had resolved it. He might have wanted to deal with it differently. She ached for someone to talk to. Not Harriet or Myf – or even Annie. She wanted Albert. But it was unfair to burden him.

She made herself a cup of green tea and turned back to the brochure on coach holidays. A few nights earlier, she had prayed for wisdom regarding Tom, Alice and Bella. When she woke the following morning, she had been given it. The words 'coach holiday' had come to her mind. It had taken her a few moments to discern the connexion. And then it was very clear. Local coach companies often ran short breaks to London. They usually included a visit to the theatre and an overnight stay. If she could find a suitable one – and it had to be convincing – they all knew her tastes – she could just say that she was coming up to London. She would tell Tom and write to Alice to explain. She had nearly finished the scrapbook for Bella and she was reluctant to trust it to the post. If Alice suggested that she should stay in the family hotel, she could say that the overnight stay was part of the deal. Tom would probably guess her motives – but she doubted that Alice would. And maybe she would get to see her grandchild. Bella was ten now and would soon be going through puberty – difficult enough for any child. Harder for Bella.

Thankfully, Hugo had died before the problem had been diagnosed. But he had been the one to suggest that they check Bella's hearing. Maybe there had been a suspicion in his mind? She hoped not.

She decided that she would make a scrapbook for Stevie and Catherine as well. For Catherine, she could add some simple activity suggestions. Stevie had phoned her the other evening – all by himself. Susan and Paul had gone out and Cindy, the girl at the nursery, was baby-sitting. There was an extension upstairs and Stevie had crept along the landing and slipped into his parents' bed.

'Hullo, Mami' he'd said. 'Guess what I'm doing?' And he had told her about his little exploit. He had packed a bag of food so that he could have a midnight feast. 'Should I clean my teeth afterwards? Or will Cindy think it's odd?' She told him to forget the tooth-brushing – just for once. She wouldn't have said that if she had been his mother. That call had meant a lot to her. To be allowed into a child's world and be part of his secrets.

There was a knock on the door, and she knew that it was Albert. She let him in and he went straightaway to sit down on the armchair. He knew that he didn't have to wait to be invited anymore. 'How are you, sweetheart?' he asked, taking her hand.

'Fine. How are you? Did the aromatherapy treatment go well?'

'It was OK. I think I get as much from the girl herself as I do from the therapy. Maybe that's all part of it. I hadn't realised how much the mind . . . I knew it in theory. But it's not until it happens to you personally that . . .' He looked at her face and stopped. 'Have you been crying?' he asked. 'You've been crying! What's wrong, sweetheart? Tell me what's wrong!'

There was a tenderness in his voice that made her want to run to him for comfort. Impulsively, she said 'I can't.'

Then she saw his eyes. They were telling her that he wanted to stay.

'Stay!' she pleaded. 'Please!'

They had a restless night. He had to get up several times – but so did she. There was something poignant about their closeness. There was a beauty in being prepared to share and expose the limited stamina of their bodies – accepting each other as they were.

She told him about the meeting with Gracie Millstone, though he hadn't said much. But he had put his arms around her – one at the shoulder that reached up and followed the circles of her hair at the nape of her neck. The other rested on her waist then slipped down very tenderly to stroke her bottom. Again, in little circular movements with the palm of his hand and the fingers squeezing gently. She was actually relieved to know that the tenderness wouldn't develop into anything – none of the expectations, disappointments or pretence. It was enough in itself. More than enough. All that she could have or wanted or needed. He respected her body as it was. With its looseness and bulges. Just two ageing human beings who loved each other. And one of them dying.

When he got out of bed suddenly, quickly, she knew the problem. He made his way back from the bathroom and, although she couldn't see his face clearly, she sensed that he was embarrassed. Instead of saying anything, she just kissed him on the mouth and let her arms caress the upper part of his body. She had been through this with Hugo, of course, but Hugo had withdrawn from her as soon as the disease had set in. He slept in the spare bedroom as if ashamed of his vulnerability. Maybe he had wanted to hide it from her. He had always been protective – scared that her depressive bouts would return. Albert was dozing in her arms when she had to get up herself. Her bladder control was weak especially at night. In spite of the pelvic floor exercises.

'I've got to go now!' she whispered.

When she got back into bed, she and Albert began to laugh. She felt so happy and she knew that he was too. Then he fell asleep.

In the darkened room, she realised that she would soon have to let all this go. Was she strong enough to deal with it? Should she have kept her distance? But no, she felt the warm glow inside. The relationship was so precious – more so because it was destined to be brief. All things pass in this life. She wouldn't have missed out on this intimacy with Albert. Not for all the tea in China.

Not for all the tea in China.

Chapter Fourteen

Megan spent the morning in the National Museum of Wales. It never failed to uplift her. The Davies sisters of Llandinam – two unmarried women who had lived in the heart of Wales – travelled and collected paintings. They had been way ahead of their time and loved the work of the controversial Impressionists. When they eventually died, their collections had been bequeathed to the nation. Wales had priceless access to these wonderful paintings in the Museum.

She had a sandwich in the little café by the entrance of the Museum and, as it was fine, she walked over to Bute Park. She managed to find a bench and she sat down. A man was sitting at the other end reading a newspaper and didn't even lift his head to acknowledge her.

She looked at the people as they passed by. A small group of young people, probably students, chatting and laughing about something. They all looked the same, these youngsters with their skinny trousers and dark jackets – rucksacks on their back or hanging down over one arm. They took up a lot of space and a man walking in the other direction was irritated that he had to move aside to avoid them. The youngsters were oblivious to anyone else.

A woman was carrying shopping. Retail therapy, as it was now called. But it never satisfied for long. That was part of its addiction. Something that the retailers relied upon. She had a bag from Zara and another from BHS – British Home Stores. There was something very dependable and old-fashioned about the name. British Home Stores. Its profits would probably go down soon and someone would invent a different name in the hope of attracting a new clientele. Or get a celebrity to market it. The woman didn't look very happy. Was she imagining it or did everybody look more miserable, oppressed, depersonalised, these days?

A few parents walked by with children, making their way to the New Theatre for a matinee performance. Some of them were with grandparents. Or so she presumed. It was difficult to tell people's ages anymore. It was easier with the men. But the women, they were the tricky ones. Dyed hair now looked natural as did extensions. Apparently, it was getting more and more common for the average woman-in-the-street to have face lifts. Bags under the eyes could disappear along with the wrinkles. But there was usually some little give-away. The more measured gait, the hands, the neck. She had never taken her own grandchildren to the theatre. And she probably never would. Stevie and Catherine lived far away from the big towns. Admittedly, there was an Arts Centre in Builth Wells and there was more in Aberystwyth. But Susan and Paul would want to take them to such rare treats themselves. Bella? Would the theatre be too much for Bella? Would she see Bella at all? Yes, of course she would. She was fortunate. Albert might never see his grandchildren again – maybe once or twice. She found herself wondering about them – the pretty little girl with perfect ringlets. Did she ever *play?* And the little boy with the white shoes? Albert would have to tell his family soon. He had given her their details, which she had written down in her address book. The Evans entry was now confusing and over-written. Albert and Doreen Evans with a RIP mark above her name. Now there was Duncan, Fiona, Heather and Jacob Evans. In the space underneath. And, crowded into the side, Charles Evans.

She began to get chilly, so she stood up. She decided to walk home along a bus route so that she could take the easier option if her back and knees gave her problems.

The man who had been sitting beside her looked up briefly then returned to his paper. The Daily Telegraph – Hugo's paper. She had always preferred The Guardian, but it was hardly worth an argument. From time to time, she had bought her own copy, but she didn't like the idea of wasting so much paper. Since Hugo's death, she had taken The Guardian.

She went down the subway and came out at Greyfriars, close to the Hilton Hotel. She crossed the road and was soon passing the shops opposite the Castle. Several camping shops close together. There was a new type of social outcast now standing outside many of the buildings. On the pavement in front of offices and shops. The smokers.

Hugo had smoked from the age of sixteen. The link between cigarettes and lung disease had come to light in the sixties and, by then, he was addicted. Young doctors were not always the first to practice what they preached.

Hugo's first hospital jobs had been so stressful – and the hours so punishingly long that he had never been able to break the habit. He never smoked in public – just at home. He had spent hours encouraging, ordering patients to give up smoking. There were posters in the surgery. More than anyone, he knew the risks. He had given it up a few times but went back to cigarettes whenever he had a personal dilemma.

Hugo had been so isolated – always. His mother had been approaching forty and childless until he was born. Elderly *primagravida*. A miracle child, she had been in the habit of saying. 'I thought it was the change.' So Hugo was the only child. Fretted about, over-protected. And then they had sent him to boarding school when he was eleven! She had never understood it. They had waited so long and then they just dispatched him to a high-achieving residential school more than a hundred miles away just as he was approaching puberty. He hadn't been very happy there – but he did fulfil the promises in the prospectus. His 'A' level results had been impressive and he had had no problem in getting into Medicine. His parents had lived to see him fulfil their ambition and then their health failed. Slowly and miserably. He had several cousins and was very close to one of them but, yes, Hugo had been isolated.

Megan sheltered in the doorway of the City Temple. It had begun to rain. It was only a shower but it had turned colder and she decided to finish the journey on the bus. The cold weather always affected her arthritis. She didn't want to risk the pain that sometimes scorched out from her joints. The smell of wintergreen. The analgesics. Paracetamol usually took the edge of it but, taken over a period of time, it made her constipated. She had been forced to resort to the non-steroidal anti-inflammatories from time to time. And they upset her stomach.

She got on the long bendy bus. Her purse was out ready so that she could show the driver her bus pass. He saw it, grunted and she found a seat. She carefully put her purse back into her bag and zipped it. She had a horror of losing her purse with its debit card and personal details. That was a disadvantage of being alone – no-one to help remember emergency hotlines. Or know the secret places where codes and PIN numbers were stored.

The woman in front of her was coughing. There was a No Smoking policy on the buses, of course. She knew the rasping, ugly cough of chronic bronchitis. The smoker's cough. Her father had had it, but no-one knew the risks then and he had gone on to develop emphysema. Coal-dust or cigarettes – or both? There had been X-rays and quibbles about compensation. All vague in her memory, muddled up with the worry of her mother's illness. And then James' tragic death.

She hadn't expected to hear the same cough in her husband. Somehow, she had nursed the comforting idea that, as a doctor, Hugo was exempt. Although Hugo had been thin and could look pale at times, he was a robust man. She had been the one to catch the colds which sometimes led to chest infections. She had been the one to get depressed. Hugo had always been there. Quietly strong. He had a tendency to lose his patience. But, on the whole, he was a considerate man.

The coughing had gone on for years.

She pressed the red button to let the driver know that she wanted to get off the bus even though she knew that it was a popular stop and there was always a queue waiting to get on.

She realised that she had forgotten to get the wine. She couldn't bring herself to go into Tesco's and give them even more custom for their greedy, grasping hands. There was a licensed corner-shop, but she didn't think that they'd have a good selection of quality wine. She'd go home, put her feet up on the footstool and read for half an hour. Then, she'd go to Ballantyne's for a bottle – or maybe two. It wasn't often that she went to visit Sam.

Megan piled the Down Manor material neatly into her shopping-trolley. Some of the files were wider than others, and she took some time to fit them all in. It was a bit like doing a jigsaw puzzle and she felt pleased with herself when the job was done. She wheeled the trolley out of the flat and towards the main door. She knew that there was a ridge there, but her mind was preoccupied. The trolley twisted and she wasn't strong enough to stop it from falling. Although she had done her best to fasten the top, the zip couldn't close it completely and some of the Down Manor documents fell out. A little book with newspaper cuttings fell onto the pathway. 'Down Manor pupils raise £250 for 'Médecins sans Frontières' – one said. Cicely Stafford had often given money to this charity and was one of the first to promote it. On the other side was a picture of a woman who had been a pupil at the school. She went on to become a fairly well-known actress and her picture had been on view in the school when Megan taught there. 'Former Down Manor pupil a West End success' boasted the headline. Underneath the cutting, Cicely had glued a piece of paper with the girl's name – in capital letters. The dates of her time in Down Manor – underlined. And a resume of her successes. The glue was old and the fall loosened the cutting on one side. Megan looked at it and was overwhelmed by sadness.

The wind was light, but it carried the book a couple of yards and Megan ran after it to retrieve it. For a moment, she wondered if she was mad. So much effort, so much emotion concentrated on the redundant efforts of a deceased woman. Even Bill and Ronnie Price had wanted to get rid of it all. But she knew in her heart that she was doing the right thing. Before she could recycle all this paperwork – a lifetime's devotion – she knew that she had to honour it. There were times when ritual held an unrivalled way of dealing with things.

Back in the flat, she sat down and rubbed her knees. It had been a mistake to run after the Down Manor book. Sudden movements like that caused her problems. The knee pain was usually the first to start and then her altered posture strained her back in the lower lumbar area. Sometimes she got away with it. And sometimes she didn't. She was too busy to go to the osteopath.

Too busy? Was she too busy? Yes, she was. She and Albert were spending a lot of time together. Sometimes, this was difficult and distressing but, on the whole, she was trying to take advantage of every day. So was he. Every morning was a gift. She didn't have the energy that she used to have and it showed in little things. The jolt with the trolley had unnerved her. Then, there was her unexpected invitation to Sam's farm after so many years. The scrapbook for Bella and the ones she wanted to make for Stevie and Catherine. She didn't want to favour Bella just because she had a problem. Indeed, her idea had spread. Harriet was beginning to make scrapbooks for her grandchildren, and she had told another friend about it. The friend thought it was an excellent idea and she intended doing the same. When she mentioned it to Albert – he saw the scrapbook on the table – he had been pensive and quiet.

'Have you heard of memory boxes?' he'd asked.

She nodded.

'Do you think it's a good idea?'

She had felt choked up – that feeling when words won't come out. She had nodded again.

And he had said 'Will you help me?'

She had nodded once more. Little Heather and Jacob

Evans needed something to hold on to. The little girl might just remember him. But, for Jacob, he would be a blank page.

'Do you ever call him Jake?' she had asked. She didn't like the use of abbreviations on the whole but Jacob seemed a heavy name for a small boy.

'Fiona won't allow it.'

'I thought so', she thought. 'I thought so.'

It was Hugo who had used the name Stevie first. He'd been helping him as he took his first steps. 'Come on, Stevie' he'd urged.

Hugo hadn't been well then and it was poignant to hear him calling out the name and taking pleasure in his little grandson. It had been Stevie ever since. Susan only called him Stephen if she was cross with him – which wasn't often.

Then there was the Cicely Stafford stuff. She was well on her way to sorting things out now. Would Bill and Ronnie Price get in contact with her again? Was the whole episode drawing to a close? She thought that there was something unfinished about it. Intuition, knowledge. Gifts which came at a price.

As if that weren't enough, she had to do something about Gracie Millstone. She had actually felt quite close to the girl – especially when the two women in the charity shop were rude. Gracie had moved to Pontypridd with her mother and two half-brothers – to get away from the jibes and pointing fingers. Neighbours had given her a hard time after the later publicity. Megan had fought with the little voice inside her that she recognised as revenge. The voice that said, 'I'm glad she had a hard time.' She had allowed the feeling to surface, she had acknowledged it as being something natural and necessary; she had toyed with it for a few minutes like a kitten with a ball. And then she had let it go. Revenge harms the avenger as much, if not more than the avenged. 'Let him who seeks revenge remember to dig two graves.' Ancient Chinese proverb. A timeless message.

What about forgiveness? She still hadn't forgiven either of them – Frank or Ethel Millstone. But she was working on it. And she wouldn't get in touch with Gracie again until she had dealt with it.

Yes, she was very busy. But, as she stood up, she thought that she might have escaped lightly from the jolt with the fallen trolley. Maybe a bruise would come out but nothing more.

She put the two bottles of wine – a classic white Italian from the Orvieto region and a red Bordeaux – in the boot of her car. The filled shopping-trolley provided them with good padding, and she made sure that they couldn't slip down to the wheels or the frame when she was on the move.

Back in her flat, she checked the route again. It was very difficult to find the way to Sam's farm, and it was the first time that she had ventured there alone and in the dark. She would have to memorise it all. She needed to leave at 5.15 so she popped into Albert's flat just after five.

He had met up with his old friend and colleague a few days earlier. The man had been shocked at Albert's news, though she was sure that he had been able to see its signs for himself. He had asked the friend to keep it quiet but, since then, there had been a steady flow of incoming phone calls.

He had met up with a few more friends though, as he became easily tired, they had not been demanding. One friend – a woman, a friend of Doreen's, had called at the flat. They all told him that he should tell the family. He, himself, realised that he couldn't put it off much longer, mainly because he didn't want them to find out about it at second-hand. He thought that the woman might contact Duncan. He had made her promise to keep it quiet as his other son, Charles, was on holiday in Vienna. He wanted to write to them both when Charles returned and send the letters out on the same day. First-class post.

To save time, she used her key in his door. Albert was looking out of the window in the twilight.

'Are you alright, Albert?' she asked, going up to him. 'I'm off to Sam's.'

He turned round to face her. 'Have a lovely time!' he said, giving her a peck on the cheek. 'Have a lovely time!'

There was a dullness in his eyes that worried her. He was trying hard to be cheerful – too cheerful. She knew that he was troubled about something.

'What's the matter?'

'Nothing. Have a safe journey! I look forward to hearing all about it tomorrow!'

'Albert, what's the matter?' It was almost ten past five and she began to panic. 'You must tell me! I can't go out and leave you like this!'

'Like what?'

She knew him so well now that she picked up his every mood. And he knew her well enough to know that he had to tell her.

'I rang the surgery just now to make an appointment.'

'And?'

'I couldn't remember the number – after all these

years. I didn't even have it down in the book because we knew it off by heart. I rang Directory Enquiries. I wrote the number down and rang it. By the time I got through to the receptionist, I had forgotten why I was ringing. . .'

'Is that all?' she asked gently.

'I was so embarrassed that I pitched my voice low and mumbled 'Sorry, wrong number.''

He looked at her appealingly.

She knew what was worrying him. Was this the beginning of a cancer-related confusion?

And she took him in her arms. 'Don't worry, my love. I've done worse things. Tried to open the door with my glasses case. Started to put cereal in the fridge.'

'But you don't have metastases,' he floundered.

'Look, if you were really confused, you wouldn't have had such a sharp reaction. You wouldn't have thought of lowering your voice.'

He looked at her and realised that she was making sense.

'Excuse me a moment. I've just got to go back to the flat.'

'Have a lovely time . . .'

She left Albert's door open and went to turn the key in her own flat. She picked up the telephone.

'Sam? Sam? Is that you?' She heard his voice though there was a fair amount of background noise. 'Sam, I've got a problem with this evening.'

'You can't come?' She didn't often sense emotion in his voice but he sounded genuinely disappointed. 'Are you ill?'

'I'm fine. But a friend of mine – a very close friend – is ill. I don't think I can leave him.'

'What sort of 'ill'?'

'He has cancer.'

'Bring him along with you then. He can manage the journey?'

'Are you sure?'

'Yes. Jack's got plenty of food . . .'

'He's on a diet so he might not be able to eat much. . .'

'That's alright. I'll tell Jack that there'll be five of us.'

'Five?'

'Yes. Maddie's been helping us and she wanted to stay.'

'See you then at about 7?'

'Yes.' He put the receiver down.

She had been desperate to solve her dilemma and was relieved, if surprised, that a solution had been so easy. But who was Maddie?

It had been difficult to persuade Albert to go with her. She was firm and said that she needed him to help her navigate. He'd refused the offer of an oxygen cylinder at the flat – it was too early for that – but he'd bought himself a small portable one. Just in case. It just about managed to fit into the boot with the bottles of wine and the shopping-trolley and, once again, the paperwork in the trolley provided a cushion.

She had handed him the directions and a little light combined with a magnifying glass that normally fitted into the glove compartment. It had been a gift from Tom.

Albert began reading the directions when Megan announced 'I forgot to mention that I need to make a detour. I have to stop at Abercynon first. It's only a mile or so out of our way. That's why I needed to leave early.'

'Abercynon?' Who's there?'

She hesitated for a moment. How could she tell him about the little shrine – sadly neglected these days? Should she tell him the story of how the boy had been lifted out of the well all those years ago by the Virgin Mary. Should she tell him about the healings that had taken place there – all recorded in The Western Mail.

'Do I ever surprise you?' she asked, lightly.

'You're always surprising me!'

'There's a shrine to Our Lady – the Virgin Mary – there!'

He didn't reply.

'I just need to visit it. Five minutes or so. Come with me!'

'You really are surprising me now. Why do you have to go there tonight?'

She spoke slowly. 'You know that I have the shopping-trolley in the boot?'

'Yes . . .'

'Well, I need to take it down to the shrine. It's got all Cicely Stafford's stuff in it. All her Down Manor documents. I need to dispose of them but I must honour them first. It meant so much to her.'

'I'm lost!'

Megan was encouraged. The conversation had taken his mind off his own preoccupations, and she was sure now that his 'lapse' had been nothing more than the reaction of an anxious mind. Stress.

She told him the story and how the miners had built steps down to the river so that pilgrims could hold services there.

'I've never heard of it before,' he said.

She smiled. 'Not many people have! It's a hidden jewel. Very special.'

She drove off the A470 and parked in the grounds of St. Thomas' Church. She turned to face him and smiled, holding his chin in her hand.

'Do you think I'm mad?' she asked brightly.

'No. But . . . interesting.' He kissed her hand. 'And I love you.'

'I love you too. Do you want to come?'

'Is it far?'

'No but there's a slope. I've got a torch in the boot, packed up in the top of the trolley. We'll be alright.'

It was an odd journey – she and Albert arm in arm, supporting each other and her trying to guide the trolley down. A couple of times, it went too fast on the incline and Albert took it from her.

'I'm still good for some things!' he said.

And there they stood – two people and a shopping trolley full of the devotion of another woman's work in front of a Statue of Our Lady that they struggled to see in the darkness. It had been repainted and the white of the robes shone. Someone had left a jar of flowers at Her feet. And a candle. They heard the river rushing below them.

Megan pulled the trolley up towards the statue, held Albert's hand and began to pray.

'I thank You so much for Cicely Stafford. For all that she did, for all that she was. I know that she is safe in Your hands now. At peace. You know that I have been entrusted with these papers and I realise that I'll have to recycle them. But, first, may I offer each one to you? You alone know the dedication that went into their making. *Requiescat in pace*, Cicely.'

She let go of the trolley and the two of them stood there for a few moments in silence.

'That was beautiful!' whispered Albert. 'I must admit, when you were telling me about it, I thought it very odd. But you've done the right thing.'

It was then that she let go of his hand and walked a few steps away onto a patch of higher ground. She asked him if she could lay hands on him.

'Salmon fish-cakes alright for you guys?'

Megan had never got used to the word 'guys' in this context. But Maddie, daughter of one of the farm managers, was such a delight that it didn't seem to matter. And she was young.

She looked across at Albert who hesitated for a moment. There was a tureen of braised leeks with carrots on the table and the fish-cakes looked delicious. Jack brought them in on an oval dish, garnished with lemon wedges and a few sprigs of rocket.

'Fine for me!' said Albert, cheerfully. He had been in the habit of checking everything recently for their basic ingredients. But, with this simple but beautifully prepared food, he didn't bother.

Jack put two fishcakes on each plate and Maddie handed them round.

'Help yourselves to everything!' said Sam, passing the tureen of leeks and carrots to Megan first.

They had already enjoyed a delicious bowl of butternut squash soup with home-made bread and the main course matched it. What could be better than eating an excellent, wholesome meal in good company?

She had never thought of Sam as being good company before, but she noticed his eyes as he watched Maddie. The same applied to Jack. They were smiling at the young woman with the kind of passive indulgence normally reserved for a grandchild. There were photographs of her on the wall. One of her on her own – a pretty girl with a mass of titian hair. And another informal one with her standing between Sam and Jack – her arms round both of them. Sam had never looked so happy. He'd changed for the better when he met Jack but there was an additional air about him now. Contentment maybe?

Albert was on good form and enjoying himself. For a moment, she forgot about his illness. He helped himself to some more leeks and carrots. He hadn't said much but this was his first meeting with Sam and Jack – and Maddie. It was the first time for him to visit the farm. And she had forgotten what a reserved man he was.

They had uncorked the bottle of Italian wine which everyone had enjoyed. Maddie offered a second glass. Megan refused as she was driving, and Albert refused too. Maddie poured more wine into Sam and Jack's glasses without even asking them. And then she helped herself.

'We've got planning permission,' she said. 'The stables will make a lovely flat for you, won't it?' she added, turning to Sam and then to Jack.

They both smiled back at her. Sam even laughed.

Megan was looking out for any sign of coercion but there appeared to be none. The two men were obviously delighted at the prospect of moving out of the farm house when the stables had been converted.

'All on the flat,' Maddie said, looking at Megan. Then she turned to the men and added, 'You're not getting any younger, are you, guys?'

Jack beamed with pleasure – as if it were a compliment. He even bent his back over to accentuate his slight stoop. This made Sam laugh – again.

'And Sam's not getting any younger either' she added pertly. 'He's seventy-five next birthday.'

Albert joined in with the smiling and Megan was awed by the power of this young woman, probably in her early twenties, with a power to captivate.

They all finished their food about the same time -

though Albert had left a little on the side. But, considering that he had lost his appetite, he had done very well.

'I'm sorry to leave a little,' he said to Maddie, who had begun to collect the plates. 'I have some difficulties with . . .'

'No problem!' Maddie replied charmingly. 'Who's for Eve's Pudding? And custard.'

Jack got up from the table. 'I'll give you a hand,' he said. 'I just want to check it's the right temperature. Eve's Pudding is awful unless it's just right. When I made it earlier . . .'

The conversation got lost as they went into the kitchen. The large farmhouse kitchen with the Welsh dresser displaying an impressive assortment of china. The pine table covered with a checked oilcloth. Red and white. The chairs – some beech and some oak. Plain. The Aga. Sam and Jack's – and Maddie's, so it seemed.

Jack carried the Eve's Pudding in. He had turned it out onto a large circular plate and it was steaming hot. 'Three cheers for Jack!' Maddie said. She began to clap and everyone joined in the applause.

Albert said that he couldn't eat anymore, and Sam pointed to the fruit bowl.

'Would you like some fruit?' he asked.

'No, really. I'm full. It's been a lovely meal.'

Megan felt a bit guilty as she ate the pudding with some custard as Albert was sitting next to her. But he put his hand on her knee under the table. Briefly. To let her know that he was happy.

'Tell me more about your plans!' Megan said to Maddie. There was no trace of suspicion in her voice. She, too, was captivated.

'We've got it all sorted.' The enthusiastic optimism of

youth. 'Craig – he's my partner – oh, I've told you that. Well, he's just finishing his course in the Business School. Taking his final exams in June. He'll do very well.' The enthusiastic optimism of youth but Maddie was probably right. 'I got my degree last summer. Hotel management. Well, I was wondering how to use it. It started out with the jam.'

Megan looked at Sam and smiled. But he only had eyes for Maddie. And occasionally Jack.

'Well, between us – Craig and me – we've got a wide range of abilities.' The enthusiastic optimism of youth again. And, once more, she was probably right. 'Farming's got to diversify – everybody knows that. Well, once we get Sam and Jack booted out to the stables . . .' She looked at the two older men with affection. They laughed together – a private joke that excluded her and Albert. Sam was still gazing at her. Jack was checking that everyone had finished their pudding.

'So how will you do it?'

Maddie needed little encouragement. 'Dad'll start winding things down here in a few years. Craig and me, well, we'll move in. We'll get people in to help us do the work. It'll be a lovely B&B. Speciality home-made food, away-from-it-all weekends, kids seeing the animals. If we get planning permission to convert the other outhouses – and we *will* – we'll rent those out for self-catering. We'll have got our name known through the jams. ''JacnSam's Jams', that's what we thought we'd call ourselves. Oh, I know it sounds a bit clumsy!' She shrugged her shoulders and winked at Sam. 'But it's hard to say, a bit of a tongue-twister. We'll start with a little promotion. Tiny jars – just a few spoonfuls. We'll say 'Can you say 'JacnSam's Jams?' without making a mistake. 'Well done, sonny. Take this home!'"

As she finished her words with a flourish, she disappeared back into the kitchen.

'Coffee?' She poured water into a kettle. Then, after a moment's hesitation, she added, 'I've got herbal tea too, Albert.'

Megan looked at the photos on the wall. Maddie. Experience told her that young partnerships don't necessarily last. Plans get crippled by red-tape. Ideals fall by the wayside. And yet she knew intuitively that she needn't have any worries about Sam. Not anymore.

The journey home was difficult. Turns in the lanes, hidden junctions, puddles and holes in the narrow roads – and no markings. She swerved when Albert's head fell on her shoulder. She had to stop. She had hit a hedge.

Albert woke up. 'I'm so sorry! What . . . ? Is this my fault?'

They both got out of the car and used the torch to check the damage. Fortunately, there was nothing major. She'd have to have the paintwork touched up. It wasn't as if it was a new car. She knew the men in the garage well.

But it had shaken her, and the two of them sat in the stationary car. She realised that she had pulled a muscle in her shoulder – probably after the incident when the trolley had twisted at the front door earlier on. It was not too bad – it would heal itself in a few days. But suddenly, she felt very vulnerable. Forlorn. It had been a lovely evening. This is how Cinderella must have felt after the Ball, she thought.

Albert kept on apologising – and it irritated her. 'It's alright!' she said, on edge.

He picked up her uneasiness and apologised all the more.

She wasn't really irritated with him. She was annoyed that the party was over. Here they were, car scratched, in the middle of the night, she with a strained muscle, him getting frailer . . .

'Let me drive!' His voice was terse.

'No, I'll be alright in a minute!'

He opened the door, got out of the passenger seat and walked round to the driver's door. 'Get out!' he said in a clear voice. 'I'm driving us home!'

She had never heard this tone before from Albert and she simply obeyed.

He was a good driver and they were soon back on the A470. They were silent. Albert was concentrating on the road in an unfamiliar car. She was trying to understand her feelings.

At the next roundabout, he turned towards the road for Nelson then took a side-street.

'Wrong way, Albert.' She was surprised at his mistake and was worried as his driving became more erratic. He pulled in at a lay-by. It wasn't a residential area and he got out of the car and walked off.

If she had felt like Cinderella after the Ball, how must he be feeling? To enjoy an evening out in lively company, to be with her, to think how things could have been . . .

'Sorry about that!' he said when he returned. 'I'll get us back on the road again. And I insist on paying for the work to put the car right. It wouldn't have happened if I hadn't nodded off like that . . .'

'There's no need, my love.' Her voice was soft again and she hurt for his hurt.

They drove for a few minutes in silence, but it was a comfortable one.

When he spoke, his words were slow and pensive.

'Sam and Jack. Are they?'

'Gay?'

'Well, yes.'

'I'm sure they are.'

'But they've never talked about it?'

'There seemed no need. Oh, Sam was unhappy when he was younger. When he got together with Jack, things got a lot better for him. I was just pleased.'

'But you didn't ask?'

'Things were different then. It must have been, well, I don't know but a long time ago. Why do you ask?'

She knew the answer. But she also knew that he had to make the statement himself.

'I think my younger son – Charles. I think he might be gay.'

Chapter Fifteen

'How much do I owe you?'

'Dunno. I bought stuff for myself at the same time. Ten pounds'll be fine.'

Harriet was a generous woman. It had cost more.

'Please, Harriet! I'm so grateful that you went for me.'

'Had to go anyway. Don't worry! If it was over, it was only a few pence.'

Megan grimaced. 'Apart from my shoulder, I've got quite a nasty bruise coming out. Just above my ankle. I told you how it happened?'

Harriet shook her head so Megan told her how the shopping-trolley had twisted and fallen on the metal ridge at the main door. But she didn't tell her what the trolley had contained.

Harriet had been down to the shops and bought Megan some glucosamine for her joints. It was worth a try. Hugo had been against alternative medicine because it hadn't been through the process of double-blind trials. Though he had approved of the arnica cream that she always used for bruises. It was applied externally, and he thought that it could do no harm. But anything taken orally was out.

She had her feet up on the stool, and she reached for her purse which was on a little foldaway table right beside her. So was the brochure for the coach holidays.

'Going away?' Harriet asked lightly.

'Yes. To London.'

She could see Harriet's eyes light up but she contained her feelings and said quietly 'Are you going with Albert?'

'No. I'm going on my own.'

The glint in Harriet's eyes shone again. 'It's ages since I've been to London. I used to love it all – the shopping, the Theatre . . .'

Megan smiled. 'There's plenty of availability. I'll spend part of the time with the family, of course. I couldn't go to London without calling on them.' After a moment's hesitation, she asked – 'Do you want to come too?'

Harriet was excited now. It made her face so much more attractive which made Megan realise how miserable her friend had been in recent months.

'Oh, I'd love to. When is it for?'

The package involved travelling to London by coach on the Friday and stopping for three quarters of an hour at Windsor en route. The theatre tickets were for the Saturday matinée performance of 'Les Misérables'. That left the Saturday morning free – 'to shop till you drop' – and the evening – 'Why not treat yourself to a meal out?' There was a list of restaurants which offered discounts to 'our loyal customers'. There was an hour and a half allocated on the Sunday morning for visiting a local market. And, after that, the journey home.

There was great pleasure in the intimacy of arranging an outing for two. They might be able to sit next to each other on the coach and the theatre. Before Harriet got too carried away, Megan told her that she had paid an extra charge for single occupancy of her room.

'Perhaps we ought to ask Myf?' Harriet had principles too and knew how hurt Myf would be if she weren't invited. She probably wouldn't go, but it was important to invite her.

Megan suggested that Harriet should ring Myf straightaway so that they could book. It was for the second weekend in December so there might be a rush of people wanting to use the trip for Christmas shopping.

Megan listened as Harriet took her time to pronounce her words clearly. It seemed that Myf was quite keen to join them, and Harriet gave her the dates with the details.

Megan pointed to the armchair. 'Would you like to stay for a bit?'

'Better get back. I told Myf to ring me back. She doesn't know I've rung from your number so . . .'

Harriet opened and closed the door behind her – she didn't want Megan to have to get up.

It was better in a way to have Harriet and Myf, she thought. When she went off to see the family, they'd be company for each other. The family? What a wonderful word family was! But how much secret pain could be hidden within it.

She had already told Tom about the trip and the scrapbook for Bella. He knew – he guessed, that it was a pretext.

'Didn't know you were interested in musicals, Mum,' he'd said.

'Some of the music in Les Misérables is very good!' And she had immediately thought of the Requiem.

'I've made a decision,' he'd told her. 'I'm not going to see Bella for a month. See how it goes . . .'

'What did Alice say?'

'She didn't understand – thought that things were working out fine.'

Megan had written a letter to Alice but was waiting for a reply. She hoped and prayed that, before the month was out, Bella would miss her Dad and ask about him. But what if she said nothing? It would only reinforce his view that he wasn't needed. Could she have a word with Alice's parents? They were more worldly than Alice herself. But would she be seen as interfering? Discernment. Discernment. Her main concern at the moment was Tom. Whatever he thought about Alice's way of dealing with Bella, it was working – in the sense that the child was settled and in a routine. Not that Alice had much of a routine. Yes, Bella was alright. Tom was not. Life was so unfair. It was just a case of getting used to that fact.

Chapter Sixteen

Megan and Albert were on their way out to post the letters, he had written several drafts, and was finally happy about them. As they were leaving, Albert went back to get a pill for his nausea, and while Megan was waiting at the main door of the complex, a visitor came up to her and offered his sympathy on Hugo's passing.

When Albert rejoined Megan the visitor looked perplexed. Time had passed – four years had gone by. At first, there had been the birthdays. And then the first of everything. The first Christmas without Hugo – the first wedding anniversary. The first time she had sent cards to the children. 'With love from Mum xxx' Now she had stopped counting when there might be more counting about to begin again.

Outside, it was drizzling. She suggested that Albert should put the two letters in his pocket so that they wouldn't get wet. After all the effort, the last thing he wanted was to have the addresses blurred. He slipped them in but the pocket wasn't big enough, so she put them in her handbag.

They reached the post-box and she got the letters out for him to post. He held them in his hand and hesitated, extending the other hand over them as a make-shift umbrella. They just stood there then he sighed. It was more of an emotional expression than a sigh – a gasp. He held on to them still and, before he posted the first one, he kissed it. Lightly. Inconspicuously. Then he looked at the other letter and he did the same. Gone. Disappeared into the gaping hole. At the mercy of the Royal Mail. First-class. Bearers of bad tidings.

She held his hand and whispered 'Well done!'

The little colour that he had in his face had

disappeared, and, for a moment, she thought that he was going to faint. Her own shoulder – though better – was still sore. There was a pub nearby. Neither of them had been in there before. It was down-at-heel – tatty. Youngsters used to gather around in the evenings, but it was the only place for them to go. Somewhere to sit down and recover.

She ushered him to a seat and ordered the drinks. A Tonic Water for him and a J2O for herself – Apple and Mango.

It was early afternoon, and they were the only customers. The cork coasters were stained. The table had a streak of plain wood where a spill had removed the varnish.

'You've *done* it.' She leant over to him. 'You've done it.'

'They'll be on the phone to me tomorrow.'

He took his jacket off and she noticed some perspiration on his forehead. Little beads of it, unusual for Albert. She put her left arm around his waist. She tightened her grip. Above her thumb, she could feel the bones of his lower ribs. Below her little finger, there was the sharpness of his pelvis. He was so fragile. And her hand was there like a rock. Steady. She had to keep it firm.

'Tell me more about the boys!' she said. She knew that the relationships were complex – he had written three drafts for Duncan. Two for Charles.

'I've not been a good father,' he said miserably.

'What makes you think that?'

'Doreen was a strong woman. I needed her to be like that. I've admitted it. I needed her to be like that at the beginning, but she took over with the boys. Said it was

her job. I suppose it was.' He looked at her pleadingly. 'I
was weak. I should have stood up for them . . .'
She moved her fingers up and down on the side of his
waist. Quickly. Feathery. Like a fan. As supple as she
could be. And then she stroked him.
'She was too hard with those boys. She drove them
both away in the end . . .'
'Duncan?'
'Oh yes. She had big plans for Duncan. Pushed him.
Wouldn't let up. She was the one to decide on his 'A'
levels, his University, his career. When he became a
solicitor, she said to me 'I told you so. I told you so.' But
he got fed-up of the pressure, the manipulation. He
lived in Scotland for a while.' He paused and then gave
a hollow laugh. 'And then he married a woman just like
Doreen.'
'Are they happy?'
'Who knows? They wouldn't tell me either way.'
'The children?'
'Oh, they're regimented into routines. I'd like to see
them out playing, getting dirty, falling over. Picking
themselves up. The rough-and-tumble of life. You can't
create a cosy little world for them. Over-protect them.
And then let them out into the harsh realities of life. It's
cruelty, posing as kindness . . .'
'Charles?'
'You know just before I posted the letters? I don't
know why I did it, why I kissed them. And yet I do
know. When I went with you to Abercynon and you
prayed about Cicely's stuff, well, I thought that I needed
to do the same. I suppose it was a kind of prayer. Ritual.
She kissed his cheek.
'Charles? Guilty on that score too. He's a brilliant
musician – I've told you that. Viola. He thought about

195

joining an orchestra. I've told you that too. But he decided in the end to go in for music therapy. You know that too.'

'What did Doreen think of that?'

'She said that music therapy wasn't a job for a man.' He started fiddling with the stained coaster. 'He got a certificate. There was a ceremony. Doreen said she wouldn't go. I said that I was going, and she sulked.'

'Did she go in the end?'

'Yes. But she went for the wrong reasons. She went because she thought it would look bad if I went alone. She didn't go to support Charles. I them . . .'

His voice trailed. She couldn't hear what he was mumbling. Then he lifted his head up and said firmly 'I heard a voice inside me when I had the letter for Charles in my hand. It said, 'Talk to me son. Talk to me.'

They were sitting awkwardly on the chairs with dark red fitted cushions. They moved them so that they were facing each other. They did this at the same time spontaneously. Enemies seek out the weakest points in the other to attack. They sought out each other's weakest points to protect. His knee. Her knee. His knee. Her knee. And then they embraced.

Albert spent the night in Megan's flat. She had persuaded him. He wasn't well. It was difficult to know how much was directly due to the illness and how much was his anxiety. There was no need to ask. Or question. Or analyse. She just had to let him be.

And, as she held him through the early hours of the night, she found herself wondering how long they'd have together. A month? Two months? She knew that things would change the very next day – from the moment his sons received the letters. They'd be down. They'd want to spend time with him. It was only natural. It was important for him. It was right. She would fade into the background. Being there when they weren't supporting.

In the past few weeks – or was it months? – they had become lovers. Not in the accepted sense of the word. But there had been tenderness and acceptance. Affection. Generosity. There still was. There still would be. Every kiss, every word, every silence spent together was so precious. The irritation they had felt towards each other after the visit to Sam – when she had driven the car into the hedge had been so painful but was redeemed swiftly by their mutual understanding. This was a deep love. She didn't want to let him go. But she would have to. And the process would begin before the next nightfall. One more dawn. One more sunrise. One more day. One more opening of the curtains in the morning to check the weather. Then – change.

He felt sick in the night, and she fetched a plastic bowl to place beside him. She reassured him when he apologised. She made him comfortable. She held his hand until he went back to sleep. Then she fetched the duvet from the spare bedroom and wrapped it around herself as she settled in the chair beside the bed.

She didn't sleep well. When she stirred in the middle of the night, at first she thought that it was Hugo in the bed. She made herself meditate. The Jesus Rosary that was recited by the Greek Orthodox. A very powerful prayer, repeated like a mantra. 'Lord Jesus Christ, Son of God, have mercy on me, a sinner.' She whispered it to herself again and again until the full phrase fell away. 'Lord, have mercy' was all that she was left with. And, as she said 'Lord, have mercy', she fell back to sleep.

When she woke, the words were still with her. They had soothed her unconscious mind and now they were still supporting her. She felt strangely uplifted. Albert was still asleep so she quietly took the duvet back and went into the kitchen.

There were some simple pleasures in life that she still wanted Albert to have. Breakfast in bed. His appetite was now very poor. He might still be feeling sick. But, after the earlier disturbance, he had slept well. She brought out the tray that she seldom used – it had belonged to her grandmother. She placed a linen cloth on it and rolled another up as a serviette. Little by little, she filled the tray. A glass of pomegranate juice in a tumbler that was sparkling clean. An apple on a little plate with a knife. A pot with a peppermint teabag. Good for the digestion. She'd pour the boiling water in when he woke. A bone china cup on a bone china saucer. A little bowl of rolled oats. And a tiny pot of dried fruits and nuts.

He was still sleeping so she made her own breakfast. She preferred it that way. It was hard to eat with someone who has no appetite. Her own bowl was fuller. She had the rolled oats too with sultanas and sunflower seeds. Walnuts and apricots. Then yoghurt with honey. And tea. She was aware of how fortunate she was. It was at times like these that she fully appreciated the wonder of what she had before her. Oats that she had not grown herself. The fruits picked and dried by somebody else. The nuts that had been shelled. Yoghurt made with care by Rachel's Dairies. Cows fed on wholesome food before they were milked.

Honey from the bees. It took the bees so long to produce just a spoonful. And there she was having a spoonful for her breakfast. Tea from anywhere in the world. And water – the wonderful gift of clean water.

After breakfast, when she went back into the bedroom, Albert was just beginning to stir. He frowned at first, trying to make sense of things. She smiled at him. He smiled at her and she held out her hand.

'Close your eyes!' she said.

And he did.

She carried the tray in from the kitchen and put it on the bedside table until she had found a place to sit on the bed. Then she lifted it up onto her lap and said. 'Open them!'

When he saw the tray, he began to cry. 'Sweetheart!' he said. 'How can I thank you? I'll never forget what you've done for me. What you are to me. Not until the day I die – which might be soon.' He said it in a relaxed way, as if it were a gentle joke.

She held onto the tray and watched as he drank the pomegranate juice. He didn't leave a drop. Then he added things to his little bowl of rolled oats. She had cut the dried apricots into small pieces and he took three of them. She had cut the prune into four pieces and he took two. They would have been too daunting for him whole – some pumpkin seeds too. He ate the bounty before him. He enjoyed it. Then she poured the peppermint tea for him. She knew how long to leave the bag in the pot. This was what love was about. Knowing how strong he liked his tea and making it that way for him – the little personal habits and needs of another. Catering for them. Providing them. Taking delight in seeing them received.

'This is the best meal of my life,' he said.

He finished everything apart from the apple. Then they just sat together – lost in time. Not wanting to move on.

Then Albert said, 'I'll have to go over to my flat in case the boys ring. They might get the letters before they go to work.'

'I'll come over with you, my love,' she said. Then, checking herself, she added – 'If you'd like me to.'

They sat tensely in Albert's flat waiting for the phone to ring. It rang just before eleven and he jumped nervously. It was his Macmillan nurse. Then, at mid-day, it went again. It was his old friend wanting to arrange a meeting.

They had a light lunch. She brought out the set of dominoes and they had a game. But he wasn't able to concentrate.

'They'll not get them till tonight,' he said. 'Though Fiona will probably open Duncan's letter. 'We don't have secrets from one another'. That's what she'll say.'

'Why don't you have a rest? There's no point worrying about it.'

'What if one letter arrives before the other?'

She stood behind him and massaged his shoulders. He always responded to that. 'Why don't you go to bed, my love? Get some rest. You'll be able to deal with the boys better if you've slept.' He didn't seem to have the energy to get up, so she moved in front of him and helped him to his feet.

They walked together to the bedroom and he sat down on the bed. She took his shoes off and put his socks inside them. 'Hands up!' she said gently, as if to a child. And she slipped his jumper over his head. His cotton pyjamas were under the pillow, and she put the top on – taking time to do the buttons up properly. It was things like this that were important to keep his dignity. She pulled his trousers down and noticed how the muscles of his legs had wasted a little more. She took hold of the pyjama trousers and, taking one foot in her hand, she eased one side of it up his leg. She did the same with the other leg and asked him to lift his bottom for a moment so that she could put the pyjamas in place. She tied the drawstring neatly at the waist. Firmly enough to keep them up. But not so tight that it would hurt.

'There!' she said. 'Can you lift your legs up onto the bed for me?' She was sounding like a nurse. Again. He was drowsy and she helped him. Before she could put the duvet over him, he had fallen asleep.

She stayed for a minute or two to watch him. She stroked his forehead and noticed the stubble on his face. He hadn't shaved. She would encourage him to do it when he woke.

She looked around the flat. There was a bit of washing-up to do. A small pile of underclothes in his laundry basket. Old newspapers to be recycled. She busied herself with the jobs in order – the washing-up first, then she took the washing to be taken back to fill her load. Rather than tidying the newspapers there, she could take them over to her flat and put them in with hers in the green bag.

Someone knocked on the door. She went to answer it. Albert was getting more visitors as the news of his illness was beginning to spread. She knew what he could cope with – and whom. She knew when to say 'No' on his behalf.

The couple at the door looked flustered. 'I'm sorry!' the man said, checking the number on the front of the door. 'I thought we had Albert Evans' flat. There must be some mistake.'

She recognised them from the photograph. This was Duncan with his wife Fiona.

'Come in!' she said. 'Albert's sleeping.'

She knew that she would have to explain herself. 'I'm a friend,' she said. 'A neighbour. Albert was very tired.' She wanted to tell them that he had had a troubled night but she didn't.

Without introducing herself, the woman went straight into the bedroom. 'He looks as if he's lost weight. In fact, he looks dreadful. He hasn't shaved,' she called out to Duncan, who followed her into the bedroom. But not before he'd had the decency to say 'I'm Albert's son, Duncan. How do you do?'

She heard them talking over Albert's sleeping body. And she resented it. She wondered how she might feel in their position and her resentment began to melt away. In a way, their conversation was giving her time to think of a reasonable story. They would assume that they would have been the first to be informed.

She heard Albert stirring. If she had been there with him, she would have held his hand and he'd have gone back to sleep. But Fiona had different ideas.

'Dad!' she said, urgently. 'We got your letter today. I rang Duncan straightaway. We've left the children with friends . . .'

'How are you, Dad?' Duncan's voice was softer. 'This is terrible news. We'll do everything we can . . .'

Fiona chipped in. 'We've got a friend in the golf club. An oncologist. Lovely chappie. We'll take you up to stay with us. He'll sort you out. We'll get the very best . . .'

She remained seated as she saw Albert walk into the lounge quite steadily. Fiona and Duncan followed him. He sat down in the chair opposite Megan.

'If you'll excuse us!' said Fiona, turning to Megan 'We've got confidential matters to discuss.'

Albert spoke firmly in a tone that was unfamiliar to

her. Perhaps she had sensed it a bit the night when he had told her to get out of the driving seat after she'd gone into the hedge. 'Megan's staying here. We have no secrets between us.'

'You mean that she knew about all this before we did?' Fiona turned to Megan with spite gleaming in her eyes.

She smiled as she tried to think of an answer but, again, Albert came to her rescue. 'Yes, I've told Megan,' he said. 'I don't know what I'd have done without her. Otherwise, I've kept it to myself. And, believe me, I agonised over that letter . . .'

Megan knew then that Albert would be able to deal with the situation. So she picked up the old newspapers and got up to leave.

'If you want anything,' she said to Albert. 'Give me a ring' and looking at his son and daughter-in-law, she added, 'Please let me know if I can help.'

Back in her flat, she began to pack the newspapers in a green bag. Albert liked The Independent but he had insisted that they should alternate. The Independent one day, The Guardian the next. Each issue had a memory. There was the paper they had both read, the one where they had tried to do the crossword together. Another had not been read at all. He'd had a very bad day. Then there was the one that they had half read – it was turned to the middle section, just after the main World News. For some reason, they had checked the weather in another one.

She made herself a cup of chamomile tea and wondered what to do next. She didn't want to begin the job of piling Cicely's Down Manor things into the green bag as well. But it was something to do. She didn't want to leave the flat. She couldn't concentrate . . .

Her knees were stiff when she got up to answer the door. There had been a frantic knock and she was not surprised to see Fiona on the other side.

'Can I come in?' she asked, bleakly. She had been crying.

'Of course.'

Megan showed her to the leather armchair with the brass buttons and asked if she would like a cup of tea. She declined – too upset to focus on anything other than her own distress.

'Dad told me to come over. I've tried to talk sense into him, but he won't listen. It's as if he's had a change of personality – illness can do that, you know . . .'

Yes, she did know. 'What's the problem?'

Fiona stared at her. 'Have you got a medical background?' she asked abruptly.

'No. But my husband was a doctor.'

'I see.' Fiona looked at her pleadingly. 'He won't let me sort it out.'

She began to cry again. Megan knew the type of personality. Harsh, forthright, a hard outer shell and, when it was pierced, there lay inside something that was soft and frothy. Fragile. Like marshmallow.

'I'm sorry if it hurt you that Albert spoke to me first,' she began, choosing her words carefully. 'He needed someone to talk it over with. And it's kind of you to offer to take him in hand – to sort it out – but he needs to do it his way. Don't forget that he was a pharmacist. He's no fool. Chemotherapy might have given him a few more months more but that's all. The metastases are extensive. He doesn't want to put himself – or his family – through the misery of what was available to him . . .'

Megan got up and put a hand on Fiona's shoulder. 'Are you sure that you wouldn't like a cup of tea?'

The woman looked at her gratefully – a lamb needing to be fed. 'Thank you. Yes, I would.'

Megan was just pouring the boiling water into the pot when there was another knock on the door.

'It's Duncan!' Fiona wailed. 'I know his knock. He'll be so upset to see me like this!'

'Go and answer the door!' Megan said kindly but firmly. 'I'm pouring your tea for you. I can't do two things at once'.

Her teaching experience served her well as she watched Fiona and Duncan talking in the doorway. She saw the uneasy tension between them as their roles were reversed. Him comforting her. She frail.

'I can't!' she heard Fiona say. 'She's . . .'

'Megan' Duncan reminded her.

'Megan's just made me a cup of tea.'

Duncan came into the flat and approached Megan. 'I've had a good chat with Dad,' he said. 'He didn't mean to upset Fiona. It's just that, well, he's adamant about staying here and he explained his options. I wonder if I could leave our details with you? Just in case of an emergency.'

'Of course.'

She watched as Duncan fiddled in his trousers pocket for some paper and a pen. Fiona rallied. 'You never carry a pen – except in your jacket pocket,' she reminded him. 'Here. I'm always prepared.' She searched in her handbag and immediately found a small notepad and a biro.

She didn't let them know that she already had their addresses and phone numbers. She turned to Fiona and said – 'Why don't you go back in? Take the tea with you. It's been good to meet you.'

She shook their hands. She saw them to the door.

And then she shut it.

She was functioning on autopilot as she continued putting Cicely's paperwork in the green bag.

By the time Albert rung her, he was exhausted. But he was pleased with his achievements. He had broken the news to his sons – and Fiona. Now he wanted to see her. She looked at the filled green bags that she'd lined up in the hallway. She passed them and felt a bit faint for a moment. It would pass.

'How are you, Megan? You must be tired. You must get your rest too. But I just wanted to thank you. I wanted you to be here. For five minutes.'

She kissed him and then went to sit opposite him. 'Was it alright with Duncan and Fiona in the end?'

He nodded.

'I was really proud of you!'

He smiled.

'Did Charles ring?'

'He did – just before they left. He's coming down on Sunday . . .'

Albert had been forcing himself to stay awake for too long. His head fell back in that uncontrollable urge to sleep. She couldn't lift him, and he'd wake before long anyhow. So she made him comfortable in the chair, and put a cushion beside his head on the other side from where it had lolled – in case it rolled back. She covered him with a warm blanket as she would do with a child. It had belonged to his mother who had nursed him in the traditional Welsh way. The blanket was still binding them together.

She let her own head rest on the blanket for a few moments in between his knees. Then she realised how tired *she* was. She took a piece of notepaper that he kept in a little bureau – and his fountain pen. He didn't like biros. The message was clear. 'Give me a ring when you wake. I tried to make you comfortable. Love, Megan.' She placed it on his lap – on top of the comfort blanket. And then she left. She remembered that the green bags were congesting her hallway and managed to get through to the living-room. It had been a very busy day. She was emotionally drained.

She poured herself a glass of filtered water and went into the bedroom. She was too tired to clean her teeth but rinsed her mouth quickly with a diluted Propolis tincture. There was no need to wash. She took off her shoes, her jumper and skirt and climbed into bed in her underclothes.

Sleep didn't come as easily as she'd hoped. She knew that, if she didn't get some rest, she'd become ill. And that would help no-one. She wanted Albert to be with her – but an Albert who was well. She found herself thinking of Hugo. Stevie was so much like his grandfather. In a few years' time . . . Susan had been so close to her father. She'd rung a couple of nights earlier. She had been very stressed. Paul was out at a meeting and the children were in bed. The problem in the church had escalated. There was now an outright battle. The parish was polarised, tugging itself in an ugly war. Someone had written to the Bishop. Paul was worried and tired. He'd been to the doctor's who'd suggested taking a holiday. But if he did that, they'd say that he was running away.

After the phone call, sleep came. And Albert didn't ring.

Chapter Seventeen

It was impossible to avoid the premature Christmas celebrations that were enforced on everyone. In the shops, everywhere. 'Away in a manger' as background music. It was all lulling people into a different state of consciousness. 'Have yourself a merry little Christmas.' The obsession with buying. Mince pies in packets of twenty-four. Two for the price of one.

The Warden had put decorations up in the complex. A tree in the hallway just beside the main door. To the side. Artificial. It was festooned with baubles and tinsel – plastic candles with plastic flames. There was a Santa on the clear glass above the main door. It would be uplifting for those who were lonely – but Megan didn't like it at all.

It was the first week of December. Myf and Harriet were very excited about the forthcoming trip to London. Harriet had bought an A-Z, and the two of them had made a note of the places they wanted to visit. She felt like telling them that they wouldn't have time, but she didn't want to dampen their enthusiasm. Brochures of forthcoming holidays had been sent with their tickets. They were thinking about other trips – for the Spring.

She didn't really want to go to London. She didn't want to leave Albert for that length of time. But she needed to see Tom. Alice had replied to her letter, but it had not been as spontaneous as it usually was. There was clearly some tension. She couldn't avoid the situation – pretend it wasn't there or that it would go away if she did nothing about it. And she had the scrapbook ready for Bella. Albert had told her how important it was that she made the trip.

She and Hugo had enjoyed going up to London to see Tom and Alice so much – and then Bella came along. It had been a happy time in their lives. Hugo had recovered from the Millstone affair – as much as he was ever going to. He'd gone back to work and settled down. Patients continued to be kind. And then, he'd had the diagnosis.

She knew that something had happened that day. When he'd come home early – as he had after the Millstone incident. He'd sat down in the armchair with the brass buttons and refused her offer of a cup of tea.

'I need to talk to you, Megan,' he'd said. She knew that it was bad news. And she had a keen idea of what it was.

A few days earlier, she had been cleaning the lavatory pan when she noticed it. A blob of sputum that he'd not flushed away – flecked with blood. She put it in a little jar. Just in case he hadn't realised and didn't believe her. Hugo was very irritable when he told her. And then he didn't want to talk about it anymore.

'I've got bronchial cancer. The cigarettes have caught up with me!' He was trying to joke it off and she realised that he must have rehearsed the words. 'It's not too bad!' he'd added. 'Adenocarcinoma. They're going to operate. The prognosis is good.'

She hadn't known what to say. She was scared of upsetting him when he had tried so hard to pass it off lightly.

'I'm so sorry, Hugo!'

That's all she had said. Then she had made a cup of tea.

It was only when he was convinced that she had absorbed the news that he expressed his own feelings. There would be surgery, radiotherapy. He hadn't wanted to say anything at all until he was sure of the diagnosis and the treatment.

He'd recovered well from the surgery, but he took early retirement. They travelled a bit. And they went up to London often. Alice's parents had always been generous, and the hotel was like a second home. They had gone to the theatre, the museums, walked along the Thames and soaked up the culture. They had been delighted to babysit for Bella. Hugo had been happier than he had been for years. It had taken a brush with death. He had been swept along by a tide that reminded him of his mortality. He was grateful for every day. And he gave up smoking.

Now she was faced with a different kind of journey to London. A mission. Trying to act as a go-between. It had to be done. Her heart wept for Tom.

Megan liked Charles as soon as she met him. He'd left Lincolnshire at six so that he could spend a few hours with his father. Albert wanted to see the sea and his son had offered to take him to Southerndown. As Albert's appetite was poor and his diet was so selective, they intended to come back to the flat for lunch. She was invited to join them immediately afterwards for a cup of tea.

Originally, she and Albert had planned to go to St. Michael's together, so she found herself walking over to the church alone. She met a few people on the way. One man – a former neighbour, hadn't seen her for a while. He and his wife had just returned from a cruise, and he enthused about it. He listed all the ports they had called at, spoke about the weather in every country – and the scenery and the points of interest. There had been a delay on their return to Southampton and they'd hit a storm in the Canaries. It was unprecedented. 'You'll have to come over!' he said. 'We've got hundreds of slides. A once-in-a-lifetime experience. Did you and Hugo ever go on a cruise?'

She shook her head gently. They had both hated the idea. The children had wanted to book them on a cruise for Hugo's sixtieth birthday. An academic one – taking in Greece and Turkey. But they hadn't liked the idea of being in a closed environment, socialising at every meal, eating and drinking too much. And the visits to the ports were so short that it would be impossible to savour the sites.

Hugo had chosen a holiday in Italy instead and they had spent a week based in Venice.

The former neighbour took his leave of her, and she promised to keep in touch. Looking at her watch, she realised that she would be late for the service, but she kept on walking. Standing outside, she heard the last verse of the first hymn. She would be conspicuous if she went in then for the Collect and the readings. She leant against the wall and felt the feelings that would have led to tears if she were not on medication. She didn't *belong*. She was an outsider. She remembered the time when she had been rejected for following the leading of the Holy Spirit. Not here. Not in this Church. She had been so hurt, felt so rejected in the house of the Prince of Peace.

She started counting the bricks on the outside of the church. Fourteen, fifteen. Each brick made from the richness of the earth, each put in place by a craftsman, coated with mortar. Then another layer and another. How many people had it taken to build the place? And how many people had prayed here since, taken their burdens to the Lord? And how many people had squabbled here? Tearing His body apart all over again. Crucifying Him. Repeating the taunts, the denials. Putting their self-centredness, their pride in the place of the Lamb?

So it seemed apt that she should be praying outside the building. She prayed for Paul and Susan – for their divided church to make peace. She asked that the world might wake up to the folly of its ways. Then, deep inside her, she heard a voice saying – 'Go inside. Take and eat.'

And she did.

Chapter Eighteen

'Yes, it's an amazing place!'

And, indeed the cliffs at Southerndown were spectacular. So were the pebbles that led down to the wide stretch of sand. And so was the dramatic sweep of the waves.

'We saw the tide come in. Savage. Ruthless. Majestic.' Charles had pulled a chair up to sit beside his father.

'It's good to meet you,' said Megan, smiling. 'Albert's very proud of you.'

She noticed the way father and son looked at each other. Charles, in spite of the circumstances, had an excited flush in his cheeks. And Albert – he just looked proud. There had been some healing between them, and she was delighted. It was so important to deal with rifts or misunderstandings, especially now. When they said good-bye to each other, she saw the affection.

Charles was intending to come down every Sunday. Duncan and Fiona said that they would come as often as they could – Thursday was a good day. Duncan had fewer commitments at work, and the children were able to sleep over at a friend's house. Albert had insisted that they contact him before each visit, and he had expressed a wish to see the children soon. The scrapbook for Bella was one of a whole series of special gifts being prepared for children. Albert was busy making a memory box for his grandchildren.

He already had the box – a large one, flat-packed for the time being. He wanted to tell them about all the things. There was the comfort blanket. And he put ready a fob watch that had belonged to his father – and his father before him. It was silver and fitted into a pocket rather than being placed on the wrist. He had taken good care of it. It still kept good time.

Megan watched him, smiling. 'Tired, my love?" she asked.

'Yes but happy. I've never felt so close to Charles. When we watched the sea coming in, it was wonderful. He took my hand.'

'I'm pleased.'

'And to be with you now, sweetheart. Just the two of us. How long will we have?'

They sat together silently. She kissed him from time to time. He kissed her and stroked her hair.

Megan set off for London with a heavy heart. Albert had encouraged her again to go and was cheerful when she said good-bye. He wanted to see the programme from the Theatre when she came back. He hoped that all would go well with her meeting with Tom. Then Alice and Bella.

Megan, Harriet and Myf took a taxi down to the bus station.

Megan found herself sitting on a seat away from the window next to a stout man who was travelling alone. He wasn't communicative – which suited her well. But Myf and Harriet were concerned about her, and Myf offered to change places after their stop in Windsor. She thanked her but said that she was fine where she was.

Her plan was to meet Tom that evening in the hotel after the evening meal. He was going to bring the laptop. The apparatus was the last thing on her mind, but it would provide a focus if there was any tension between them. Tom would probably find it difficult, and she would leave it to him to bring up the subject of Alice and Bella – or not. She had to be strong for him. She could feel the feelings later.

The arrangement with Alice still hadn't been clarified. 'Call over!' she'd said. That was all. She needed to see how Tom was first anyway. If a meeting with Alice was going to make things worse, she'd give him the scrapbook. Somehow, sometime, he'd give it to Bella. She wanted to entrust it into his keeping. He was totally reliable.

The journey was tedious. She didn't join the others on their 'comfort breaks'. She said that her knee was painful, which was true.

Her room at the hotel was small but clean and pleasant enough. There was one chair so, when Tom came, she'd sit on the bed. By the chair was a tiny side table. He could plug the laptop underneath. And Windows and Mouses – or was it Mice – would provide a useful distraction.

She hadn't been on her own with him in such a small, enclosed, area for years. There was the time when he had shut himself up in his bedroom after disappointing exam results. 1985? 1986? She had kept away for hours, letting him be. And then she felt – an intuitive insight – that the time was right to talk to him. She had knocked on the door. His face was ashen and he'd been crying. She had gently put her arms around him. He didn't say a word at the time. But he didn't brush her away and, as she left the room, he whispered 'Thanks, Mum'.

'I can plug it in here. I've written down a few instructions, tried to simplify it. But watch.' And, slowly, he turned the machine on, explaining every step.

He had aged. But would she have thought that if she hadn't known about the problem? His hair was receding. She could see his scalp on the crown of his head. He was greyer. But men do grow older. It's the natural progression of things – even with her son. It was a strange feeling. The wart on his finger was still there. And he'd been biting his nails. His hands were expressive – long and slim, ready to hold and support.

He carried on setting the laptop up and spoke through the instructions. 'I can't deal with the situation. I'm waiting till after Christmas. I've bought Bella a present of course but . . .'

'I've made her a scrapbook.', Megan ventured. Perhaps you can pass it on to her when you give your own present?' She lifted the book out of her bag to show him. He left the computer to look at it.

He smiled as he turned the pages. 'It's beautiful, Mum'. He was struggling with his feelings. She put an arm on his shoulder.

'I shouldn't be burdening you like this.'

'It's alright. It's alright.'

As she held him, she remembered the adolescent who'd had disappointing exam results. She remembered the schoolboy determined not to cry after he'd fallen and badly sprained his ankle. She remembered the toddler who loved to play hide-and-seek under her skirt. She remembered the months when she had carried him inside her. Watching him grow inside her own belly.

'I just don't get anywhere with Alice. It's as if she doesn't relate to reality. Oh, I love her – I always will. But it's so infuriating trying to live with her. I want the best for Bella. When I say that, she just says that she wants the best for Bella too. It's just that our ideas of 'best' are poles apart. I can offer them everything. I know that she's not short of money, herself, but I can offer them security. I can offer them love. And common sense . . .'

He cried in her arms.
The laptop was still switched on.

Chapter Nineteen

There was something comforting about toast. With butter and jam. Admittedly, it was not wholemeal bread. And she had no idea how the butter that she had unwrapped from its little gold-coloured rectangular envelope was sourced. The coffee was not fairtrade.

But, when she had called Reception and asked for breakfast in bed with fairly traded items, they had apologised. If people kept on asking, the message might get through. There was a questionnaire in the room for visitors to fill on their departure. She would suggest that guests should be given options. She would make a few specific suggestions.

Tom had been with her until almost eleven the night before, and she realised how physically tired she was. She had slipped a note under Myf and Harriet's door. They were aiming to get up early and shop in Oxford Street. She had no energy to join them. No desire. No need. She had simply said that breakfast in bed was her way of treating herself.

There wouldn't be enough time to visit a museum – the matinée began at 2.30. She thought that she'd wander around outside when she was ready – somewhere near the hotel. There were always interesting little places in London – everywhere. Asian shops that sold every variety of spice, a bit of parkland, newsagents with papers in a multitude of languages. It was easy to guess the local ethnic population by those papers. A bundle of Arabic ones or Spanish or Irish. There were the shops that were boarded up. What had gone wrong? Were they up 'For Sale'? Or would they just be left to decay, plastered with graffiti and out-of-date posters?

Yes, she would wander around and search for a little café for some lunch – a baguette perhaps. Somewhere that looked clean. They had booked a meal out after the show in one of the restaurants recommended by the coach company – with a discount.

She thought there must have been a mistake when the phone rang in her room.

'Mrs. Megan Roberts?'

'Yes?' she said, slowly. Her blood ran cold. Something had happened to Albert! She knew that she shouldn't have come!

'I have an outside call for you. Will you take it?'

'Of course.'

She sat on the small chair by the desk where she had folded her clothes the night before.

It was then that she heard Tom's voice. The words came hurtling out. Disjointed which was unusual for him.

'Mum . . . I didn't know what to do. I know you're going to the show this afternoon. I thought I'd leave it. But it might be too late by then. So I . . .'

'Tom, what's wrong?'

'Alice's mother's in hospital. She's been there since yesterday. Alice tried to get in touch. I wasn't at home and I had my mobile switched off. It was when I was with you. Oh, she's alright, her mum. Well, she's not alright. But they know what it is. They thought it might have been a heart attack. But it wasn't.

'Angina?'

Yes. They've done a few tests on her and she'll probably be out tomorrow.'

'Angina responds very well to treatment. Once she's

on the medication . . .'

'Yes. I know. Alice has been to see her. She overheard her parents talking. They've told her that it'll have to go – the hotel. This means it's going to happen sooner rather than later. The angina attack. They're going to retire. Kent. A bungalow. Alice has gone to pieces.'

'And Bella?'

'I'm looking after Bella.'

'Where?'

'At the hotel. I wondered if, after the show, you might ... As he was still talking, she looked at the folded clothes. She could wear the same ones today. Just change her pants and tights. 'I'm coming,' she said firmly. 'I'm coming now.'

'But, Mum, you can't. If I'd known you'd . . .'

'See you as soon as I can get there.' And, before he could protest, she put the receiver down.

She dressed as quickly as she could, picked up the scrapbook and used the back of the questionnaire to explain the situation to Harriet and Myf.

As she walked down the road outside the hotel, she was still buttoning up her coat. In her haste, she had put the third button into the hole meant for the second one. Not that it mattered. It was more important to find a taxi.

Bella didn't smile when Megan entered the room. She didn't run up to her for a kiss. She didn't look at her. She just stayed where she was and then continued arranging some flash-cards that Alice had made.

Tom took the scrapbook from her and put it on the floor. 'Look, Bella! Look at what Grandma has made for you!'

The child looked across, then at her father. She

carried on sorting the flashcards. Tom sat beside her and helped with the flashcards.

Megan sat at the edge of the room unobtrusively as she waited.

Tom had to spend some more time with Bella and the flashcards – playing a repetitive game that had no rules except in Bella's head.

Then, quietly, she walked over to the scrapbook and sat on the floor. Tom joined her.

'Look! Feel this bit of bark, Bella. Do it like I'm doing it.' He stroked the bark, gently, again and again.

The child looked at Tom and hesitated. He put his hand over hers. They touched the bark together. Bella smiled. A private smile for herself.

'This bark comes from a tree near Grandma's home,' he read. 'This bark comes from a tree near Grandma's home.'

From the corner of the room, Megan watched. And she felt so proud. Proud of Bella, such a pretty girl with long eyelashes. She wore patchwork trousers and was struggling to understand the world around her.

'Bark,' she said.

'That's right, Bella. Well done! Bark. Shall we turn to the next page?'

'No.' She wanted to stay with the bark, and she began touching it again on her own.

If Megan felt proud of Bella, she was overwhelmed by Tom. So much love and patience. Every minute she had spent on the Scrap Book had been worthwhile. Just to see her touching the bark. Saying the word 'bark' with Tom teaching her and gently holding her. She remained where she was, spellbound. Bella turned the page.

'Megan, I'll lose my home. This place means so much to

me. And poor Mummy!' Alice flung her arms around Megan.

Bella had gone to bed. Alice's father, Alice, Tom and Megan were waiting for a take-away to be delivered.

'She'll be home tomorrow,' her father said.

'But she'll have to rest. We mustn't let her get stressed. We'll all have to help. Oh, I don't want to let this place go.'

Tom was right. Alice's world had fallen apart. Tom and her father were trying to help her piece it together again but it would never be the same. And Alice had to take responsibility for the change eventually.

Before that, she had curled up in a little ball beside Megan on the settee. It was almost a foetal position. A delightful privileged young woman who needed to grow up without losing her charm.

As Tom and Alice's father talked, it was obvious that they had discussed the subject before the couple split.

They agreed that the most sensible thing to do was to find a manager for the hotel – someone with good references and experience. Then employ him – or her – for a trial period. And, if it worked, make it permanent. Alice's parents would move into their bungalow in Kent as soon as possible. Her father would come up to oversee things until they became settled. And he wanted Tom to be involved. Tom was the one with the financial expertise. And, although neither of them said it, he was the one with the common sense.

'I want to keep it in the family,' her father said. 'You and Bella' – and he looked tenderly at his beautiful daughter. 'You can both stay here. I don't want anything to undermine the improvement that she's been making.'

Alice stretched herself out even if it was only to get up and kiss her father.

Keep it in the family. Keep it in the family. What beautiful words. She wouldn't have wanted to miss hearing them.

The coach trip really had been an answer to prayer.

Tom dropped her off at the hotel after their take-away meal. He wouldn't stay. He had to return to the hotel, make plans and prepare for the day ahead. With Bella. With his family.

She blew him a kiss and walked into the hotel jauntily. When she asked for her key, there was a note in the little cubicle where it had been hanging.

'There's a message for you, Mrs. Roberts,' the receptionist said. It had come from Charles.

Harriet and Myf had been very kind and invited her to sit with them at breakfast – 'but we'll understand if you want to be alone.' She did sit with them as they ate from the self-service buffet. Myf had returned with a bowl of Corn Flakes, orange juice and a boiled egg. Harriet had taken Muesli with Orange Juice and a small tub of fruit yoghurt. They were both going to have a cup of tea from a machine. Megan looked at it all and had no appetite. But not eating wouldn't help. She had muesli and a plain yoghurt.

Myf and Harriet didn't mention the show so she brought the subject up herself. 'It had been quite good' – they'd said in muted voices. She asked them to be honest. She knew that they had enjoyed themselves. She could see it on their faces.

She didn't want to wander round the outdoor market

after breakfast – she just wanted to get home. The arrangement had been for the driver to leave them on a nearby street and pick them up there at 10.45. They had all entrusted their luggage to him and were free to enjoy themselves. 'Don't forget. Everybody back here by 10.45. I need to set off by ten to eleven.' He'd repeated the name of the street and checked out that they had all heard.

She decided to start off with Harriet and Myf as she had no real alternative. They wouldn't have left her if she had decided to stay on the coach and she didn't want to spoil things for them. With a small gathering of them in a crowded market street, she could wander off – give an excuse. She liked looking at book stalls and knew that they didn't.

She quickly found one and they stayed with her for a while. Harriet was interested in Child Development and Gardening – even though she no longer had a garden to care for. Myf liked crime fiction. Good quality stuff. Ruth Rendell. Patricia Cornwell. Agatha Christies. Megan pretended that she was searching for more and encouraged them to make their own way through the rest of the market. She said that she'd see them back on the coach. She watched as the two of them went on to a china stall. The man was haggling and an overt entertainer.

She disappeared up a side-street. She leant against a wall. It was probably ill-advised to be loitering there but she didn't care. She would soon have to be making conversation – or listening to it – on the coach. She couldn't blame Myf – or Harriet. They were trying so hard to be sensitive and caring.

The week-end had been surreal. Firstly, there had been the time she spent with Tom in her little hotel room. She had wanted him to open up to her. And he had. But she was left with the burden of his pain even though she had tried hard to let it go. She knew that worrying was a waste of time. It would make her less able to deal with the situation – whatever the outcome had been.

On the Saturday morning, she thought that her prayers had been answered. And they had. It was a pity that Alice's mother was ill but she had been assured that the angina would respond to treatment. It had probably been something waiting to happen for months. She couldn't measure the joy she felt on the Saturday when she had seen Bella. She had liked the scrapbook. She was with Tom. There had been a reconciliation as Alice had to face reality. No-one could possibly know the happiness she had felt.

And then she had received the blow. Charles had been trying to get hold her. At the very same time when she had been so delighted with the way things had worked out, Charles was trying to get in touch. He and Duncan had agreed that she should know. Albert had been admitted to hospital. There was not a lot of information. They were doing tests. He had been in a great deal of pain. The pain had made him breathless. He was frightened and had called for an ambulance. The two sons had gone down immediately. They were still there. They were going to stay until they knew the results of the tests. They wanted to see the doctor who was looking after him. On the Monday, if it was possible. Things had been complicated because Albert had been admitted on a Saturday. The consultant wouldn't be in until Monday so they might have to wait longer. Charles asked if he could stay in the guest room in the sheltered housing complex. Duncan had signed into a hotel.

No, there's nothing you can do,' Charles had said. He's not critical. Just enjoy the rest of your break. Visiting isn't until the afternoon. They would be going in to see him on the Sunday. She could see him on the Monday. And maybe they'd have some news by then. Yes. He promised that they'd be in touch if he deteriorated. And, yes, they'd give him her love.

He'd been in great pain, and she'd not been there. She knew how he panicked when his breathing was laboured. She could have held his hand. She could have driven him to hospital. But this wasn't about her. Duncan and Charles needed to be there. They had probably not worked together so closely since they were boys. There could be a lot of healing between them. They both needed time to be with their father. Duncan would be freer without Fiona, who was with the children.

And, if she had been with him, maybe he wouldn't have called the ambulance. He'd have held on a bit longer. Perhaps hospital was the right place for him to be. The words thudded in her brain. Perhaps hospital was the right place for him to be.

A little gang of boys sauntered into the alley. They looked about fourteen, maybe fifteen, maybe younger. Hooded jumpers, trainers, jeans. Chewing gum. Provocative. Shouting obscenities. Aimless. Powerful.

They looked at her and laughed. One of them said – 'Got a problem, missus?'

And she thought, yes, I have.

It occurred to her that she was the only one to have Albert's key. She turned it in his door and filled a bag with a few items. Pyjamas, underpants. He had two dressing-gowns and he had taken neither with him. Although it was winter, she folded the silk one. Paisley. It would be hot in the hospital.

It was strange to be in his flat without him.

She could see what he had been doing just before he'd rung for the ambulance. He had taken a cup of tea – maybe an hour before. Unless there was a problem, he did the washing-up after lunch and again after his evening meal. Only the mug of tea was unwashed. Peppermint. He must have been worried about his digestion. Pains in his gut. The box of arachis oil suppositories was still out on the shelf below the bathroom cabinet. Constipation. He had been having a problem with this for some time. The newspaper had been half-read and was on the table – on the crossword page. He must have felt fairly well to have considered looking at it at all. He had completed two of the clues. He had scattered the letters of an anagram at the bottom of the page. The radio had been left on – Classic FM. As she turned it off, it felt like a symbolic act. She was saying goodbye to the life that they had shared together. Extinguishing it.

Duncan and Charles were already there when she arrived at the hospital. At first, she only saw his sons. Charles was sitting on the near side of the bed. Duncan was standing. Awkward. Uneasy. It was Duncan who noticed her first and he told Charles, who turned round and smiled. He stood up and beckoned for her to join them. And he kissed her gently on both cheeks.

A man looks very different in a hospital bed with drips and a catheter. An oxygen mask and a line on the back of his hand for morphine. She couldn't get close to him. Because she wasn't supple, she was scared of her movements. She didn't want to dislodge any of the apparatus. Charles offered her his seat. She refused. He insisted.

'Any news?' she asked gently. Scared at the question. More scared of the reply.

Albert was trying to talk through the mask.

Charles stood up at the end of the bed. 'Dad, I think Duncan and I could do with stretching our legs. Get ourselves a coffee. Is that OK?'

Albert smiled.

'There's no definite news yet,' Charles said. 'as we thought. But we've got an appointment to see the Consultant tomorrow'. And, turning to his father, he added – 'Haven't we Dad?' The sensitivity of knowing how important it was to refer to the patient and not talk as if he weren't there.

The two men left the ward and Megan pulled her chair up as closely as she could.

'How are you, my love?' she whispered. 'Sorry I wasn't with you on Saturday.'

Albert lifted the oxygen mask. 'Did you see Tom?' he asked.

His first question. About her and her family.

'Yes, I did.'

'And Bella?'

Part of her felt guilty at telling him what had happened. On the other hand, he had asked. And she knew that he would be happy about the situation. For her sake.

She slipped the oxygen mask back on his face and told him what had happened. The joy of his smile overwhelmed her. He fumbled with his hand to try and reach hers.

'I know what'll happen.' His words were muffled by

the mask. 'They'll give the results to me and tell the boys. It's more important for them than for me. They'll keep me here for the hydraulics and then they'll find me a place in the hospice.'

He said it in a matter-of-fact way. And then he closed his eyes.

Her hand seemed to be offering him comfort so she kept it there. She looked at the face that was distorted through the mask, the hospital pyjamas that demeaned him. Even his nightwear had been smart and elegant in an unobtrusive way. She knew that better than anyone. Except Doreen?

On the floor by the end of the bed, there were two new pairs of pyjamas and a dressing-gown. He won't like them, she thought. They're not his style. But he'll love the gesture.

Chapter Twenty

There is something very wrong with a society where two full balls of wool can lie in a charity shop for 20p – unsold for weeks. White, gently twisted and held in place by a paper label that described its ply. Maybe someone had used less than they needed when knitting a garment. They had brought it along with some unwanted clothes. It had just sat in a basket of odds-and-ends – belts, caps, a foldaway waterproof hat, some padded coat hangers. A plastic bag of pot-pourri. Chiffon scarves.

If the balls were left there much longer, they would get dirty and then it was certain that no-one would buy them. Even at 20p. She had given the volunteer 50p and asked her to put the change in the box for Cancer Relief.

Wool. Taken from the sheep, cleaned, carded, spun, and there were no buyers.

She had done a lot of knitting in the past and kept the needles, thinking that the gentle, familiar exercise would loosen up the stiffness in her hands. She had made little jackets for the grandchildren. Then Stevie developed an allergy to wool.

There is something very wrong with society altogether. Processed food transported across thousands of miles. Artificial fertilisers, pesticides scattered down from helicopters, blown by the wind. Soil over-used and stripped of nutrition. Intensive farming, cheap flights, pollution. Cheap foreign labour, exploitation. What have we done? Every generation has a collective guilt – a collective crime. Lord, have mercy.

She used to go to jumble sales and looked out for woollen garments, bought them, unravelled them and made them into new things. Her first gift to Hugo had been a woollen V neck sleeveless jumper. Grey with flecks of red.

There had not been an immediate attraction at first. He heard her accent and told her that his grandfather was Welsh. He had asked her name.

That was how it had started. She had always been interested in medicine. As the daughter of a miner, she was very aware of the damage that can be done to the lungs from spending hours a day in the dark, damp and dusty conditions underground. She read books on mental illness to help her understand her mother's illness. These had, in turn, helped her to understand what happened to James. And they had helped *her*.

Hugo was more than happy to talk about his studies which fascinated her. She was aware of a vulnerability in him though she didn't mention it. It would have made him withdraw. Young men didn't like to show any weaknesses – not then.

He had loved the jumper and wore it often. She could see him now in her mind's eye. Hugo – a young doctor with a tweed jacket. Her jumper underneath it in the winter. She had later bought him several shirts that blended . Ties that brought out the red.

She gasped. For a moment, the image of Hugo's face had merged into that of Albert's.

As she looked down, she realised that she had been knitting. On autopilot – all done by the working of the hindbrain.

In front of her, she saw the beginnings of a baby's jacket. But there were no babies to knit for anymore.

Then she remembered Gracie. Gracie Millstone.

Albert was inundated with visitors. His brother had flown in from Australia and she had been shocked to see the resemblance. Doreen's sister and brother-in-law came over from the Isle of Wight. There was an odd mood about his bed. Combined with the distress of the news and seeing him so ill, was the excitement that came with the meeting up of relatives. His brother hadn't seen the sons since Duncan's wedding. Doreen's family hadn't seen Albert since her death. They had intended to visit and he had been invited to stay with them on holiday. But it had never happened.

Duncan and Charles had seen the registrar – the consultant had been called to an emergency. As Albert had predicted, the results were not good. They would keep him for a few days before transferring him to the hospice.

She called in every day but they had never had the chance to be alone. She was aware that the extended family was wondering who she was.

A close friend? She thought of the loneliness of the close friend in times like these. Not family. Not next of kin. Yet it was often close friends who had shared the deepest intimacies. But they had to know their place. A seat in the middle of the church.

Of course, there were people who arranged death-bed marriages. But there was no point. They were what they were to each other. That was all that mattered. And, with such a marriage, there was always the problem of the will. Not that he would have time to change it. Not that she would want him to change it. He had told her that his effects were to be shared equally between Duncan and Charles. He had asked her advice on this – conscious that he had two grandchildren. But he worried more about Charles. His salary wasn't high, and he didn't have the securities that Duncan had. That was when the idea of the memory box had surfaced.

Duncan returned on the Wednesday. Albert's brother had gone on to visit some other members of his family but was keeping in touch on a daily basis. Doreen's relatives went back to the Isle of Wight.

On the Wednesday evening, she was finally alone with Charles at Albert's bedside. Charles had arrived earlier and saw the look on his father's face when Megan arrived.

'I need to pick a few things up from the late-night shop,' he said. 'I'll be half an hour or so. Is that OK?' He looked at them both, smiled – and winked at Albert. And then he left them alone.

'You mustn't tire yourself, sweetheart!' Albert whispered. 'You've been coming every day. I love to see you but please don't wear yourself out.'

'I'm fine!' she assured him.

His lips were cracked and dry. There was a bottle of cranberry juice on his locker. She didn't need to ask him. She just knew. She poured some into the glass that was provided with the water jug – slightly less than half full. He removed the oxygen mask, and, standing up and leaning over him, she put the glass to his lips. He sipped some of it and, when a little dribbled down onto his pyjamas, she quickly tried to lift the stain with a moistened tissue. He was wearing the pyjamas that his sons had bought him. They were striped – grey, white and red.

'I've brought your pyjamas from home,' she said. 'Did you see them?'

He smiled. He struggled to make his words clear and took her hand with a surprisingly firm grip. She was still standing.

'If I were to have a miracle cure, Megan, would you marry me?'

'I would.'

Charles had asked if he could ring her every day. He needed something more than the brief hospital statement. He wanted to know if he had colour in his cheeks – personal details. He was coming back on the Sunday – sooner if there was a problem.

Back in the flat, she tried to get as much rest as she could. She didn't want to be surrounded by people but it was difficult. Residents asked how Albert was every time she walked along the corridor.

She told Harriet and Myf how tired she was. They were good friends. They acted as go-betweens. They called in to see Albert briefly and, within 48 hours, people were asking *them* the questions.

Susan and Tom had picked up that she was under some kind of strain. So she had told them the truth. It was only fair to them. And it would stop them worrying too much about her. At least they knew what the problem was.

Every time the phone went, she turned cold. She took all of the things that Albert might need from his flat into her own flat. She could wash the clothes and take care of them. She fetched the flat-packed box – the items for the memory box. And then she decided that she wouldn't go back there anymore. It made her feel desperately sad.

She kept his set of dominoes in the hallway. Maybe he would value a game. It was a simple thing to do. Matching up the little blocks. They wouldn't score. The pleasure would be in the simple task of putting one block next to the other. Sharing the game. A little miracle really. Brains that could tell what the numbers were by counting them by seeing the way they were spaced. White rounds on black. Knowing whose turn it was. Hands that could lift each little piece and place it down on a board with precision. For a while.

'Teach us delight in simple things.' Kipling had said in 'The Children's Song'. Their love had been child-like. It was a characteristic that she had always held on to – something that she had taught Albert. And it had enriched him. It would help him to blow into the wind of the Creator when the time came.

She looked at the things he had chosen for the memory box. The set of dominoes – kept from childhood in a box that was held together through layers of Sellotape. The comfort blanket. The watch. Three bottles that he had kept from his early days as a pharmacist. Two china tea-sets – one from his maternal grandmother, the other from his paternal grandmother. Two medals that his grandfather had earned. A coin collection. Old letters. Family photographs.

The wedding-ring he had given Doreen. The wedding-ring that she had given him – he had already taken it off, knowing about the swelling of fingers. Jewellery. Some of his old student notes – it would be interesting for the children to see how times have changed.

The memory box. He had asked her to put the things together if he didn't have a chance to give them to the children himself. He had wanted to show the things to them when he was still fairly well – for them to identify the items with him as a healthy person. To know the stories behind them. It didn't look as though that would happen now.

Who knew how important this little collection would be? It was certainly helping Albert now. It could have untold influence on the children who would have few memories of him. Just like Hugo.

She got off the bus in Pontypridd.

Megan had been struggling with the Millstone memories, more so since she found herself automatically knitting the baby jacket. There was no-one else to give it to but Gracie's baby. She realised how much internal searching she had to do. To get beyond the anger and those dreadful months that still haunted her. She had decided that she wouldn't go to see Gracie until that was done.

She was weary. It seemed the wrong time to be working on such difficult emotions. But life's journey is not neat. The situation had come at the same time as Albert's decline in health. It was meant to be.

They had just moved Albert to the hospice, and both sons had come down to be with him. His brother was paying a final visit before returning to Australia. She was going in most days. Trying to fill the times when other visitors had gone. She had asked if she was tiring him. She knew that she wasn't but it had been important to ask. To know that she was doing the right thing for him, especially during those dark moments of the night when she couldn't sleep and she doubted her judgement.

Duncan and Charles had asked about the timescale. Who knows times and dates? Not always the doctors. But they had said that a month would be optimistic. And Christmas was in the middle of it. Plans were being altered. The sons wanted to be close at hand. They were with him as she walked along the street in Pontypridd.

When she had seen Gracie in the shop the first time, the

hardest words to say had been – 'How's your mother?' But she had asked even though she felt like a child who has been forced to say sorry when she doesn't mean it.

Back home, the struggle had continued as she completed the baby jacket and sewed the pieces together.

The only concession she had made to Christmas was to have her wooden Nativity set out on the hall table by the telephone. She looked at the baby lying in the cradle and his mother, Mary. How she had suffered! A sword had pierced her heart.

A sword had pierced her own heart too. On the day when Hugo had come home and sat on the armchair with the brass buttons, broken by what had happened. She had felt broken too. And the pain went on for months. Years. Comfort had come from so many sources. Everyone had affirmed Hugo. In a way, he had had more affirmation because of the Millstones. But the self-doubt had been persistent, lurking near the surface. And she had been the one who had to deal with those uncertainties even though he had tried so hard to protect her. She could see any disturbance in his face. In his eyes, in little mannerisms. A slight tic. Fiddling with the brass buttons. Smoking again.

He had finally regained his confidence. Then he had the diagnosis. It was so cruel. Logically, she could tell herself that the cancer was the result of cigarette smoking – just something that had happened. But was it possible for emotional pain to be so intense that it surfaced as physical disease? Of course, she knew that it was. Hugo reckoned that a large proportion of his patients presented with psychosomatic problems.

But cancer? Could it be a contributory factor? If it could, then the Millstones were little short of murderers.

The Millstone murderers. The Millstone murderers. She said it to herself again and again vehemently. And then, through the open door, she noticed the Mother and Child. The little figures were free-standing and she noticed how she had placed them this year. Joseph was a little distance away. So were the shepherds and the Wise Men. Mary was seated very close to her baby with the angel looking on. Placed near the front of the little stable, they looked frail and exposed.

Whatever damage the Millstones had done to Hugo – and to her and the family – they could never harm the soul that is eternal. And it was nothing to do with Gracie. It was then that she realised that she was well on the road to forgiveness.

She went into the shop. Gracie looked up puzzled.

'Hello?' Her voice was apprehensive.

'Hello. I thought I'd call by to see how you are.'

Gracie was still wary.

'How's the baby?' She was heavier now – maybe six or seven months into her pregnancy.

Gracie smiled ruefully. 'Busy. Keeping me awake at night.' There was a man browsing through the books, but, otherwise, the shop was empty. 'Why did you come back, Mrs. Roberts?'

She couldn't say that she had been crossing over from Wood Street to the main bus station when she saw a bus about to leave for Pontypridd. And a voice within her had said – 'Go now. Go now.'

'I wanted to wish you a Happy Christmas,' she said.

'Oh.'

'How's your mother?'

This time, the question did not hurt. Not as much.

Gracie had said before that her mother was alright, but she spoke more freely now. As if she could sense that it was safer territory. 'Mum's in a home. She had a massive stroke. I couldn't look after her. Sometimes, she doesn't know me.' Her voice broke in mid-sentence as she added – 'She won't know about the baby. Her grandchild.'

Megan took hold of her hand that was resting on top of the counter. There was no need for words. She liked Gracie. Her touch would pass on that message.

The man came to the counter with a couple of books about the Great War. She served him and wished him a Happy Christmas.

'I'm knitting something for the baby – your baby!' said Megan. 'I won't give it to you now. But perhaps you could let me know when it happens . . .'

'I don't have your address.' Gracie stumbled with her words. 'I don't know how to get in touch . . .'

Megan had decided to give Gracie her address – but not her phone number. But now that seemed mean.

Gracie reached into her large bag and brought out an address book. It was elegant and attractive. And it had some luscious Renoir women on the front.

She had refused the offer to stay with Susan and Paul over Christmas. And she had refused the offer to stay in Alice's parents' hotel. She was glad that she had told them about Albert. It helped them not to persist. Myf was going to spend two days in a hotel with a cousin and Harriet was going to stay with her daughter.

Megan had struggled to send out most of her Christmas cards. She usually added a few words to them – enquiring about people's health, giving a little of her own news. This year, there was just a signature.

Instead of presents, she had sent money for her three grandchildren, for Susan, Paul, Tom and Alice. It wasn't something she liked doing, but she didn't have the energy to look for presents. She didn't know what to get them anyway. Friends would all be getting vouchers. Otherwise, she would let go of Christmas. Charles had booked into a hotel, and Duncan was still deciding what to do, torn between wanting to be with his father and pleasing the rest of the family.

Albert had a lovely room overlooking the sea. The staff were kind and cheerful. The atmosphere was so tranquil that she sometimes had to remind herself why she was there.

An old friend had just left, and she and Albert found themselves alone.

'How are you, my love?' she asked.

'Alright.' He seemed serene and she leant over to kiss him. On his head that still smelt of sandalwood. Or cedarwood. Or both. And, as she sat down, she kissed his hand. Still sensitive.

'Happy?' he asked.

'Yes.' And it was true that she was happy to be there. He had taken a few steps further along the journey that would separate them. She could see that. A fading away. A heightened delight in the simple things. Ordinary things. He had watched the tide come in. A bird had perched on a bench outside. The clouds had been so wonderful. And constantly changing.

They sat quietly together. With few words. Smiling.

They were both surprised to see Duncan and Fiona coming into the room with the children. She looked at his face as Heather gave him a drawing. He was overflowing with joy and pride. Jacob gave him a little plastic train as a Christmas present. Fiona helped him to climb onto the bed gently.

'What a lovely present, Jacob. Thank you so much. And that's the best drawing I've seen for a long time, Heather! Duncan, can you put it on the wall for me, please? I want to have it in my own special gallery.'

Duncan did as he was told and left the room. Megan saw his tears. She had wanted to leave them alone but, before she kissed Albert good-bye, she reached into her handbag. Then, as she took his hand, she saw him frown at the cold, round metal object that she passed to him. Concealed. As soon as he realised what it was, he laughed with joy. Yes, joy.

She had brought his grandfather's watch in her bag. Just in case. He hadn't had time to put it in the memory box.

In the corridor, Duncan was blowing his nose. She went up to him with a smile.

'Sorry about that!' he said. 'It just got to me – seeing the children with Dad like that.'

'You don't know how much it means to him', she said. 'Heather and Jacob – and Fiona.'

'Fiona was against the children coming, But she asked her friend on the PTA. Her husband's a psychologist. He told her that it would be a good thing to do. 'Let them take him a present,' he had said.

Back home, she sat down on the chair in the hall to listen to her phone messages. 'You have five new messages' – she was told. She was surprised but then realised that she'd been out for most of the day.

She had left Albert with his grandchildren and couldn't settle afterwards. She went to have a bowl of soup in a café. It was warm and nourishing but the staff were busy with tired and hungry last-minute Christmas shoppers. She was asked rather abruptly if she had finished.

She had wanted to find somewhere else that was cosy and comforting. Relaxed. She couldn't bear the idea of hearing more recorded carols. A collective mania that felt as though it had nothing to do with the manger rude and bare.

So, she had gone back to her flat. Home.

The first message was from Annie. The second was from Ronnie Price. 'Hullo, Mrs. Roberts' – it said. 'Ronnie Price here. Thank you for the card. I hope you're well. I know it's a busy time of the year, but I wondered if you could give me a call please.' It didn't sound like a Christmas message. There was something wrong. The third message was from an old friend. She had been into hospital to have surgery on her varicose veins and hadn't got around to sending cards. The fourth message was from Bill Price. 'This is Bill Price. Thank you for your card. Sorry to trouble you, Mrs. Roberts, but I wonder if you could give me a ring sometime?' There was a problem between father and son. Had they fallen out? Sorting out an estate often brought up tensions within a family. Which of them should she ring first? If there was some dispute, she could get either of them when she rang. Maybe Ronnie had rung from his mobile, but she had no record of the number. The fifth message was blank. From someone who had rung and been unnerved by the idea of leaving a message. Or someone from a call-centre who'd rung off because somebody else had answered the phone before her.

She went into the kitchen and put the kettle on. She was still unsettled, tense, restless. In spite of her tiredness, she needed something to do. Something to focus on other than Albert. She didn't want to leave the flat in case the hospice rang.

She slipped her shoes off and drank her tea. Chamomile. Soothing. Not that she wanted to rest. She was too agitated. It was too early for an evening meal. She wasn't hungry anyway. She knew that she had to eat to keep her strength up. But there was no point in cooking herself something until she was ready for it. She picked up the Italian book but couldn't concentrate.

She made her way back to the chair in the hallway. She had a mobile phone – which she never used except for emergencies. She had given Charles this number in case they needed to contact each other. So she turned the mobile on, making sure that it was charged.

She'd leave Annie till later. The other friend hadn't sounded as though she wanted an immediate answer. She had just been anxious to explain. Before she had finished dialling the Prices' number, she put the receiver down again. She did it awkwardly so that she failed to replace it properly on its ledge. It slid sidewards towards the Nativity set. And knocked the figure of Mary to the floor and tipped the baby Jesus onto his side. If she had had any doubts about the wisdom of getting involved in other people's problems, they lifted. What do we do every Christmas but ignore its essential message? Knock the main characters to the floor. Hurt. Wound. Ignore. Again and again. She picked the figures up and put them back in place. For her, this Christmas was going to be an offering of herself. To Albert – whenever he needed her, night or day. To poor Gracie Millstone, to Ronnie and Bill Price in their moment of need.

She dialled the number, having no idea which of the two men would answer.

It was Ronnie's voice that said 'Hello. Cardiff

385936.'

'Hello, Ronnie. It's Megan Roberts here. I got your message'

'Thank you so much for ringing back.' He sounded a bit guarded.

'I need to tell you that your father has been in touch too . . .'

'I thought he might.'

She hesitated for a moment. 'Is there something wrong?'

'Not as far as I'm concerned. You see, Donna's come back into my life . . .'

Was he hesitant because Donna was in the same room? Or maybe Bill was within earshot.

'Is it hard to talk?'

'It is a bit.'

It was then that she heard the baby cry.

'I'm going out with Donna and Poppy. Christmas shopping!' he said. 'Can I get back to you?'

'Of course.'

She wrote the number down and asked – 'Is your Dad in?'

'Yes. Do you want to speak to him?'

At the other end, she heard the mother trying to calm the baby. There was a sudden silence. A dummy, she assumed. Ronnie called out to his father – loudly but not unkindly. Before Bill got to the phone, there was the sound of laughter and the closing of a door.

'Bill?' She was gentle with him.

He only needed that one word. His Christian name. In a tone that was full of concern. He poured his heart out. Donna had got herself entangled in another relationship after Ronnie. The couple had been together for a few months when she became pregnant. Her new partner had behaved badly. Deprived of his 'rights', he had slept around. Donna got to hear of it, challenged him and he screamed at her, telling her to mind her own business. And then he left.

'She's using him again,' Bill moaned. 'But he can't see it. They say that love is blind . . .'

Poor Bill! As she listened, her mind was filled with a mass of conflicting ideas. Was Bill jealous? Could Donna be after Ronnie's money? And then there was the reality of the situation. Bill would have to let Ronnie do things his way. He was an adult.

'I said that I'll support Ronnie – and I will. But I'll support you too,' she said.

'He'll just tell you that she's learnt her lesson,' Bill complained. 'He wants to move out, and in with her and the baby.'

'You'll have to let him do it,' she said simply, expecting a backlash. Peacemakers usually receive the anger of both injured parties.

'We got so close when we were helping Miss Stafford. And we've been close trying to do our best now that she's gone. A third of her money went to Down Manor with that other school. We never told her that the old school had gone. We had to sort things out with the solicitor. We thought that she'd like to have that money invested so that there could be a cup every year and a prize. For the pupil who'd tries the hardest. That's what she'd have liked . . .'

Megan was so shocked that she asked the question directly. 'You and Ronnie weren't beneficiaries then?'

'Oh, Miss Stafford was very generous to us. Her money was split three ways. A third to Down Manor, a third to Médecins sans Frontières . . .'

She would never dream of humiliating him by

repeating the name of the charity with the correct pronunciation.

'The other third was to be split equally between me and Ronnie. The money's not sorted yet, but I think Ronnie'll blow it all on a deposit for a mortgage.'

She said again that she would keep in touch with Ronnie. Maybe meet up with him, Donna and the baby.

How dangerous assumptions are! She remembered telling Annie that Cicely had left her bungalow to Bill and Ronnie. Assumptions are so easily made and, when they are wrong, they are the cause of so many misunderstandings in the world.

Under different circumstances, she would have met up with Bill. She could feel his pain – aggravated by the jollity of consumerism at Christmas.

'Ronnie's all I've got!' he said.

She needed to explain her circumstances. 'Bill, we'll meet up soon. I can't offer a lot at the moment. A close friend – my closest friend, is dying.'

'Oh, I'm so sorry to have taken your time.' His voice was full of shame. 'I hope that she doesn't suffer too long.'

She woke early on Christmas Day to the silence of her flat. She was determined not to turn the radio on or the television.

She helped herself to a simple breakfast. She allowed herself an extra spoonful of yoghurt with a generous dollop of honey.

Then she made her way to the hospice. Charles was staying for a few days and he was already there when she arrived. Duncan was spending the day with the family and driving down after Christmas dinner.

Albert was in good form. Happy, smiling, chatty. Free of pain.

'Happy Christmas, my love!' she said, leaning over to kiss him as best as she could.

He put his hand on her shoulder and let it slide up to her neck. 'Happy Christmas, darling!'

'I've brought my viola in,' said Charles. 'We're going to take Dad into one of the other rooms. He wants me to play for him.'

Two members of staff came to help Albert into a wheelchair. He could still walk but he was weak and the chair was much easier. They were so tender with him. Like a king, she thought. They're treating him like a king.

Several people gathered in the room as Charles stood apart from them and took his instrument out of its case. She saw his fineness as he tuned it and placed it under his chin. His nostrils quivered. His bow slid along the strings with an exquisite dexterity. The sound was perfect.

He played 'Silent Night'. That beautiful, familiar, tune had never sounded finer or more relevant. When he came to the second line of the refrain, he looked directly at his father. Albert seemed mesmerised by the performance. Full of pride. Charles was struggling to hold back the tears.

No-one sang the words. But everybody knew them. 'Sleep in Heavenly Peace. Sleep in Heavenly Peace.' Words intended for the infant lying in the manger. Words that could be sung for any honest human being who is looking forward – with a little fear, to that most mysterious of journeys.

Back in his own room, Albert talked to Charles as she pinned some of his cards onto a board opposite the bed. She tried to balance a few more on the little narrow ledge above its wooden frame. They fell down, so she tried again. She busied herself with things that didn't need doing.

She looked out at the sea. Stared at it. The tide was coming in. It would reach a certain point then flow out again.

'Megan, I'm going out to walk along the prom,' said Charles. What a sweet man. Giving them time to be together. He found it far easier than Duncan who didn't quite understand how she fitted in. But Charles belonged to a minority group. He knew exactly how important it was to let them be.

'Charles is wonderful!' she whispered as soon as he'd gone. 'You must be so proud.'

'I am.' He paused and said, without emotion – 'I've given the boys instructions for my funeral. At St. Michael's. Do you think the Minister from Ebenezer would lead the prayers?'

'I'll see what I can do.' It was not the time to speak of the differences between the Anglican and the Nonconformist services. 'I'll see what I can do.'

'I asked Duncan and Charles if they would read.' He spoke firmly now. A man with a message that could not wait. 'Duncan said he'd do it but Charles felt he'd be happier playing something on the viola. Will they agree to that?'

'I'm sure they will.'

'So I need someone else to do a reading. Would it be too much for you . . .?'

It was a question that she had dreaded. But also one that she had hoped for. The effort of explaining everything had made him tired and he leaned back.

She nodded at him, smiling. 'I'll do it for you.'

'Come here!' he said softly in a voice that she could hardly hear. 'Sit on the bed.'

She took her shoes off and looked for a place. He moved as much as he could to one side. She settled beside him. It was not comfortable with all the medical paraphernalia, but it was where she wanted to be. She felt the body that she loved. Smaller. Frailer.

They held hands. And they watched the sea.

She moved the little Nativity set into the living-room. It was warmer there and more comfortable. It was just a gesture. Room for them in the inn. She placed Mary and the baby further inside the wooden stable. She moved the other figures closer. And, to their right, she lit a candle. It was a scented candle in a gilt container– a birthday gift. The fragrance of vanilla filled the air.

She began to pray. For Albert – that he may sleep in heavenly peace, when the time was right. For Charles and Duncan. Fiona, Heather and Jacob. For herself – that she would be given strength. For Tom and Alice. That they could work to rebuild a future together. For Bella. Alice's parents. For Susan and Paul. Stevie and Catherine. For peace to come to Paul's troubled church. For peace in the world. Was it too much to hope for?

She counted the days. After Christmas, there were five of them when Albert seemed to be quite well. Duncan had taken him out – well-wrapped up – in the wheelchair to see the sea and breathe in its air. He had been so excited about it. Charles went home to rest for a couple of days then returned. He stayed at the guest room in the complex. There was not a great demand for it immediately after Christmas. They got quite close to each other and he offered her lifts. She cooked for him a couple of times and he cooked for her. It gave them something to do. The basic routine of boiling vegetables and grilling a piece of fish.

Seasoning. They talked about herbs. Should it be dill – or parsley?

New Year's Eve was another time of enforced heartiness. Myf and Harriet had returned from their holidays but they kept at a respectful distance, speaking politely and in hushed tones as if she were ill herself. Residents who wanted to stay up until midnight were invited into the common room for sherry, nibbles and the singing of Auld Lang Syne.

Duncan rang her at one thirty in the afternoon of the first day of the year. Albert had deteriorated. There were three people who were prepared to stay with him in shifts. Three people whom he had named. Duncan, Charles and Megan.

Charles picked her up at four o'clock. He had been with his father all the afternoon and gave her a lift in before returning to the complex for a rest. She would stay there until the early evening when Duncan was due to take over.

Albert was sleeping when she got there. She sat down on a chair and looked at him. It was beginning to get dark. It seemed wrong to put the light on. She didn't want to disturb him. She remained there in the twilight. A nurse came in and checked on him and then turned to her, smiling. Would she like a cup of tea? Would she like to use the muted light from the table-lamp beside her chair? She hadn't noticed it before. Its glow was soft. She took the cup of tea without remembering that she had asked for it.

As he slept, she spoke to him from time to time. Gentle assurances. Words of love and comfort. Lines from poetry.

He stirred. She went up to him to hear any words. 'Doreen' – he muttered. She held his hand and stroked it. She wanted to tell him that it was her – Megan. But she didn't. The most important thing was to support him – to accompany him on his journey. And, if he was thinking of Doreen, she wouldn't let her ego intrude.

But it was a painfully hard thing to do. She deliberately avoided saying anything and just stroked his hand.

He opened his eyes. 'Megan'. She caressed his forehead and saw that his mouth was dry. She took a little spatula and soaked it in water. Then she gently opened his mouth and let the water moisten it.

He smiled at her then fell asleep again. She struggled to keep awake. Hugo had insisted on coming home for the last few weeks. He had been keen to stay in hospital until then. Always believing that there was something else they could do. But one day, he just said that he wanted to go home. There had been help, of course, but she had paid for 24-hour nursing, seven days a week. He had told her how awkward he'd felt having older parents. He'd been teased. She didn't know that. He'd never forgiven his parents for sending him to the boarding school. He wasn't good at sport so he'd put everything into his studies. And the questions had come. Had he been a good husband? Had he been a good father? Had he been a good doctor? And she had replied yes to everything. 'Hugo' she muttered as she dozed.

Duncan woke her up gently. He drove her home then

returned to the hospice.

She was wide awake then and wondered what to do. A beautiful image came into her head. Of a raindrop. A raindrop sliding down a window-pane and merging into another. They slithered further down the pane together and were separated by a fault in the glass – a little whorl. She remembered the words of Keats – 'life is but a day: A fragile dewdrop on its perilous way – from a tree's summit.'

It was a bit like that. She and Albert had shared their journey for a little while. It was 'but a day' whether it had been a matter of months or years. They had travelled together, slithered down the windowpane together. For a bit. And she thought of the immensity of the universe, the greatness of God, the littleness of humanity – though so treasured. The dewdrop against the mightiness of a mature tree. The drop of rain that is nothing in the grandeur of the ocean, but it was Mother Teresa who said that the ocean is made up of drops.

She wondered what to do. The area in the hall just above the place where she had removed the figures from the nativity set, looked bare. She went into the spare bedroom and brought out the frame. She carefully lifted the little brass triangles that held the hardboard in place. She took out the hardboard and the print that she didn't want. She dusted the glass and set the Berthe Morisot print in place. She lay down the hardboard on top of it and re-fixed the brass triangles. The string to hang it up was rather loose so she undid it and fetched some more from her bureau. She was about to put a pencil mark on the wall to show her where to knock the picture-pin when the telephone rang.

Printed in Great Britain
by Amazon

30787954R00146